Twinship

ALSO BY LAURIE FOOS

Ex Utero

Portrait of the Walrus by a Young Artist

Twinship

Laurie
Foos

HARCOURT BRACE & COMPANY
New York   San Diego   London

Requests for permission to make copies of any part of
the work should be mailed to: Permissions Department,
Harcourt, Inc., 6277 Sea Harbor Drive,
Orlando, Florida 32887-6777.

This is a work of fiction. All the names, characters,
organizations, and events portrayed in this book are
either products of the author's imagination or are used
fictitiously for verisimilitude.

Library of Congress Cataloging-in-Publication Data
Foos, Laurie, 1966–
Twinship/Laurie Foos.—1st ed.
p.   cm.
ISBN 0-15-100417-X
I. Title.
PS3556.0564T95   1999
813'.54—dc21   99-25609

The text was set in New Aster.
Designed by Lydia D'moch
Printed in the United States of America

First edition
A C E F D B

For my mother

Acknowledgments

I wish to thank the following people, who were instrumental in the writing of this book:

My agent, Tony Gardner, for his unflagging belief in this book; Bobara Pendergrast for her invaluable information on the world of Persian cat breeding; and my editor, Kati Steele, for her keen insight helping to bring this book into its final form.

My beloved friend and champion, Cody ("Trish") Collett, whose friendship fills my life with endless blessings; and Ann Bauer for all of the laughs and for always understanding.

Kerry Madden-Lunsford and Carol Magun for their encouragement and friendship and for reading the manuscript in its various stages; and Susan Segal, kindred spirit, for all of the wonderful E-mail, talks, and brilliant notes.

And, of course, thank you to my best friend and "sister," Lauren Hayes Fonte, for sharing my childhood and adult life, and to my husband, Michael Giannetta, for the love, support, laughter, endless patience, and . . . everything.

I also wish to thank Coffee House Press—especially Allan Kornblum for being a gifted editor and friend—for rescuing me from the slush pile.

And the MacDowell Colony for the time to complete this book.

And this was my worst guilt; you could not cure nor soothe it. I made you to find me.

—Anne Sexton, "The Double Image"

I gave birth to myself on a Thursday. Thursdays had always been lucky for me, until that fateful day. I met Jerry on a Thursday; and Red Duchess, my prize Persian, became a grand champion on a Thursday. To Mother's best recollection, I was also born on a Thursday. Perhaps that should have been enough of a clue, that I should go into labor on the same day of the week I was born. But days in the week were nothing but insignificant marks on a calendar. They held no inner meanings or harbingers of doom. Mother said Thursday was her lucky day. And, as with most things she told me, I simply took her word for it.

Beginning in the eighth month, Mother came to my house on Friday nights to rehearse.

In her spare time she'd written a script for me to follow, complete with spaces for heavy breathing and bearing down from the pelvis, and even rigged my dining-room table with mock stirrups. She perfected the snapping of rubber gloves.

Mother had my dried umbilical cord fashioned into a necklace as a lucky charm. Everything had gone so smashingly well for her at my birth that we had no reason to believe there would be any setbacks for me. Because she'd had such luck having me for a daughter, Mother hoped she could reproduce that luck for the birth of the grandchild she'd spent half her life waiting for.

"Now remember," Mother would say, snapping on her rubber gloves and holding one hand on my belly, "if we follow the script to the letter, you'll have yourself a daughter just as wonderful as you."

Then she'd press her lips to my forehead and signal for us to begin:

The Birth: An Excerpt

Doctor stands at the foot of the table, hands out, gloves ready. Mother, with mask on, stands (in place of the father) to the side.

Cue overhead lights. Cue doctor. Cue exiting fetus. Maxi begins to moan.

MAXI: Oh please, Doctor, I've got to push! Let me push! I've just got to see my baby.

Heavy breathing. Mother blows air in daughter's face with rounded mouth, smooths back daughter's red hair.

DOCTOR: OK, Maxi. Crowning! Crowning! Go ahead and ...push!

Mother and Maxi hold on to each other as Maxi bears down.

MAXI: Aaaaaahhhhh! Aaaaaahhhhhhhh!
MOTHER *(weeping softly in sympathy):* That's my girl.

One final push and the baby is out. The ringing sound of applause.

DOCTOR: It's a girl!
NURSES, IN CHORUS: It's a girl!

Mother and Maxi stroke the beautiful red-haired baby on Maxi's belly. They kiss.

MOTHER AND MAXI, TOGETHER: It's our little girl!

And so, when the time came and the nurses wheeled me, with my heaving white belly, on the gurney covered in blue sheets smeared with fluid, I wasn't ready for surprises. Dr. Norton had told me time and again that all birth experiences are unique; and certainly I'd assisted enough feline deliveries to know that no two could be identical. Yet, our endless rehearsals and the story of my own birth had become so ingrained in me, I turned my back on logic and believed that I would give birth in the exact way that Mother had delivered me.

I closed my eyes and waited for the lights to come on, for the nurses to appear in their blue masks and rubber gloves, for the pain that locked in the middle and wouldn't let go until the fetus was out. I waited for the doctors and nurses to hit their marks and play out the scene I'd rehearsed over and over again. Mother had even taped Xs on the floor to block the birth scene. But when the baby started to descend through that most marvelous of openings, I opened my mouth and

screamed out of turn. I kept on screaming, even after
Mother dropped the script pages on the floor and her
face went white with shock, after the baby came flying
out in a liquid splash and left me hanging open in the
breeze.

"It's a girl!" Dr. Norton said, the only line any of us
got right. He pressed the gray shape onto my chest, coat-
ing me with blood and paste.

My legs were shaking and the scene went on and on;
this time there was no sense of closure. I tried to press
my thighs together to hold myself in, to keep the other
parts of me from falling away; and I cried, staring into
the milky bulging eyes and trying to use my hand to
close up the gap between my legs. I cried heavy, thick
tears while Mother clapped and the doctor reached in to
pull more of me out, as if my body had opened too wide
and would never close up again.

This wasn't the way it was supposed to be. Instantly I
knew. After all the months of rehearsal, something had
gone terribly wrong. Or perhaps terribly right. Even
Mother had forgotten her lines, had leaned over me
when she was supposed to be at my feet to watch the
crowning. She'd missed several of her cues. Later the
doctors would tell me that there was no way I could have
known, that this was the secret knowledge of life, the
thing that all women hoard inside and only talk about
once it's over; and then they can't seem to stop. I couldn't
have known until it happened, they'd said.

As they held the baby up for me to see, I stared into
the infant's squinched face, the flattened pink nose and
wiry fluff of red hair, the curving fingers, and the birthmark in the shape of a comma over the right eye. I rec-

ognized that comma and those bluish eyes. In that face I saw myself.

I pressed my legs together, trapped the umbilical cord between my thighs, and screamed. The pain had passed, but now was the time for screaming. I took a deep breath and let my lungs open up, felt my tonsils shaking with the force of it. At the same instant—that millisecond when I'd drawn in a long breath and braced myself to let it go—the baby started to scream, too.

"Maxi," Mother whispered, her eyes brimming with tears, "this is where the curtain falls. This is where we take our bows."

She glared down at me as she glided her hands over the infant's pasty back, smearing the fluid in thick swirls like finger paint. This was the moment she'd been waiting for and she wouldn't have anyone spoil it.

"Put it back," I said, shaking my head. My tongue flapped at the roof of my mouth. "It's all wrong. Something's gone wrong."

I grabbed at the baby and tried to slip it from Mother's hands, but she gripped its legs and slapped my hands away. The nurse wiped my face with a washcloth, begged me to calm down.

"You're a mommy now," the nurse said. "Pull yourself together."

"That's what I'm trying to do!" I shrieked, saliva sputtering from my lips and landing on the nurse's cheek. I thrashed on the bed, pulled myself up onto my elbows, and grabbed the cord from the doctor's hands.

"Let go, Maxine, let go," Dr. Norton said, gently at first, then gritting his teeth as we each yanked at ends of the cord, my fingers over the broken end and his

somewhere in the slippery middle. The baby was
screaming, too, and I felt racked by the effort it took to
get so much air into those tiny lungs.

"It's a mistake," I sobbed. "Can't you see?"

Two of the nurses held my arms to my sides. I fell
back, weeping, in a pool of my own sweat. They placed
the baby under billy lights and slid a long tube down her
throat, sucking out mucus in thick slurps. I gagged, and
jammed my hands between my knees. Mother shook her
head at me as the gas mask descended over my face and
I swallowed the first fits of gluey air. I could no longer
play the part, I thought as I sank into the anesthetic, the
sounds of our screams ringing in my ears.

It came as a shock, initially, this notion of having delivered a new self out of my body, as if part of me needed
discarding, casting off. Later I realized that I should
have known what was coming, that in fact Mother
had been working toward the creation of a new me since
I'd been born. All my life she'd said that she could never
have hoped for a better daughter than myself, and
lamented the fact there was not more of me for her to
love.

"A daughter's a daughter for the rest of her life," she
would say, her favorite refrain. "If only there were more
like you somewhere."

If only I had listened; if only I had taken her seriously: all of the birth stories she'd told, all the years
she'd spent preparing for the arrival of the new me. Perhaps I could have spared us—all three of us—a great
deal of pain. But then again, I tell myself over and over

as a consolation, there was no way I could have known.

I'd always thought that giving birth would be like a dream: bright lights and voices overhead, mind floating, sweaty thighs and white-hot pain. Mother had told me everything. She'd recounted the story of my own birth the way some mothers hand down secret sauces or tips on the shaving of legs: a very practical hands-on story, a kind of how-to. The storytelling began the day I started to menstruate. When I first saw that flowery stain on my cotton underpants, Mother began the lesson—from conception to that final push in the delivery room—sparing not a labored breath or a splash of brown fluid. I heard horror stories—from women in gym locker rooms after aerobics, in the kitchens at dinner parties, with yet another story of a record-stitched episiotomy and forceps up to the navel—but Mother warned me not to be scared off by stories of torn flesh and sore nipples. Giving birth was an accomplishment, she said, and no great success came without moments of pain. For Mother, giving birth was the beginning of a whole new life for both child *and* mother. That was what I'd chosen to believe. If I could think of birth the way Mother had, I had nothing to fear. As far as I was concerned, she'd told me everything I needed to know. I understood what birth would be like before I'd even had sex. She'd spent my whole life preparing me.

Childbirth was the laying out of your life, she'd said, and the sooner I prepared myself for exposure, the better off I'd be. She told me what it felt like to expand, for your skin to etch itself into patterns, for your swollen vulva to open in a scream. From varicose veins bulging through the groin to nipples caked over with a crusty film, she left no stone unturned. In Mother's stories, pain was always redemptive.

"The best thing a woman can do for her daughter," she said, "is to let her know what's waiting for her when she splits wide open to let some new thing into the world. It's the greatest thing a woman can do."

I'd known immediately what it took the doctors nearly a week to recognize. Such a rarity as it was, I no longer blame them for their frantic uncertainty—even for the straitjacket they put me in while I was being wheeled out of recovery. They were unprepared for something so shocking. Of course, I'd been unprepared as well, but as the "mother" of this child it was my duty to be prepared, I later told myself. They needed a battery of genetic tests; all I needed was one look.

Despite following Mother's recipe for conception, the fastidious prenatal care I had lavished on my expectant body, and despite (or perhaps because of) the endless preparation for childbirth as prescribed by Mother, I had not given birth to a baby; I had given birth to myself.

At first Dr. Norton wouldn't listen. He said I was suffering from postpartum depression, the letdown after nine buoyant months of expectation. (The fact that I was never buoyant did not seem to deter this theory.) It was only natural, he said, that I should be so disappointed. I kept telling him that this wasn't hormonal—it was the shock of seeing my own face descend from between my legs. Try to imagine the horror.

"Look at her face," I demanded when they brought the infant in for nursing. I folded my arms over my breasts and refused to let her suckle. Milk formed thick rocks in my chest that begged for release, but I wouldn't give in. "That's no baby," I whispered. "It's me."

Dr. Norton came and sat at my bedside when I refused to calm down. Mother had handpicked him from a directory of obstetricians that featured photos of prominent physicians in the area. Of course, it would have been best to have Dr. Green, the obstetrician who had delivered me, but he'd died of an embolism the year before. We were forced to find the next-best thing. Norton was a dead ringer for Green. We'd simply had to have him.

A paunchy man with thick hands that smelled of cigarette smoke and liquid soap, Dr. Norton had promised to buy three of my pet-quality Persians when this was all over; and for that reason alone, I trusted him. Anyone who loved cats could not be all bad. He pressed a hand on my arm and said I'd have to be moved out of the maternity wing if I couldn't behave myself, that I was upsetting the other mothers, that I should try to be rational.

"Go ahead and move me," I said, "because I am not a mother."

He pressed his hand to my wrist to feel my pulse and shone lights in my eyes. Perhaps I'd had an allergic reaction to the anesthesia, he said. This was not uncommon for asthmatics and cat lovers, as a matter of fact. Or perhaps my maternal instinct had yet to kick in. I'd seen this myself, many times. When a Persian queen rejected one of her litter, leaving the poor squirming soul in the corner while she lapped tentatively at the others as if not sure this was what she really wanted to do, I'd always felt a certain disdain for the queen then. But as a breeder I'd learned to make up for these mothers' lack of affection. Now I understood.

Mother stood behind Dr. Norton, frantic, running her hands over the front of her blouse and sucking her teeth. He told her that maybe I wasn't ready yet to transfer to this newborn my love of the kittens I bred.

"After all," he whispered to Mother, "sometimes it takes mothers a long time to bond. She's got to work at it."

Mother nodded and thanked Dr. Norton for his concern. She pulled her chair close to my bed and sighed. None of this was in the script we'd rehearsed for so long. And neither of us was very good at ad-libbing.

"Come on now, Maxi," she said, reaching over to tuck a strand of hair behind my ear. She wiped her cheek with a tissue, smearing her rouge in circles. "It's not as bad as it seems. Things happened that we couldn't have planned for. We didn't have Green; you went into labor two weeks ahead of schedule. But the important thing is, we have the baby now; and that's what all this has been about. We finally have the baby."

She removed her glasses and set them down on my bedside table, beside the pink water pitcher. I reached for her hand and held it in both of mine, staring into her blue eyes ringed in mascara, eyeing the spots of rouge left on her cheeks. As I stared at her, I saw a flicker of rage in those eyes, just for a moment, and struggled to pull my hand away. But she held on tighter, smiling now as she moved her thumb in circles over my knuckles, down the slopes of my fingers. I thought of the years she'd spent coaxing me toward this moment, the belief she'd had in me, that I could actually replicate my own birth. Now that we'd actually done it, she had to think of what to do next.

"It's not a baby," I whispered, but I could see she was already somewhere else, dreaming of bassinets and playpens, cloth diapers and frilly bows. She had a baby all over again. Only, this time the baby wasn't really hers.

Dr. Norton began to come to his senses when the baby and I had our first simultaneous asthma attack. He was sitting at the edge of my bed, trying to coax me into holding the baby, to at least have a look at her through the nursery window; but I wouldn't hear of it. If I wanted to see myself, I told him, he could just as soon bring me a hand mirror as drag me down a hallway, with a rump full of stitches and my sagging uterus.

"I don't want to hold her," I said, pulling a pillow over my face. "And you can't make me."

Mother came running to my side just as the breath squeezed in my chest. Throwing the pillow off my face, I sat up and reached frantically for my inhaler. We'd left it at home in our hurry to get to the hospital, and Mother'd forgotten the spare.

"She can't breathe," Mother said. "She needs her inhaler."

Dr. Norton reached inside his pocket and pressed an inhaler into my open mouth, squeezing a cold blast of air into my throat.

A high-pitched beeping rang through the room. The intercom buzzed with the names of pediatricians being summoned to the nursery. I knew right away it was her.

"It's the baby," Mother shrieked, as she took off running, leaving me there alone, wheezing, with the inhaler between my teeth. Off she went behind Dr. Norton and a team of nurses, to find that the infant had been seized with an asthma attack at the exact same moment. I sucked air down into my lungs and waited for them to come back after finding the infant blue and wheezing in her receiving blanket.

It took them three days to realize the depth of our similarities. We had three simultaneous asthma attacks within a day and a half, wept uncontrollably every four hours, and slept at the same intervals, from which we both awoke wet and cranky. Above all, we were calm only when Mother was nearby. She ran from my bed down to the nursery and back again, beaming from our need. Yet, I felt terribly alone. I begged her to get into bed beside me and rock me.

"You've got a baby now," she said. "You've got to pull yourself together."

But how was I supposed to pull myself together, I wondered, now that I'd been split in two?

On the third day, when I still refused to feed or hold "the infant," Dr. Norton came to my bedside and peered down at me while I clamped my hands over my swollen breasts.

"We're going to run some tests," he said, looking more at Mother than at me as he spoke. "Routine, really, but just to set her mind at ease," he said, patting Mother's arm.

He sat on the edge of my bed and fingered the long tube that pulsed warm Valium into my veins, making me thick with sleep. They had to do something, he told Mother, to keep me from trying to shove things up between my legs: a pillow, a pair of socks, even the plastic cup that held my daily Jell-O. Since I wasn't healed yet, they were afraid I'd tear myself open with my frantic search for wholeness. Sedation seemed the only way to stop me. As soon as they turned their backs I was at it again. Much as the pain shot through me—up my abdomen and down my legs—I didn't care. At least with the Valium I could tell myself through the haze that all of this was unreal, that I'd never been stupid enough to get pregnant, that I was back in my cattery, surrounded by bicolor Persians, my only worry the constant threat of hairballs.

When they moved me into a private room out of the maternity wing, I was relieved, really, since the sight of all the new mothers with their collapsed middles made me sob almost constantly. Although the Valium did make me calmer, they put me back into a straitjacket because I still felt the need to replace what had been delivered from my body. I sat with Mother and talked in singsong about the bicolor Persians I'd been raising. Red Duchess, my grand champion, had two weeks left before she'd give birth.

"When I get home," I whispered to Mother, "the Duchess will be ready to go at any time."

Mother, for her part, pretended that all of this was a normal reaction to motherhood, that it was something she'd experienced herself in the first twenty-four hours following my birth. "Sure you're a little afraid now, Maxi," she said. "All new mommies go a little nuts. That's part of the fun."

Why hadn't she told me about the terror I'd feel? I wanted to tell her that I wasn't a mommy in any conventional sense, that something about all this was not normal. Maybe all the inbreeding had finally caught up with me. The Valium left me so groggy, I could do nothing but lie there and listen to her prattle on and on about our little girl.

For days Dr. Norton kept me heavily sedated, and poked and prodded at me with gloved fingers, shining lights between my legs and feeling along the incision there as if reading braille, as if looking for some clue to how such a phenomenon could have occurred. I refused to see anyone, even Jerry, the father of "the infant," who was supervising the cattery until I was discharged. When he called I let Mother tell him that everything was all right, that we had delivered a healthy little girl.

"She's all right, Jerry," she whispered, cupping the receiver over her mouth. "You've done your part."

I slept thickly, with my eyes half open, watching specialist after specialist peer at me through goggles. They performed a sonogram of my vacant uterus and took vials of blood from my arm and the arm of the newborn (after which we both wept uncontrollably and bruised at the exact same points in our forearms) and studied the blood under microscopes. Finally, under the pretense of checking for an extra asthmatic gene, they summoned Jerry to the hospital and coaxed him into delivering a helping of semen into a paper cup. After forty-five minutes of watching footage of Joe Namath in Brut commercials, the test was a success, confirming what the doctors had insisted was impossible: Jerry, the cat-groomer "father," who had planted his seed in me on the floor of the cattery, was unequivocally sterile.

There was no explanation left to be found. She was me and I was her; there were no two ways about it.

A team of doctors met me covertly in a conference room at the far end of the maternity wing, the room that I later learned was used for breaking the news of deformities and of C-sections gone awry. I was wheeled in, still strapped into my straitjacket.

"Just put it back," I moaned as they wheeled me down the hall. It was all I could think to say.

Mother sat beside me in a straight-backed chair. Her eyes were puffy beneath her glasses, her bright red hair hanging loose at the roots, rouge caked on either side of her face. She scowled at the doctors and tapped her fingers on the table. All of this nonsense kept her from spending time alone with the baby. The more I carried on, the longer Mother had to wait to get her hands on that baby.

"What kind of problem could there be," she demanded, "when I told Maxi exactly what to do?"

Dr. Norton and the team of geneticists sitting next to me at the table narrowed their eyes at her. I twitched uncomfortably in my wheelchair, the stitches in my episiotomy stabbing at my swollen flesh. I could feel her disappointment and wished I could stop them from saying anything more. But it was too late.

Dr. Norton lit a cigarette and blew a cloud at the No Smoking sign. He exhaled, with his lower lip protruding slightly, a puff of smoke drooling from his lips. The fact that I was asthmatic never stopped him from soothing his nicotine fits. He leaned close and turned his head to the right and left. I stuck my neck out and held my face in profile, scornfully revealing the telltale birthmark over my right eye.

"Maxine," he said, dribbling out more smoke and shaking his head, "it appears from the exhaustive genetic testing, which revealed the sterility of the father in this case; from the uncannily mirrored behavior between you and your infant"—at this he shook his head and blew a full cloud of smoke in my face—"from shared DNA to blood-type A, that you have given birth to a baby who seems not really to be a *baby* but an exact genetic replica of yourself."

I let the words hang in the air and closed my eyes, seeing again the pink face with the comma over its right brow, the blurred glare of recognition when the infant had opened its filmy eyes, Mother's face hidden behind the blue mask. The careful script of my birth, repeated to me over and over again with not a detail out of place, I'd followed the script so completely that I'd actually cloned it. Produced a veritable clone.

"I just did what you told me," I said to Mother, shaking my head all the time. "I wanted it to be perfect."

Of course, she was not ready for this news. The veins in her forehead pulsed and she lashed out at Dr. Norton, her finger pointed at his face.

"Oh no," she said, her face twisted with anguish. "Oh no, you don't. You won't do this to me. You will not take this away. I've waited too long for this."

She lifted her hand as if to slap him, and then collapsed in the chair, her shoulders slumped like a wounded bird. I tried to lean over to comfort her, having forgotten the straitjacket that bound me.

"Let me loose," I said, and the doctors came running

behind me to untie the knots that had kept my arms across my chest. The jacket fell to the floor and I threw my arms around Mother, my swollen breasts smashing into the bones of her shoulder.

"It's a mistake," I said, rocking her and laughing giddily. The effects of the Valium lingered, and in my half-delirious state, I thought they could simply sew the infant back in and let me go on as if nothing had happened. Put me back together again, like the nursery rhyme said. Then I would be rid of the emptiness inside, the loss that pulled at my breasts and my womb.

"Now, if you'll just put it back in," I said; and as the words came out of my mouth, Mother's hand hit me square in the face. I landed on the carpet, facedown. The gown opened in the back and my buttocks stuck up in the air. The doctors grabbed Mother by the arms and held her back. Later I would look in the mirror and remember that fateful slap—a slap I would never forget—which left its mark on the new me, a tiny squirming body that had come out of me and into the world, something neither Mother nor I had ever intended.

 It had all been Mother's idea, even the act of conception. I was thirty-four and had been trying for five years to produce a Cat of the Year—a Persian so perfect that *Cat Fancy* would proclaim its virtues. For several years I'd worked nights at an all-night veterinary hospital, where I helped minister to everything from German shepherds hit by cars on dark streets to parrots whose beaks had become stuck in the bars of their cages, sending feathers and seeds flying in their efforts to shake themselves loose. Finally the sight of such injuries became too much for me. To foster my maternal instincts, Mother bought me a Persian cat and suggested I let the animal have kittens. She said that watching a queen give birth and holding the tiny bodies in my hands would awaken the mother in me.

"Your clock is ticking," Mother said the day she bought me that first Persian, a white-tipped beauty with copper eyes and a lovely receded nose. "I hear it in my sleep."

I began to learn about breeding while dating Roger, a

periodontist who wanted to shave down my gums and a whole lot more. Mother didn't like him, so she encouraged me to breed the cats to keep me from becoming too attached. I even shipped several Persians in from England to get the right crossbreed. Roger hated cats, said the sight of their rumps and sandpaper tongues reminded him of the worst kind of gingivitis, though I never did see the connection. Mother said Roger was not the sort of man who would give me a baby and then let me go, clear out of our way. And a man who spent his days elbow deep in people's mouths, his tools scraping the gook from inside people's gums, could only mean one thing: low motility.

"He's not the one," she said. "Mothers know these things."

Within four years I had my own cattery, Bicolor Bliss, and had produced a grand champion, Red Duchess, the red-and-white bicolor Persian I'd bred from a mother-son coupling. On the campaign trail for Cat of the Year, I'd met Jerry. A groomer and part-time hairdresser, he cut my hair and taught me all the grooming skills I'd ever need to know. Although the Duchess never won the title, it wasn't long before Jerry and I were spending a great deal of time together, talking about Persians and hair products, things that previously only Mother and I had shared.

Jerry had always been unsure about his sexuality, but I'd grown quite fond of him just the same, and Mother saw him as the perfect candidate for helping to produce a grandchild. He was unattached, with a strong feminine side, and had been to every cat show in the country at one time or another. Best of all, he loved the Duchess of York, Sarah Ferguson, whom Mother and I had named Red Duchess after.

Mother had always been fascinated by the royal family and felt great affinity for Fergie because, like us, she had bright red hair and freckled skin. As much as Mother loved Di—she'd gotten up at 4 A.M. the day of the funeral and thrown roses at the television as the onlookers threw them at the hearse—she'd always felt that Fergie had somehow been overshadowed by Di's blond winsomeness and dazzling smile. With Di gone, Mother believed Fergie would emerge as the royal family's star personality and could show the world a thing or two about being a fiery redhead in every sense of the word. And as Fergie's daughters' red hair had softened to brown, Mother felt it was time for me to produce daughters of my own.

The day Fergie's daughter Beatrice was born, Mother called me on the phone weeping.

"She has tons of red hair," she said between sobs, "and looks just like her mother. Why can't you give me a princess of my own?"

I wasn't sure I wanted to be a mother, though I did want to please Mother. Partly I raised the kittens to make up to her for my childlessness; that much I admitted. And for a time it worked. Every time she felt grandmotherhood calling to her, I studded a bicolor and produced a litter of kittens that would squirm in her hands. They were some of the best-quality Persians I'd ever seen, with short boxy bodies, and noses so receded they nearly disappeared. It wasn't that I didn't try—cats were just not enough, red-haired or not.

She talked me into the pregnancy, using a variety of tactics. First, it was true that I was approaching thirty-five and that my recent onslaught of asthma had weakened me physically. I was a mere cat lover who spent half her days opening and closing cages and disposing of cat droppings with a plastic scoop. Since I already spent so much time cleaning up after cats, why not change diapers instead? At least if I were a mother, my work would have some meaning beyond the scope of my little world—but with kittens, what did it all really matter? I could just as well produce a litter of my own, she said, as stay up nights waiting to help ease the sacs off of kitten bodies and clean up bloody placentas before the mother had the chance to eat them. No good breeder ever allowed her queen to eat placentas. The cats were fed so well, there was no need for all that mess. Second, Jerry and I had been friends for nearly a year, which Mother felt was more than time enough to get a baby out of him. Although we'd never consummated the relationship, he was the closest to being a boyfriend since Roger. Prospects, Mother reminded me, were not looking up.

After Roger I'd dated a few men casually but had never really enjoyed anyone's company the way I did Jerry's. Although Jerry admitted he sometimes dreamed of steamy showers with Joe Namath, I'd also caught him staring at my breasts as I leaned over to lift Red Duchess. He glowed when assisting in deliveries while I sweated in my tank top, lifting the kittens gingerly and twirling them around for air. Occasionally he'd developed crushes on men he'd met at cat shows or at the gym where he worked out, but for the most part he was devoted to me.

"He's as good a man as any," Mother said. "Let him plant the seed."

The truth was, I wasn't in love with Jerry but thought maybe Mother was right, maybe time was running out. He had a great sense of humor and an above-average IQ, and he loved Persians nearly as much as I did. Jerry had a way of including himself in my relationship with Mother without interfering or pulling me away from her. She said he had a fine head on his shoulders and a wonderful pair of hands, which she occasionally allowed to massage her scalp with hot oil to ward off dryness.

Mother and I planned for me to conceive on a Monday. I invited Jerry to dinner on the pretense of having him comb out one of the Duchess's matted knots and provide advice on whether I should cut my hair in a shag or let the layers grow out. Jerry loved this kind of thing and agreed right away to come. His hair color changed week to week—sometimes black or a shocking platinum, other times a soft citrus gold. Mother sent over several bottles of Beaujolais and a box of chocolate-covered strawberries, which had been lucky charms for her in my conception. She said I should serve roast beef and julienned carrots, and play Tom Jones records during dinner. She bought me a bright red teddy to wear under my sweatshirt and jeans, and said that we had to conceive on a carpet, just the way she had.

"You make sure he eats three helpings of roast beef," she said, "and keep those Tom Jones records playing. At the end of the main course, you'll have yourself a baby, just like I did."

The fact that Jerry was a vegetarian posed something

of a problem. I made a tofu stew, instead, with the julienned carrots, and bought a Tom Jones *Greatest Hits*
tape on sale at the record store. The strains of "She's a
Lady" rang through the house when Jerry arrived with a
hairstyling magazine under his arm and a bag of wire
brushes. His gold hair was tightly permed, the curls
frizzed at the ends. I was mating one of the Duchess's
daughters—Bea, after Fergie's oldest—with a stud who
was also the Duchess's nephew. They'd been in the cage
together for several days. You could hear the growling all
the way in the kitchen.

"Don't mind the hair," he said after kissing me hello
on the lips and pinching my waist. "I left the Zotos on
too long, got caught up in Di's interview with the BBC."

I laughed and crossed my arms over my chest, con-
scious of the teddy pulling at my breasts as Tom Jones
launched into "Delilah."

"What did Minnie have to say about it?" He snorted.
"You know, she's right. Fergie has always gotten the
shaft."

"You know Mother," I said. "She says that Fergie's
two girls are better stock than Wills and Harry any day
of the week. All because of that red hair."

I laughed and told him to have a seat at the table.
Jerry sipped at his Beaujolais as I spooned the tofu stew
into a large ceramic bowl. I'd never made tofu before
and could see that some of it gripped the bowl like wet
sand. The carrots, however, were perfect. At least I'd gotten something right.

"This is absolutely delicious, Maxi," he said, stabbing
the carrots with his fork. "And who knew you were a
Tom Jones fan?"

I tried to smile and pulled at the collar of my sweat-shirt. Was I playing the right songs? I wondered. Mother couldn't remember the name of the album she'd been lis-tening to when I'd been conceived, but she knew it con-tained several of Jones's big hits.

"Don't you like him?" I asked. "I can change it if you want."

"Oh, no," Jerry said, scooping up the last of the tofu stew, "with that curly hair and those painted-on pants, are you kidding? I adore the man."

As he ate his tofu stew, Jerry hummed a few bars of "She's a Lady," bobbing his head up and down as he ate. We both laughed, then did a little impromptu dance, Jerry twirling me around, as we went about the business of clearing the dishes. We'd each had two glasses of Beaujolais by that time (though maybe Mother had said we should have had three), and I still needed to get Jerry to eat some strawberries. When I offered them, though, he slapped his tight belly and shook his head.

"I couldn't eat another bite," he said. "The tofu really did me in."

What should I have done—force-fed him strawber-ries and roast beef until he gagged? I did the best I could. If Mother was disappointed, I thought, then she would just have to live with that.

I led the way down into the cattery in my basement, the red teddy bunching up my rear as we descended the stairs.

"Here we come, Duchess," he sang, digging in his duffel bag for a thick wire brush and a bottle of cream rinse. "Tom Jones is playing our song."

We both giggled as he set down his bag and held his brush in the air. The Duchess sauntered across the room toward us, her long coat dragging on the floor, her copper eyes burning, as if she knew what I was after. Jerry reached down and lifted her onto the grooming table, his thin biceps shining under the overhead lights. He had on a red spandex tank top and bike shorts with blue trim, a sheen of sweat on his brow. I tugged at the strap of the teddy under my sweatshirt and held my breath.

As he held the Duchess's haunches, his fingers dipping down beneath her hips to feel the matted knots I'd described, I felt myself go dizzy with arousal. In the cage at the far end of the cattery, the Duchess's daughter Bea began to moan, the low growls rumbling in her throat. The Duchess broke free of Jerry's grip and ran for the cage, her red-and-white tail swishing in the air.

"Ooh," Jerry said, feeling for my hand, "I forgot you had a stud in the house."

We tiptoed over to the cage to watch. I wrapped my hand around Jerry's bicep and squeezed as the stud circled Bea, his coat shimmering as he lapped at the top of her head. A thin line of saliva lay across her forehead as she dug her tail into the bottom of the cage. Every time the stud advanced, lunging forward on his front paws, Bea let out a piercing howl. Over and over the stud circled, lifting his face in the air and sniffing.

"There's something very erotic about watching cats screw," Jerry said, and that was all I needed to go on. Before he could protest, I slid the sweatshirt over my head and threw it, in a ball, near his feet. One of my breasts bounced free of the underwire cups. Jerry stared down at the nipple and glanced back at the cage where the stud had finally managed to subdue Bea, his teeth in her neck, hips pumping.

"Oh, Maxi," he said, "this is one hell of a cat show," and then we were on the carpet, his lips pressed to mine, his long salty tongue dabbing at the corners of my mouth. I pulled him on top of me and slid my hands under the waistband of his bike shorts, the cats screaming above our heads. As we rocked our hips together I thought frantically of the strawberries and Beaujolais, how I'd forgotten the key props. But as I struggled to free myself from his grip, his bike shorts finally gave way and he entered me with a swiftness I'd never expected. In all the time I'd been imagining this scene, I realized I hadn't left much room for Jerry's reactions, never gave much thought to the possibility of his arousal.

As he thrust into me I thought of all the black-and-white baby pictures Mother had sent me in a white cardboard box, how each night I'd stared at them and closed my eyes against the guilt I felt at my own childlessness. My back scraped the carpet, the stud moaned low in his throat. The Duchess peered at us from the corner of the room, her copper eyes narrowed, back arched as if she were about to choke up a hairball.

The cats' screaming reached a fevered pitch. Jerry lifted his head from my shoulder and bit his lower lip, his eyes glazed over.

"Do it for Mother," I whispered, as he suddenly pulled out of me, his seed dripping down the tender part of my inner thigh.

"No!" I shrieked, reaching to pull him back in, but it was too late. The seed had spilled out of me and lay in a blob on the carpet. I wiped it away with a blue sponge and Clorox.

The cats quieted to a low purr. "What's new, pussycat?" Tom Jones sang. "Whoa-oh, whoa-oh, whoa..."

Later as we sat cross-legged on the kitchen floor, eating the strawberries and drinking Beaujolais out of paper cups, we laughed at the thought of the four of us coupling together, he and I on the carpet, with Bea and her stud in the cage above us.

"Here's to conception," he said, raising his paper cup in the air.

At the time, I'd laughed it off, knowing that Jerry had pulled out of me as an act of responsibility, that fatherhood was not something he'd banked on. When he left I examined myself in the mirror, hoping against hope that a bit of seed had been left in me before he'd frantically receded, leaving me with nothing to bring to Mother again but a litter of kittens and another sad story. I hoped Mother would understand that you couldn't feed red meat to just any man, that Jerry had his own tastes. Three weeks later I urinated on a stick and watched in amazement as the purple plus-sign appeared inside the tiny white box. I went down into the cattery and stroked Bea's fur as she perched triumphantly on the basement steps.

"It worked," I told Mother on the telephone.

I lifted Bea up to my face and kissed her open mouth. She raised her ears and stared deep into my eyes as if to tell me she knew she was pregnant, too, and could feel herself expanding—the swimming of new life.

"I knew it would," Mother said. "Aren't you glad you listened to your mother?"

The fact was, up until the moment during delivery when I'd recognized the infant's face as my own, I had been glad.

I was moved from the private room to isolation. The orderlies came for me at midnight and wheeled me out of the room and into a service elevator at the end of the hall.

"We want to keep the media out of this if we can help it," one of the orderlies whispered as the doors of the elevator opened. "It's not every day that a clone is born."

I just nodded and pulled the blankets up to my chin. Another team of orderlies followed close behind us, wheeling the incubator, covered in a dark mauve blanket. The halls were quiet as they steered us into an open room with machines in every corner. The infant whimpered; I wiped away tears with the back of my hand.

They settled us on either side of the room, lifted the blanket from the top of the incubator. Dr. Norton came in a side door and waved a gloved hand in the air at me. I tried to push myself up onto my elbows to peer into the incubator, but the orderly raised the side of my bed and clucked his tongue at me.

"Believe me," he said, "sometimes there are things you just shouldn't see."

They hooked us up to matching IVs and EKGs, swabbed my temples in ointment, and pasted electrodes to my head. Dr. Norton stood over the incubator and busied his hands inside. I felt a tingling through my chest and reached for my inhaler. The baby wheezed.

"Keep those bronchial tubes open," Dr. Norton

barked at the residents filing into the room. "One's asthmatic," he said, "and so, of course, is the other."

They placed an oxygen tent around me and seeped air through a long yellow tube that descended into the plastic sheeting. I wanted another look at her, to see that birthmark again, to look closely at the comma over her right eye that matched my own. The residents surrounded me, shone lights down my throat and into my eyes. I felt saggy and used, as if my body had emptied itself of promise.

"Where's Mother?" I said, trying to see over the elbows and fingers poking at me, to see if she was out there beyond the crowd, waving at me through the tent. But no one answered. I closed my eyes and waited for her to come and find me, to bring me a bottle of Beaujolais and let me start all over again, though I knew it was too late.

Although we were surrounded day and night by a team of round-the-clock specialists, the "baby" and I were alone in the world. This thought came to me as I lay there propped up with pillows and oversize sanitary napkins, the waxy oxygen tent above my head. The infant across the room lay swaddled in blankets, the blips of her heartbeat ringing in my ears. Mother had been barred from visiting us after the slap; and they wouldn't let Jerry in to see us for fear of our freakdom being leaked to the public before Norton and his team had carefully planned what they wanted to say.

"Telling the world you've cloned a human being is not something to be taken lightly," I heard Norton telling one of the specialists. "If we let this woman's mother get the best of us, there will be pandemonium. This is our show."

He came over and reached under the oxygen tent and lifted my gown over my left breast. With his thumbs he pressed into the fat of my nipple and squeezed. Bluish milk spat out and ran down the oxygen tent. The infant screamed.

"How did this happen?" I asked, wiping at my breast with the palm of my hand. "I did everything by the book, right down to the letter. Just ask my mother."

Dr. Norton pulled the oxygen tent down over me and shook his head.

"We're working to find that out," he said. "You're a one-in-a-million woman to have given birth to yourself."

I nodded and forced a little smile, but sadness welled up in my throat and held there. I shifted in bed, a pillow under my buttocks to ease the burning stitches between my legs. Across the room doctors swabbed ointment on the infant's scalp and pasted electrodes between the tufts of her reddish hair. Every movement I made was scribbled on clipboards, a camera above my bed hissing as it filmed every breath. I wanted to tell them that Mother hadn't meant to slap me, that she was just so overwhelmed by this sudden twist of fate that she'd struck out at me in her time of need. Sometimes mothers were known to do that. No Visitors signs glared out at me from every corner of the room.

I lay there under the oxygen tent and tried to piece together the events of the last nine months: sex with Jerry in the cattery on the carpet; rehearsing lines in the evenings with Mother; sifting through the endless array of baby pictures Mother had given to me, wondering whether the baby would look like me or Jerry, who Mother thought was unattractive despite his fine hands. Every night for nine months I'd studied those photos, which I'd had blown up and covered in plastic for safekeeping. I thought of Jerry's seed, how it had run down my leg in a thick knotty stream, which had landed in a small glob on the carpet, and how I'd run to wipe it up before one of the kittens got to it. I hadn't thought much about Jerry or the lovemaking, even during conception. The enjoyment of the act was incidental; only the results mattered. All I'd thought of were the black-and-white laminated features of my infancy, my dimpled thighs with Mother's hands around them, holding on as if she'd never let go.

Maybe in the act of wiping away Jerry's seed I'd wiped away any input he'd had. Or maybe breeding Bea while her mother, the Duchess, watched had been a grave mistake. Bea's stud had been her brother after all, the Duchess's son. The kittens had been show quality—I knew it the minute they were born—but doubts still plagued me. Maybe my quest for the perfect cat had gone too far. Even Jerry had suggested I lay off inbreeding for a while, saying that linebreeding was the way to go.

"Inbreeding may be the best way to get good quality," he said, "but think of the horror of all that incest."

I tortured myself with chicken-and-egg theories night and day. The infant wailed almost constantly, as if she, too, was tormented by these unanswerable questions. Her high, pitiful shrieks rang in the air between us. I couldn't see her face from across the room, and the doctors insisted I stay under the tent, with the electrodes up and down my arms and between my legs. Even if I were able to go to her, I knew there was little I could do, even as her mother, to comfort her.

I found myself unable to sleep, except when curled up in a fetal position. At times I wept uncontrollably, stopping only when they pulled more blood from my arms and fed me Jell-O from plastic spoons. The nurses tried to comfort me. They adjusted the oxygen level and brought me blankets, but warmth was not what I needed.

"I just want to be held," I moaned, rocking myself back and forth on the bed. "Please," I said, reaching for one nurse's arm, "I want my mother."

The nurse looked down at me with tears in her eyes. Her name was Selma. She was a redhead, like Mother, a buxom woman with cool hands and ice blue eyes. She lifted the tent and sat beside me on the bed.

"Oh, honey," she said, "you need a little mothering, is that it?"

I started to sob then, loud hiccuping snorts that reverberated against the walls. The infant wailed, too, our cries competing for volume. Selma stood up and unfolded one of the blankets, wrapped it tightly around my middle, pinning my arms to my sides. Then she lifted part of the blanket and draped it over my head like a hood.

"There, there," she said, and I settled down a bit and wet myself under the sheets. Selma set the oxygen tent back over my face and walked across the room to change the infant's diaper. Within minutes we were both content, nuzzled in our blankets, Selma keeping a watchful eye from her post at the door. In the haze just before sleep I realized how similar we really were. When the infant cried, I was racked by needs I'd never felt before. Her hunger pangs shot through my middle with a fierceness that no amount of Jell-O or chicken soup could satisfy. I wondered how much she shared my symptoms, my emotions. I wondered if she felt an emptiness in her middle, if her tiny uterus the size of a lima bean now felt the vacancy her birth had left in me. If she missed the smell of fresh litter the way I did, or sweet, milky kitten breath wafting up her nose. And if she wondered when Mother—my mother, *our* mother—would come to take us away.

The media converged on the hospital. I knew it would happen. The reporters showed up in droves, parking their vans, and shining lights and pointing cameras up toward my fifth-floor window. One news station even asked a sixty-five-year-old man being wheeled into the emergency room what he knew about my case.

"I don't know anything about any clone business," the man had said, clutching his chest. "I'm having a heart attack, for crying out loud."

Norton and his colleagues had come rushing in once it was clear the media had been informed. He turned on the television with the remote and flashed the other doctors a giant smile. After all his talk about keeping the media from getting wind of this, he didn't seem upset in the least. I half expected him to hand out cigars.

One of the orderlies—a young guy with a curly red beard, who seemed to feel a certain pity for me—helped raise my bed so that I could sit up and watch along with the others, though I really wanted to be left alone. Norton upped the dosage of Valium in my IV, and I watched the commotion through a cloud.

I glanced over at the incubator on the other side of the room and sighed. I wondered if the infant knew what a frenzy she'd set off in the world. She hadn't cried for hours, as if she'd sensed something was about to happen. Or perhaps she, too, felt herself sink into the Valium haze. We had sympathetic asthma; why wouldn't she feel the warmth of the Valium up her arms and through her tiny chest? I had a strange sense of foreboding—not foreboding exactly, because the Valium kept me in a state of numbness—but inevitability, as if this were part of the script Mother had written for me.

When the reporter came on, Norton shushed everyone and smoothed the front of his lab coat. The reporter was young and attractive, with wisps of blond hair that blew across his forehead in the breeze. I recognized him from the late-night local news. Jerry had a crush on him, in fact, and often stayed late to catch the news at my house when his television reception was out. Despite myself, I leaned forward on my elbows to get a better view.

"Today marks the beginning of what may well be the most important medical event in history. I'm standing outside MacArthur Hospital, where it appears the first human being has been cloned," the reporter said. "Our station received a telephone call this morning from a Mrs. Minnie Dublin, who claims to be the mother of the woman who delivered the clone," the reporter continued. "At this point little is known about the woman involved in the actual cloning. Her name, as we have it, is Maxine Dublin, owner of Bicolor Bliss, a cattery specializing in the breeding and selling of bicolor Persian cats. She is presently under the care of a Dr. Charles W.

Norton, an obstetrician at this hospital. So far we have
been unable to determine exactly how the clone was produced, though sources tell us the clone was delivered
through natural childbirth. Hospital officials have said
that we can expect a formal statement very soon, though
no exact time has been pinpointed. In the meantime we
will update our viewers as any new information becomes
available."

The other doctors slapped Norton on the back at the
mention of his name. I felt a chill run through me at
the thought of Mother calling a news station, telling the
world in a breathless voice how I'd let her down. What
would Jerry think now that he knew his seed had been
a mere afterthought? And that the man to expose him
was someone he'd fantasized about while eating Cheez
Doodles on my couch? I sat up even higher in bed and
cleared my throat to get Norton's attention, but his eyes
were fixed on the television.

The camera cut to a close-up of the entrance to the
hospital, a pair of orderlies in their yellow hospital
"scrubs," waving at the camera from behind the reporter's head. The reporter kept his gaze focused on the
camera, stray curls brushing his forehead. I imagined
Jerry wishing he could spray those curls with gel to keep
them tame.

"Once again, ladies and gentlemen, we interrupt
your regularly scheduled programming with the ground-
breaking news that the first human clone has been produced at MacArthur General Hospital. Although we are
not yet sure of the circumstances surrounding the
cloning, it has been confirmed—I repeat, it has been

confirmed—that a human clone was produced here sometime in the last few days."

The camera cut to the anchorman, who thanked the reporter, as he shuffled papers on his desk. Norton and the other doctors let out a loud whoop, which startled me. It must have startled the infant, too, because she squawked, then long hiccuping gasps came from her incubator. The anchorman droned on about the other news events of the day, promising in a tight voice to bring the audience further details as soon as they emerged.

I sat there in bed, staring at the backs of all of the lab coats. I thought of Mother being forced out of the hospital, the sharp look in her eyes when she'd slapped my face. The infant's wails echoed through the room, through my ears, down into my chest. I wished that someone would help her. A terrible sadness came over me, and I began to cry, softly at first, my grief deepening with every second. In a few minutes I was sobbing, my shoulders heaving in my white cotton gown as I tried to catch my breath; but Norton and his cohorts didn't seem to hear either of us. No one even bothered to turn around as our cries rang through the room.

Norton decided to hold a press conference from the front steps of the hospital. The chief of staff hired a public-relations adviser, Gus Vassy, who suggested the front steps as the best location for the interview, to afford the audience a shot of the hospital sign at all times. The news of the cloning would prove to be such a tremendous medical coup, Vassy said, that grants would soon pour in of their own accord. Vassy had apparently been the mastermind behind the selling of Desert Storm, I heard one of the orderlies say under his breath. The yellow ribbons had been Vassy's idea.

"We're talking Nobel Prize here, Charles," Vassy told Norton, "more research money than you can shake a stick at."

Norton took his responsibilities as spokesperson seriously. He wore a Pierre Cardin suit and a striking black necktie beneath his lab coat, his hair gelled around the ears. He didn't seem to be angry with Mother anymore, perhaps thinking she'd done them all a favor by leaking the story.

"This way, it comes from an outsider," I heard Vassy tell him, "and won't appear as if we're trying to capitalize."

Vassy turned to me then and smiled. "Which, of course, we're not, Maxine. This hospital has your and the infant's interests uppermost in its mind. I want you to be assured of that."

We stood at the window, peering down at the crowds of reporters below. They aimed their cameras at the venetian blinds of my window, hoping for a glimpse of my stringy red hair, my pale freckled arm bruised by needle pricks. Despite the Valium, my heart pounded in my chest at the sight of all those cameras; the infant's cardiac monitor showed her own pulse racing.

"I don't care who knows," I said, as I stepped away from the window. "Everyone makes mistakes. But what about my mother? When is she coming back?"

Vassy pinched my sleeve with his manicured hand and laughed.

"Mistake? You've made a miracle. As for your mother," he said leaning in closer, "we're all on the same side in this, of course. We'll get her in to see you. Right now we've had to tighten security. It will only be a little while."

With that, Vassy called to Norton from across the room.

"It's show time, Charles," he said; and before I could say anything else, Norton was off with his entourage, a group of armed guards holding the door open for them and then closing it behind them.

I padded back to my bed, glancing over at the incubator. The closed-circuit camera above my head recorded my every move. I tucked my hair behind my ears and smiled up at the camera's lens. My heart rate had slowed, and I could see from the infant's monitor that hers had as well. I wondered if she could feel what I was feeling, whether the same sense of anxiousness and dread came over her whenever Norton and his team came into the room. Once they were gone, we were calm again. Perhaps I ought to offer to hold her when he returned, but the thought of cradling an expelled part of myself sent chills through me. I sat with my arms folded over my chest as Norton's face appeared on the screen, bigger than life.

Flanked by two men in lab coats, whom I couldn't recall seeing before, Norton cleared his throat and looked straight into the camera. Beneath him in white letters appeared his name and title: CHARLES W. NORTON, M.D., OBSTETRICS AND GYNECOLOGY. A dozen microphones were thrust in his face.

"On behalf of the medical staff at MacArthur

General," he began in a booming voice, sending a piercing reverb through the microphones, "I am pleased to announce that we have achieved a human clone—a female—from the ovum of a healthy thirty-four-year-old Persian cat breeder. Mother and clone are resting comfortably as we speak. Both specimens are being monitored for vital signs and have undergone extensive testing to determine the facts of their exact genetic makeups. So far we have witnessed several phenomena, including simultaneous attacks of asthma. Though we cannot offer specifics as to the actual procedure, we are willing to take other questions from the press at this time."

Selma came over and adjusted the electrodes pasted to my chest and belly.

"Who is this 'we'?" she whispered. "It's *your* baby they're talking about."

One of the doctors shushed her and turned up the volume. I didn't say a word.

"Do you mean to say the clone was produced?" one reporter asked. "Was it produced under laboratory conditions? Will there be others?"

Norton smiled and pointed to the reporter.

"One question at a time, please," he said, puffing out his chest. "And no, we have not ruled out the possibility of others at this time."

All at once the reporters began shouting questions: What did this mean to the world of genetics? Did Norton think cloning was a moral issue? How would this affect the balance of nature? Would this mean greater independence from male bondage for lesbians dying to be mothers? How did it feel to have discovered the forbidden fruit of biotechnology? And finally, what was the reaction of the mother in this case?

Norton cleared his throat.

"We cannot think of the woman in this case as a normal mother," Norton said, reaching up with one hand to smooth his hair back. "This was not a traditional birth."

"Then how will this affect the patient's medical insurance?" one of the reporters called out. "What do HMOs have to say about covering a birth like this one?"

For a minute Norton and the others laughed, until Vassy stepped forward to announce there would be no more questions.

Selma sat beside me on the bed and shook her head. She didn't look at me, just reached for my hand and held it. I stared at her, at the glints in her red hair, and wondered what Mother would say when she returned, when she found out how desperately I'd failed her.

"I knew I wasn't a real mother," I whispered to Selma, squeezing her hand and closing my eyes against the light of the television. "Motherhood doesn't feel like this."

Selma reached for the remote control and switched off the television. She sat there holding my hand for a long time; and with my eyes closed, I could almost pretend that it was Mother sitting there with me—holding my hand through this as she had through everything else in my life—as if she hadn't abandoned me in the face of lights and cameras to hear her name on the nightly news.

Norton could lie all he wanted about the circumstances of the birth; I didn't care about that. I'd let him take the credit for "producing" this infant, if that was what he wanted. I certainly didn't want to be the one responsible.

Jerry was finally allowed to visit, after a tabloid reported rumors that Mother had threatened to break the baby and me out of the hospital. Mother's face appeared on the cover, her rouge striped like war paint over her cheeks, her teeth bared. Beneath her photo were the words: MOTHER'S WAR CRY: LET MY DAUGHTERS GO! One of the nurses slipped the tabloid under my dinner tray one night, though Norton had given strict orders that he had to approve any media coverage to come my way. I nearly choked on my mashed potatoes when I saw Mother's face blown up on the front of the paper, a small picture of Fergie in the bottom right-hand corner with a new hairdo and a polka-dot dress. At first I thought the *s* in "daughters" was a typo, but then I realized what Mother was driving at. I hid the tabloid under my pillow and dreamed of Mother and Fergie coming for us, their red hair flowing in the wind.

If they let Jerry in, the doctors reasoned, this might placate Mother for a time. Jerry could report back to Mother about our condition and try to keep her quiet. Besides, Norton had been told by a civil-rights attorney that he could not keep me against my will.

"We want you to be happy here, Maxine," Norton said, when he told me he'd allow Jerry to visit. "We want you to stay for as long as you'd like."

I sat up in bed and pried my arms out from under the blankets. A guard had been posted at the door. I'd agreed that it was necessary to keep the reporters out, but I couldn't understand why Mother was still barred from visitation.

"What about my mother?" I asked. "When will she be coming in?"

Dr. Norton tapped at my arm and pressed his fingers to my wrist to check my pulse. He scribbled numbers on my chart and refused to look at me. "She's in a highly emotional state," he said. He shook his head and stood up from the bed, staring down at me. "Twice she's assaulted members of the staff and she says that there's nothing we can do to keep her from this infant. Once we've completed observations, we'll decide what to do where your mother's concerned. Right now there are much more important things to consider than your mother."

I sank down into the bed and closed my eyes. Images of Mother with her fists drawn ran through my head, her red hair flying, rouge like flames surging up her cheek. I knew how terribly angry she must have been to have been kept out like this, to have the door slammed in her face. I imagined her pinning a security guard to the wall, moving her hand in a flurry of slaps across his face. Maybe they were right to keep her away.

"The father's the one who's important at this point," he said. "If he can be called 'the father' in a case like this."

Before I could answer him, he crossed the room and peered into the incubator, cooing to the infant in a low voice. From a scientific standpoint, he was right, I supposed. Jerry was the one to study. He'd supplied the seed—or failed to—after all. But it was Mother who had orchestrated the conception; it was Mother who had given me the road map of childbirth. Mother had always had all the answers.

Jerry arrived surrounded by a team of specialists, with security guards bringing up the rear. He'd cut his hair and dyed it in short blond spikes, with a long red curl that hung low on his forehead. He smiled when he saw me, and I started to cry right away, which sent the infant into a fit of wailing that even Selma couldn't calm.

"Maxi," he called over the screams, "what in the world has happened?" He rushed forward, breaking free of the guards. I held my arms out as he tore the oxygen tent off me, clucking his tongue at the electrodes taped up and down my arms. The tears streamed down my face as I reached for him, needles pulling at my skin.

"I thought you'd never come," I said, and went to wrap my arms around him; but he ducked his head and went straight for my hair.

"Good god," he said, running his fingers over my scalp. "What in the world have they done to your hair?"

I struggled to say something, but he shushed me and tilted my head to one side. "I saw a picture on the news and I said to myself, they've got to have the wrong woman, that can't be my Maxi. Her hair is so much brighter than that." He took fistfuls of my curls and then let the hair fall limp on both sides. "We've got to highlight as soon as possible. The redness has just dulled away like you've been sitting with your head in the sand."

Since the birth, I hadn't bothered to look in the mirror at all, given the fact that my own image was alive and in diapers. The infant bawled.

"You've disturbed the baby," one of the doctors said. All at once they huddled around the incubator, the camera on the ceiling buzzing as it moved in for a close-up. Jerry sat frozen for a moment, his hands falling to his sides as the enormity of fatherhood seemed to hit him all at once. He reached out for my hand and squeezed it, my shoulders crunching as I struggled to sit up taller in the bed. We leaned against each other as one of the doctors lifted the infant out of the incubator and onto a small metal table and poked at the tufts of her reddish hair with his gloved hands.

"Is that her?" Jerry asked, turning toward me, his eyes frighteningly blue against the shock of the red curl on his forehead. "Is that our baby?"

I reached up to stroke the curl and sighed. He took a deep breath and puffed out his shoulders the way he had when I'd met him that day at the cat show and he was given a blue ribbon for grooming. There was no gentle way to tell him, I thought, no kind way to shoot a hole in his pride. I looked away from him and blurted it out.

"She's a baby," I said, rubbing his palm with one of my thumbs, "but we can't say for sure that she's ours."

His eyes drifted over my face, to the birthmark over the right eye and down my neck to my engorged breasts, beneath the white paper gown, the curdled milk pressing at me from inside like a betrayal.

"What do you mean?" he asked. "You don't really believe this clone business." He lowered his voice and looked right into my eyes. "I was there that night, Maxi. I heard Tom Jones singing our song. I know."

For the first time since I'd known him I saw a flicker of jealousy in his eyes. For a fleeting moment I was glad, thinking of the times we'd walked down the street together when I was pregnant and I'd caught him stealing glances at men in tank tops and walking shorts. But then I felt a stab of guilt at having duped him to start with. He'd taken the news of the pregnancy in his stride. In fact, it had brought us closer together.

He moved his hands to his lap and scowled at me. His eyes had never looked so blue and wide. His mouth hung open, lips trembling.

I felt the warmth of Valium come up through my chest. It left a tinny aftertaste in my mouth.

"It's the truth," I said softly, "as crazy as it sounds. She's not yours. She's mine."

For a long time he said nothing, just sat with his head turned toward the incubator and watched as they lowered the infant back inside. The blond spikes shone so brightly, I wondered if he'd changed shampoos. When I reached for his hand, he pulled it away.

"It's not what you think," I said. "Something very odd has happened. Something terribly wrong."

When he didn't answer me, I kept on.

"Maybe you were right, I should have stopped all the inbreeding a long time ago. I shouldn't have gone so far. But you know how close I came, I almost had Cat of the Year. It was the only way to get good quality. You said so yourself."

When he didn't respond, I went on.

"As for that night, I only did what Mother said; I only did what she told me to do. Maybe I shouldn't have played the Tom Jones record. I was supposed to give you roast beef, you know, but I made tofu instead. I wanted

it all to be perfect, don't you see? I thought everything
would be all right if I did it her way."

He just sat there on the bed, his shoulders slumped. I
reached forward and plucked at one of the blond spikes,
but he still didn't respond. Finally I sank back against
the pillows and sighed.

Dr. Norton came over from where he'd been standing
and pulled a chair up beside us.

"Of course there's one way you can satisfy yourself in
that department," he said, squeezing Jerry's knee. "We
have all the medical facts that we need. This is one miracle woman, cloning herself before our very eyes. She's
made herself all over again, if you can believe it." At this
he blew out a long breath as if he'd forgotten there was
no cigarette in his mouth.

He chuckled and slapped Jerry on the back.

"But," Dr. Norton went on, "for a man of your per-
suasion, I can see why you might want to put your mind
at ease. Minnie tells me you're a little unsure of yourself
in that department—and with all the Joe Namath commercials, and now well, we have our evidence."

With that he chucked me under the chin and headed
back over to the incubator. Jerry sat up straight and let
one of his hands drop between his legs. I thought of all
the times he'd told me how he loved the slope of a
woman's back and yet thrilled at bunches of muscles just
the same. The day I told him I was pregnant, he'd said,
had been a landmark for him. Although we'd never slept
together again, he said he'd loved the act of lovemaking
itself, complete with cat screams and all.

"Does he mean what I think he means?" he asked. He

wiped his hands on the front of his tank top and held his shoulders high. "You've made yourself a clone, and my manhood's as useless as a wooden nickel."

I smiled at him and took his hand in mine. His bracelets jingled.

"Is it true what they say about Mother?" I asked. "Is she really that angry?"

Jerry nodded.

"I've never seen her this pissed, not even when the tabloids printed those pictures of Fergie poolside with her toes being sucked. Compared to this," he said, "the Fergie episode was a day at the beach."

I remembered how grief stricken Mother had been when those photos surfaced. She'd marched down to the grocery store and bought up all the tabloids, burned them one by one in the kitchen sink, her chest racked with sobs. I felt a deep sadness at the memory. The tears came all of a sudden and I let them drop on the front of my gown. The infant wailed in sympathy.

"Maxi," he said softly, leaning forward, "look at me."

The infant's screams grew louder and louder. Why weren't they doing something for her? The doctors just stood there watching us and scribbling on their clipboards. I let out a loud snort as I tried to catch my breath, to stop the crying for both our sakes.

"What?" I said, lifting my head to look at him.

He reached forward and wiped a tear from my eye. Then, without looking back at me, he walked over to the incubator, leaned down, and pressed his face to the glass. Dr. Norton patted him on the back.

"It's really her," I heard Jerry say. "It's a little Maxi."

After a time he came back to my bedside and reached inside his pocket. He slipped a piece of paper into the palm of my hand and kissed me on the forehead.

"Let's go show you those results, old boy," Norton said as he grabbed Jerry by the upper arm. He eyed the piece of paper, but I stuffed it inside my gown, and he pulled Jerry toward the door.

"I'll take care of the kittens," Jerry called as Dr. Norton pushed him out the double doors into the hall. "You keep a lookout for your mother. She's really upset."

He waved at me as the doors closed behind him. I reached inside the gown and held the piece of paper in my fist, watching through the portal in the door. His blond spikes bobbed up and down as they hurried him down the hall. When the infant finally stopped screaming, I unfolded the piece of paper and slid it under the pillow, lifting the corner of the pillow up to read it.

"She's mine as much as yours," it said in Mother's fine scrawling print.

For a minute I wasn't sure what to do. The doctors stared at me from different angles of the room, their pens scraping charts. I had still hoped that something would happen to make everything right again, for Mother to rush in and take over the way she always had. Yet, as much as I yearned for her, I began to feel afraid of her wrath and that somehow I was going to pay for reneging on our deal. I hadn't given her a grandchild as I'd promised; I'd given her a piece of myself, which was what I'd been doing all my life. We both knew that had never been enough, no matter how much I'd continued to give.

I decided to call the infant Millicent because the doctors said she needed a name. The media had begun calling her Baby X, which confused people because of its similarity to Baby M. This clone was no offspring of a surrogate, reporters said. The least I could do was give her a name before they made one up themselves. It seemed foolish to call her anything at the time because I felt no connection with her at all except biologically. There was no love there, no emotion, just flesh and bone and body.

Millicent seemed as close a name to Mother's and mine as I could find without duplication, and I wanted a name Mother would like. She was Minnie and I was Maxi—we were a couple of sanitary pads, my friends used to joke, though I'd often wondered why I was made to be the larger of the two. Millicent seemed somewhere in the middle.

I lay propped up on pillows, wondering if Mother would approve of the name. Electrodes pinched my scalp to monitor brain waves, and a belt over my middle produced a constant sonogram of my ovaries, shown on a large screen above my bed. Instead of hearing about my life on television, I watched the slow spinning of my eggs on a black-and-white screen. They pulsed and swirled as if they knew somehow that I was watching, turning this way and that in the flat of my ovaries, as if trying to give me a better view. I couldn't help thinking how much Mother would have enjoyed this, how she needed to be in on everything. Missing out on close-ups of my ova would cut her straight to the core.

We'd always been close; I was the only child. When I was a little girl, we looked so much alike people would say it was as if my mother's face had been brought down to size and pressed over my own. We had the same porcelain skin, freckles over the bridge of the nose and down the slopes of our arms. Even our hair was always in synch. When I was in high school my red hair had softened into a shade of strawberry blond; Mother had hers dyed to match.

As mother and daughter we'd shared everything: secrets, makeup, romance novels. My friends were always friends with Mother. When we were teenagers, my best friend, Anita, and I would ride in the car with Mother, singing Top 40 songs and talking about boys we liked.

And Mother had included me in her life just the same way. Although she'd never actually had a boyfriend after my father left, she'd occasionally go on a spurt with the personal ads. Her ad read:

> *DWF seeks man who likes redheads,*
> *the royal family, and teenage girls.*
> *Smokers and banjo players need not reply.*

This last part was a reference to my departed father, of course. He had played the banjo in a local group called the Mummers and had tobacco-stained teeth. Though I remembered little of him, Mother assured me the smell of Camels and the tinny sound of a banjo were the only things that remained with her after he'd left. She'd been repulsed by the permanent indentation of strings on his picking fingers. His leaving her didn't pain her the way it might have other women, she always said. All she'd ever wanted was a baby.

"I was ready for him to go," she said. "He was always in the way. I only regret I didn't get more daughters out of him before he left."

Inevitably the ads would cause some confusion with the men who responded, because of Mother's lack of good syntax. Many of the men, who met with us in coffee shops—I was always dragged along for the initial dates—hoped to score with a redheaded teenager, not a flaming-haired woman approaching forty with crow's-feet and a daughter for a best friend.

Images of these men floated through my mind as I watched my eggs turning on the screen, the Valium warming my chest and head.

Selma came in to fetch my morning urine sample and to have me sign the birth certificate with Millicent's name on it. I propped myself up in bed, loosening some of the electrodes on my scalp. Selma laughed as the wires popped free, and handed me the birth certificate and a fountain pen.

"Some women have all the luck," she said, and smiled up at the image of my ovaries. "Not only to have the whole world know all about you but to have your womanhood up close and personal on a TV screen."

I held the fountain pen poised above the paper as Selma reached over to reattach the wires. A shock of her red hair hung down over one eye, and I imagined Mother outside the hospital, shut out once and for all.

With a quick glance I saw that father was listed as "unknown." Millicent's measurements were carefully typed in the boxes. I had pressed the pen to the paper and scrawled my signature, when we suddenly heard a terrible noise coming from the incubator.

A horrible stretching sound, like the creaking of a wood floor, came from the corner of the room. I felt a sharp stab in my middle and cried out, grabbing hold of Selma's hand. The room echoed the sounds of splitting, a tearing of paper, the ripping of cloth. Something squeezed at my ribs and arms, then moved down through my legs. My head swam.

"Call Dr. Norton! Stat!" Selma shouted to one of the residents, who was sitting outside the door reading a car magazine. "Something's happened to the baby!"

Alarms sounded through the room as Millicent started to scream. I held my hands over my ears and huddled under the blankets. Part of me wanted to run over to see what had happened, but my limbs felt rubbery, as if I couldn't get up if I tried. The screen of my eggs went black.

Dr. Norton came tearing in with an unlit cigarette bobbing between his lips, a trail of residents in lab coats following close behind.

"Are you all right, Maxine?" he called, but didn't wait for my answer. I nodded at his back as he lifted the incubator. Selma stood in the corner biting her nails, her bangs hanging low over her eyes.

"Good god!" he yelled as his hands grabbed handfuls of his gelled hair. "She's grown!"

The room fell silent. I inched myself up to sit and let my legs hang over the side of the bed. This was not the time to look away, I thought. Think of what Mother would do. Pressing myself up with my hands, I stood for the first time since giving birth, my legs shaking from the coldness of the tile floor.

Dr. Norton reached in with both hands and lifted Millicent out of the incubator. A collective gasp filled the room. I shuffled toward the incubator, the crowd of doctors blocking my view. My heart raced in my chest, blood thumped in my ears. I reached forward and grabbed one of the doctors by the shoulder, pushing him out of the way.

"Let me see!" I shrieked.

One of the doctors tried to steer me back toward the bed, but I pushed him back, the electrodes hanging loose from strands of my ratty hair. I took a deep breath and held it as Dr. Norton turned toward me.

Millicent lay in a torn receiving blanket, her diaper ripped at the seams, exposing a juicy thigh. Her eyes were open and she gurgled a bit in her throat, the red tufts of hair now a full crown. In a matter of minutes she'd grown to the size of a six-month-old. For a moment the baby's eyes caught mine; the birthmark over her right eye twitched in recognition. The image of myself at six months flashed before me, a photo Mother had of me with my diaper hanging loose at my hips, a receiving blanket falling away from me, just before a bath.

"Wait till the press hears about this," someone said. The last thing I saw were faces smiling at me as I hit the floor.

When I came to, the room was dark, the screen above my head hissing static. The electrodes had been removed, and I felt the warmth of a sedative up and down my arms. I blinked several times, trying to get my vision to come clear. The room was quiet except for a low humming from the far end of the room, where a silhouette stood against the venetian blinds. My mouth felt cottony and bruised, my arms and legs heavier than I'd ever felt them before.

Suddenly the person turned and reached inside the incubator.

"There, there," the voice whispered. "Mommy's here now."

I tried to pull myself up onto my elbows but couldn't muster the strength. It must be Selma, I thought, coming for a late-night feeding. Images of a growing Millicent flashed in my mind, but I couldn't remember whether it had all been a dream. Maybe none of it had happened, I thought as the silhouette lifted the infant in her arms and carried her away. If I could relax into the dream, then maybe I'd wake up and find myself whole again, the constant flashing of bulbs outside my sealed window would finally stop, and all the reporters camped downstairs would disappear. I'd open my eyes and find myself back in the cattery changing litter and holding the Duchess in my lap. Life would be the way it used to be, before the pregnancy and birth, before all of Mother's hopes had been dashed.

I lay back against the pillows and heard the tug of a window being pulled open. Moonlight flooded the far end of the room, a sheen of redness spilling into the light.

"Mother," I whispered, craning my neck, "is that you?"

But there was no answer, only the sharp slamming of the window as it fell closed and a laugh that rang through the darkened room.

4

CLONE KIDNAPPED, GRANDMOTHER SUSPECT

Winfield, NY (AP)—The world's first human clone was reported missing from MacArthur General Hospital at approximately 3 A.M. Hospital officials claim the female clone, who at press time is known only as Millicent, was last seen late last evening in a highly guarded isolated room at the hospital in upstate New York.

Dr. Charles W. Norton, the obstetrician who delivered the clone by vaginal birth, reported the alleged kidnapping to police and federal officials early this morning. Norton told police he was about to announce yet another phenomenon to the public, when the clone was stolen from the hospital before the news could be broken.

When asked about the nature of the newest phenomenon, Norton said cryptically, "She grows."

Federal officials believe that the infant's grandmother, Minnie J. Dublin, is responsible for the kidnapping, though police have no leads yet as to Ms. Dublin's whereabouts. Hospital staff and personnel claim that the woman was barred from the hospital because of erratic behavior shortly after the birth of her granddaughter. Apparently the news that her granddaughter was actually a clone came as a shock to her. In the words of one hospital employee, "The lady freaked."

Norton, who brought the news of the clone to the world in a press conference and who was recently rumored to have been placed on the short list for the Nobel Prize in genetics, was reported to be under heavy sedation following the loss of the clone.

Dr. Hans Glimmer, a prominent biotechnologist at UCLA who has openly criticized the possibility that the infant now known as Millicent is in fact a clone, expressed further doubts about the reliability of Norton's latest report.

"What little we know of clones precludes their simply growing in leaps and bounds," Glimmer said. "This is a fairy tale foisted on the public to frighten them with the possibilities of DNA duplication."

The mother of the clone, Maxine Dublin, a thirty-four-year-old Persian cat breeder and owner of Bicolor Bliss, a cattery in Winfield, is still residing at the hospital, though she could not be reached for comment.

Police officials describe the suspect as a red-haired Caucasian woman in her mid-fifties. She was last seen driving a maroon station wagon, with a large stroller visible in the backseat.

Officials have created a telephone line for any information regarding Dublin and the missing clone. Anyone with pertinent information is urged to call 1-800-SEE-CLON (733-2566).

I realized the next morning that Mother had stolen the baby. I didn't need any newspaper to tell me. She'd been waiting for the perfect opportunity to sneak in at night, had been planning it since being expelled for slapping me the day Dr. Norton had broken the news. It was as if Millicent's magnificent growth spurt had spurred her on, as if she'd somehow sensed that time was running out for her and she'd better seize the infant now. Of course, it was also possible that she'd been the one to sedate Norton. He lay prostrate in a hospital bed, his eyes glazed, though I'd overheard one of the guards say that he'd been known to medicate himself when the pressure of hospital duty became too much for him to bear.

"When the going gets tough," the guard whispered, "the doc scores some Valium."

To assure the hospital that something this drastic hadn't happened on his watch, Gus Vassy assembled all of the security guards and fired a barrage of questions at them.

"Which one of you told her the infant doubled its size? How did she know to kidnap her now, when we are on the brink of yet another medical phenomenon? Who let that woman get past them, when we all knew she was capable of something like this?"

The guards stood with their heads bowed, and delivered the same version of the story, one at a time. Apparently a woman had traipsed past security, dressed in a nurse's uniform, with a stethoscope around her neck. The security guards had thought it was Selma and waved to her between hands of pinochle while she made her way through the double doors and into our isolated room.

"We thought she was coming in to check on the baby," one of the guards said. "She looked as much like Selma as anyone I've ever seen."

The orderlies stripped down the incubator and my bed, and entered the sheets and blankets into hospital evidence. Guards pasted long sheets of aluminum foil over all of the windows to prevent photographers from scaling the walls and trying to snap photos. I sat alone in a chair, staring at my warped reflection in the aluminum foil, wondering where Mother might have gone.

One of the residents leaned forward and whispered in my ear, " 'Hell hath no fury like a mother scorned.' " He tied the ends of his mask behind his head and laughed at me through gauze.

I sat silently while Norton and Vassy argued whether the hospital should sue for damages, since Mother had robbed them of their most precious source of research. Vassy paced back and forth, fists clenched, jaw set tight. Apparently Norton had just sent for the foremost growth specialist in the country, who was due to arrive in the afternoon to test the infant's pituitary gland in comparison with my own. The findings were to be discussed on that week's special edition of *Hindsight* with Sophie Sussman and Hy Brown.

"The hospital will be disgraced," Vassy said, "when this man gets off the plane and finds that not only is there no growth spurt to test but the clone has done a disappearing act right under our noses."

The throbbing between my legs had finally eased and my breasts seemed to have shrunk down to size. Even without Valium, I was calm, no longer driven by the urge to shove something inside myself to fill the emptiness. Mother had taken it out from under me.

As I sat listening to various theories on what could have caused the infant to double her size in a matter of minutes, I felt a complete dissociation from my body. When I looked down at my hands, they seemed long and strange, the half-moons of my fingernails flecked with pieces of cuticle I could not remember chewing away. Norton had once said that the cloning could very well be my body's way of throwing off mutations of itself, which would account for the rapid growth rate. Then, maybe this new me was trying to catch up to the real me, I thought.

While Vassy barked orders to the hospital staff, I shuffled over to my bed and sat down. With my hands folded in my lap, I picked at the dead ends of my cu-ticles, tearing bits of them off, until the nail beds were red and swollen. Although they throbbed, the pain was distant, like a scream from far away. I wiped my hands on the bedsheet, leaving a thin line of blood behind.

Suddenly I became aware of someone saying my name.

"Maxine," one of the doctors said, taking my hand and patting it, his fingers tapping deliberately on my torn cuticles, "if you knew it was your mother in here taking the baby, why didn't you stop her?"

Without looking away from him I shook my head and pulled my hand back to my lap. How could he possibly understand what it was like to be a mother or a daughter—or a mother and a daughter squared—to repeat the same mistakes instead of giving your mother hope? That's what children were for, and I'd gone and botched it despite all my best intentions.

"I don't know," I said softly, bowing my head and staring down at my feet. "Because she's the mother, I guess."

The doctors groaned. Vassy opened the lid to the empty incubator and shook his head. With his index finger, he traced a pattern inside the incubator and cleared his throat.

"We'll find a way to get her back," he said more to himself than any of the others. "We can't allow the hospital to be damaged like this."

They talked into the night about the best plan to get the baby back, how to save the hospital from humiliation and still get to the bottom of the "Rapidly Growing Clone" (or RGC, as they began to call her), how to bring Norton out of his shock. Norton was particularly photogenic, they agreed. The camera loved him, even though he knew little, if anything, about genetic engineering.

"He was supposed to be on Sophie Sussman, for Christ's sake," someone said. "Sussman has even confessed that she's a fan."

When the room was quiet, I read the newspaper

article over and over again. Even as I stared at the words and pictures that described myself and my life with Mother, I felt utterly abandoned.

As I lay there, I thought about the first litter the Duchess had given birth to. After I'd shipped the white-tipped Persians over from England, I'd studied genetic charts on the best way to cross the Duchess's recessive piebald gene to produce red-and-white stunners just like herself. When the kittens were born, Mother had plucked one of them from the nipple to stare at its red-and-white face. Before I could warn Mother, the Duchess hissed and tore a streak down Mother's arm, a red line that would swell up in a purple welt. Mother had been so surprised that she nearly dropped the kitten, but I scooped it into my hands and set it back among the other squirming bodies. Even now I thought of the look in the Duchess's eyes when Mother took one of her babies away, the terrifying quickness of her claws.

I pulled the blanket tight around my shoulders, the way Selma had swaddled me, and let the newspaper fall open on my lap. No matter how hard I tried, I couldn't bring myself to feel that same fierceness at the thought of Mother stealing the baby from under my nose. What got me, what hurt me straight to the core, was not that she'd stolen my baby but that she'd left me here alone.

With the infant gone and no new leads on Mother's whereabouts, several reporters took to the streets in the vicinity of hospital to assess public opinion.

When asked whether they felt it was medically necessary to keep me in the hospital now that the clone was gone, people responded in a variety of ways.

"I guess if they can't get the baby back, they have no other choice, right?" said a trucker from New Jersey as he waited at a red light. "I mean, what if this never happens again? They'll have to take more of her—whatcha-call-em?—eggs and try it again."

An elderly woman in an overcoat smiled sadly at the camera and looked down at her shoes.

"I'd do it if they asked me," she said softly, "now that I'm widowed." She smiled at the camera, the cataracts clouding the blueness of her eyes. "It would be nice to have some company."

Several women in long flowered dresses staged a protest outside the hospital and demanded I be released.

"Anyone who has given birth knows that a doctor takes everything she has," said a woman in sunglasses and walking shorts. "Give Maxine back her life."

Since Norton remained somewhat disoriented, I was able to persuade the staff that I be released on my own recognizance. They had all the information that they needed, so there was no further need to keep me. Without the infant, this could border on a hostage situation, I told Vassy. My eggs had been captured in freeze-frames at various stages, a videotape playing the inner workings of my fallopian tubes day and night. Besides, I said, the only one, who could find Mother was me.

"If all else fails," the chief of staff said, pumping my hand as we said our good-byes, "we can always try to get you to do it again."

I just laughed and thanked him for doing his best to keep the reporters at bay. He'd arranged for twenty-four-hour guards at my house, and for a decoy to distract reporters when I left the hospital. The last thing I wanted was to give my fragmentation any more attention than it had already had.

"Mother will turn up," I said, though I felt the uncertainty in my voice even as I said the words. "She's always been known to come through in a pinch."

Several of the orderlies asked me to autograph bedsheets for them on the chance that either one of my selves ever became famous or decided to write her memoirs. I obliged, scrawling my name in black Magic Marker, and thanked them for the boxes of sanitary pads they'd given me for good luck. As I turned away they called out my name and waved.

"I hope you find yourself, whoever you are!" they shouted.

A security guard led me to the service elevator, where I could exit the hospital without being spotted. Jerry would be waiting for me in the back parking lot while the decoy left from the front entrance. The doors to the elevator opened, revealing Selma standing there with her finger pressed to her lips. I slipped inside and quickly pressed the button to the basement. The doors closed with a bang, and the elevator began its rattling descent.

"I thought you might want to have these," Selma said, handing me the torn receiving blanket and diapers stamped with the hospital logo. "If anyone should have them, it's you. You're the one who's been taken away."

The doors opened to the basement. I could see Jerry waiting at the end of the dark hallway, the blond spikes now dyed black. Before the doors closed, Selma wrapped her arms around me and squeezed. Her rouge left a dark red stripe on my white blouse.

"Maxi," Jerry called, waving his arms, "I'm over here."

I held the receiving blanket tight to my chest and whispered a thank-you; but the doors had snapped closed behind me. I walked down the hallway, my chest sinking as Mother's words echoed in my mind: "Once you have a baby," she'd always said, "you're never just you again."

The guards had formed a wall around the front of the house by the time we arrived. For the time being, the decoy had taken the reporters on a wild-goose chase, so I was guaranteed to have at least a few hours of relative peace. I'd given the hospital permission to search the house as part of our agreement, provided they didn't disturb the Duchess, who was due to give birth any day.

Mother would not come to my house so soon, I knew. She'd wait until the excitement died down before resurfacing. After years of studying Fergie, she knew there were ways of slipping about undetected. There had long been stories of Fergie giving the royal slip to her bodyguards, much to the queen's dismay. Rumor had it that Fergie occasionally tied back her red hair in a blue kerchief and passed herself off as a commoner. Following Fergie's lead, Mother would know what to do.

With a black wig and a shopping cart filled with Pampers, Mother could pass as anyone's grandmother. She'd visit juvenile furniture stores and order layettes in every color of the rainbow. Then she'd come for me in the night, and together we'd decide how to raise the new me. We'd done everything together, I thought. This wasn't something she'd attempt on her own, no matter how angry she'd been at being shut out of the hospital.

Dr. Norton would write her a glowing letter of apology, which she would laminate and hang on her wall. She'd dye her hair a pale chiffon in celebration of the new me.

"There's no trace of your mother here, ma'am," one of the guards said. "We searched the whole place, top to bottom. Nothing in there but a bunch of longhaired cats and maternity clothes."

Jerry brushed past them into the kitchen and dropped my overnight bag on the floor. I held the torn blanket and diapers under my sweatshirt. As the security guards moved aside to let us through, I pressed the shredded Pampers against my bare skin and couldn't help smiling to myself as I remembered the night that I'd hidden the teddy under this same sweatshirt. If only I'd had the good sense to keep that sweatshirt on, I wouldn't be motherless and childless now.

Since they'd finished searching the house—including under the sink and inside the kitchen cabinets, even going so far as to sift through litter boxes—Jerry escorted the guards to the door. The most they'd found was a clump of red hair in a wire brush, which they thought was a great coup but which I quickly squashed, pointing to my own head of thick strawberry curls.

I stood watching Jerry at the door as he leaned forward and brushed his arm against one of the younger guards, who had a heavy blond mustache. He laid a hand on the guard's shoulder and moved his lips near the young man's ear.

"You tell Norton whatever you have to," he whispered. "Let him think the baby's gone to Timbuktu. We've got to find this baby ourselves. Maxi doesn't know how badly she's going to need it."

The guard winked at Jerry and shook his hand. Their shoulders touched as they said good-bye. My stomach flipped over on itself in a squeeze of jealousy. Seeing him talking so closely with another man always unnerved me, but the fact that they were talking about me in the third person—as if I weren't there—underlined all the emptiness I'd been feeling since Millicent's birth.

Once the guards assumed their posts outside the house, Jerry and I went to the cattery without another word to each other. On the way down the stairs he took my hand. His fingers were cool and smooth, his palm moist. I gripped his hand and thought of him poised above me that night, cats howling above our heads. Mother's voice in my ear.

"Don't be alarmed when you see her," Jerry said, stepping in front of me as we approached the Duchess's cage. "She's gained an ungodly amount of weight; and her fur lost all its sheen, no matter how many times I brushed it out. If I didn't know she was once a grand champion, I'd swear she was pet quality at best."

He squeezed both of my shoulders before he stepped aside, bowing his head low, the black spikes parting to reveal a road map of scalp. I leaned forward and held my breath to look.

"Oh, my god!" I gasped at the sight of her, the red fur dulled to a brownish rust, her copper eyes dim and slanted, not wide-eyed at all. Her tongue hung from between her parted lips, the ridges gray with wanting. I reached over to open the latch, a signal that usually sent the Duchess into a mewing frenzy of excitement, but she just lay there listless, kittens pooching out from her swollen belly.

"My god, she's huge," I said, reaching in to stroke the Duchess around the neck. I poked at the bulging kittens with my thumbs. They twirled away from my touch. The Duchess winced. "I've never seen a Persian carry so heavily," I said to Jerry. "Have you?"

He tapped at the cage with a brush and smeared hairball remedy onto the tip of his finger. Extending his hand into the cage, he held the malt-flavored ribbon under her nose, but she just raised her receded nose in the air and closed her eyes.

"She's a shadow of her former self," he whispered, wiping the hairball remedy away with a handkerchief. "Just like her mother."

Since the Duchess was due to give birth in a matter of days, I had to shave her belly. Shaving was not so much medically necessary as practical. With all that long hair out of the way, the kittens could suckle more easily. I reached in to pull the Duchess toward me, but she growled low in her throat, something she'd never done before.

"She won't let me near her," I said. Jerry tried to lure her closer with a dried fish from the bag of treats I kept, but she wouldn't budge.

"I've got an idea," I said, turning away to tiptoe over to Bea's cage. Bea leaped at the door of the cage as I came toward her, her red paws flying out between the Formica bars of the cage. Normally I didn't keep either Duchess or Bea caged, but with the Duchess about to give birth and my absence, I'd felt it was best. Bea was about to go into season again and purred voraciously as I lifted her in my arms. Jerry opened the other cages except for the two studs', Bea's nephew and the Duchess's cousin, who were too lusty to be trusted around the ripening females. I carried Bea over to the Duchess's cage, hoping the sight of her daughter might spur some life in her.

"Look who it is, Duchy," I said, holding Bea up to the door of the cage. "Come say hello to your girl."

Bea leaned forward in my arms and hooked her claws in the loops of the cage, opening her mouth in a resounding meow. The kittens squirmed in the Duchess's belly, bunches of her fur jumping from the inside as she turned to stare at Bea, her eyes wide. The ends of her ears turned down as she let out a terrible hiss, lips pulled back with rage. I scrambled to keep hold of Bea, but she leaped from my arms and darted across the room, between Jerry's legs, and under the grooming table.

"What was that?" Jerry called from the opposite end of the room. He came rushing toward me, carrying a box of torn sheets that I used for birthing mothers.

"It was the Duchess," I said, taking the box from Jerry and throwing the torn articles inside. "I can't shave her in this condition. She just rejected her own daughter, her own flesh and blood."

Before he could answer me I locked the Duchess's cage and climbed the steps to the kitchen. He must have sensed that I needed time alone, because he didn't come upstairs for at least an hour. I could hear him downstairs talking to the cats and whistling show tunes through his teeth as I sat eating one of the pink cupcakes my friend Anita had sent over with a card as a welcome-home present.

Dear Maxi,

Saw you on the news. Will you really be on
Hindsight? *You know how I've always adored So-*
phie. If I hear from your mother, I promise you'll
be the first to know. Candy and Sandy can't wait to
see the baby. How do I explain?

Love,
Anita

P.S. Can't believe you've been on TV!!! How did
you get so lucky?

I smiled to myself at Anita's note, at her reference to
celebrity interviewer Sophie Sussman. As my best childhood friend, Anita knew what Sophie meant to Mother
and me. Sophie had brought Fergie into our lives. Anita's
twins, Candy and Sandy, were nine years old now. Her
husband had left them some time ago, and since then
Mother had been counseling her about divorce, assuring
Anita that she was better off without him, that now as a
mother alone she could do what she wanted, have the
girls all to herself. In recent years Anita had become
more Mother's friend than mine, but still I was glad to
see she hadn't forgotten me. Slowly I peeled back the paper from another cupcake and held it up to my mouth as
I thought about where Mother might have gone. I imagined Mother behind the wheel of her maroon Taurus, the
baby bouncing in the car seat, as Mother sang songs
from my childhood at the top of her lungs.

Mother placed her first personal ad on my fifteenth
birthday. I had a crush on a boy named Pete, a lanky

clarinet player with wavy blond hair, whose voice hadn't changed yet For my birthday Anita had asked Pete if he would play Minuet in G in the hallway by my locker after eighth period. When I came down the hall after my social-science class, Pete stood by my locker, with his hair hanging in front of his face and his eyes closed, while he blew out a series of whiny notes.

"He said, 'Happy birthday,'" I told Mother at the kitchen table when I got home. "And he played the clarinet."

She'd made me fifteen pink cupcakes, which Anita and I dived into right away. As I bit into the first one, Anita giggled and kicked me under the table. She raised her eyebrows at Mother as if she were in on some secret.

Mother applied a thick smear of coral lipstick to her lips, then smiled at me.

"I have a big surprise for you," she said, getting up from the table and clapping her hands. "Wait until you see what I've done."

She ran for the bedroom, her high heels clicking on the floor.

"What is it?" I mouthed to Anita, thinking Mother might have bought me a new miniskirt or treated me to a perm to celebrate my blossoming womanhood. Anita smirked at me and pressed a finger to her lips, leaving a dot of icing just under her nose.

"You girls," Mother called as she came back in waving a newspaper in her hand, "you girls will just not believe what I went ahead and did!"

Anita squealed as Mother spread the newspaper open in front of me and pressed her painted fingernail to the box with her ad inside. Anita's mother was widowed and rarely left the house except to go to morning mass or volunteer at the home for the blind in the center of town. The thought of one of our mothers actually being interested in men was a thrill for Anita, because the only man in her mother's life was the Lord.

I read the ad, with a cupcake poised in one hand, lips smacking as I peeled frosting from the roof of my mouth with my tongue.

> *DWF seeks man who likes redheads,*
> *the royal family, and teenage girls.*
> *Smokers and banjo players need not reply.*

When I finished reading the ad, I dropped my cupcake and stared up at Mother. She was beaming, hugging Anita around the waist.

"What do you think of your mother dating, Maxi?" she asked, twirling Anita around in a little dance. "Finding myself a man who likes redheads and teenage girls. Like being a kid again, don't you think?"

She reached for my hand and pulled me into an embrace. I hugged her and closed my eyes, images of Pete and me kissing to clarinet music being erased by Mother and a stranger tangled on our living-room sofa, her red hair caught in the nest of his fingers.

Of course, the dates never lived up to Mother's initial excitement. We met more than a few men in the nonsmoking sections of coffee shops or diners with mini jukeboxes on the tables. It was in those places, while sharing bagels with cream cheese and sipping diet sodas as we waited for the next prospective date, that Mother would tell the story of my birth over and over again.

"It all started with a squeezing around my middle," she'd say, her eyes going starry as she sipped at her diet Coke and took bites of my bagel between sentences. "Like being hugged from behind, but really the hugging comes from inside."

I kept one eye on the door at all times, half expecting Pete to appear there, with his clarinet case under his arm and a mouth full of love. Once she started the story, she wouldn't stop, going on even after the men arrived and sipped coffee while staring at me from across the table, their lips wet. The next morning, after the men left with rumpled hair, Mother would inevitably complain about their lack of interest in her.

"He didn't say one word about our lovely red hair or the royal family, or even what a wonderful mother I was," she'd say, her lips pressed tight in mock disappointment. I wanted to tell her that of course he'd never mentioned any of those things with her going on all the time about the sight of me all cheesy between her legs, the meat of her placenta. Looking back, I realized that she must have known this, that the personal ads were another way of grooming me for motherhood, of searching for suitors for both of us while she did the seducing. When she finished the birth story, she'd make a long sucking sound with her straw, the corners of her mouth turned up at the edges.

She never really wanted a boyfriend. She wanted me to hear the story again and again, with men drifting in and out of the scene to discount the importance of fatherhood. It had certainly done the trick, I had to give her that. Millicent was as fatherless as they came.

5

Jerry agreed to spend the night, in case the Duchess gave birth ahead of schedule and to help me ward off any crazed reporters in the event that one of them got past the guards.

I could have called Anita, who had been with me the day the Duchess was born and had assisted at several other births, but I was afraid that Mother had gotten to her first. She'd been Mother's surrogate me, coming over on weeknights to watch *Wheel of Fortune* while I was off helping to euthanise old dogs and cats. When I got home late, with fast-food burgers spilling grease out of a bag and a heart full of grief, Mother and Anita would be curled up on the couch, eating popcorn and watching pretaped soap operas they'd been too busy to watch during the day. Once Anita got married and had her own twin daughters—blue-eyed blonds, which irked Mother because they reminded her of Di—she'd become less available to either of us. I didn't even tell Anita I was pregnant until after the end of the first trimester. When I was pregnant it became just the two of us again—

Mother and me—with Anita off in the distance, wrapped up in the world of Brownies and 4-H. But now that I'd let Mother down, I thought, she'd probably go running to Anita with the infant in tow and I'd be left out again. Besides, Anita had always been a sucker for media attention. Even if she hadn't already heard from Mother, I couldn't be sure she wouldn't sell my story to the *Enquirer* if the price was right.

While Jerry was getting ready for bed, I went downstairs to the cattery to use the telephone in private. Jerry said Mother had gone off the deep end and I should avoid all contact with her until we devised a plan. I stood on the steps of the cattery, with the receiver in my hand, staring at the swollen Duchess, twirling the phone cord between my fingers.

"Duchess," I whispered, dragging the cord over to the cage, "you're a mother. What would you do if you were me?"

She lay curled up in the birthing box, her eyes averted. I laughed a little at my own foolishness and dialed Mother's number, holding my breath the entire time. It rang once, twice, three times before her voice came on the answering machine.

"This is Minnie Dublin," she said, a giggle stifled in her throat. "I'm sure that many of you reporters out there—you, too, Sophie—and especially my daughter, Maxine (good god, I've got two of them now!), you are probably wondering where and how Middle and I are doing. All I can tell you at this time is that we are fine and growing by the minute!" At this, her laughter became hysterical. "It's hard to believe, but—"

A beep abruptly cut off her voice in midsentence. I screamed, "Hello? Hello? Mother, are you there? What have you done with Millicent?"

The beep sounded again in my ear, telling me I'd run out of time. I sank down on the steps of the cattery and slid over to the Bea's cage. She peered out at me. I opened her cage and she leaped into my arms. I hugged her to me and scratched under her chin. She responded with a plaintive meow, as if to tell me she understood how it felt to be deserted. Before going upstairs I peeked in at the Duchess one last time, but she just lay there, her body bulging as if it couldn't wait another day to let the kittens out.

The three of us slept upstairs in my bed—Jerry in his boxer shorts and I in my nightgown and Bea between us. Jerry and I lay on our sides, facing each other, both of us stroking Bea with one hand. Occasionally our fingers met as we passed our hands over her luxuriant fur. His black spikes cast a shadow on the down pillow, the veins in his arm taut as he moved his fingers over Bea's fur. I let out a long sigh and turned to set the alarm clock, to get up for the first watch of the Duchess's labor.

"I called Mother," I told Jerry, with my back turned to him, as I set the alarm. "I just couldn't help myself."

Jerry sat up in bed and grabbed my arm. Bea howled and tunneled under the blanket.

"You did?" he asked, his blue eyes wide. "What did she say?"

I lay back down and pulled the covers up to my chin.

"I got the machine. She's calling her Middle," I said,

"and she says she has two daughters now, like the baby is hers."

Bea tunneled farther under the blanket; her head rested heavily on my thigh.

Jerry was quiet for a minute, ran a hand over the wilting spikes, and looked right into my eyes.

"How about you?" he whispered. "What do you think?"

The sound of Bea's purring was muffled under the covers. I shifted a bit, my leg grazing the wiry hair of Jerry's thigh. Instinctively I drew my leg back from the shock, but part of me wanted to roll over on my side and enfold myself in his sinewy arms.

"I don't know," I said. "I don't feel like a mother." I took a deep breath and let it out through my nose. "All I know is that I don't feel like myself anymore, like something's missing."

Jerry reached under the blanket and took hold of my hand. He drew himself up onto one elbow and leaned over me.

"Something is missing," he said, "and it's yours, not your mother's. That's why we've got to find it."

He kissed my forehead and reached over to switch off the light. I lay there a long time with my eyes open, waiting for the alarm to ring so I could go downstairs and wait with the Duchess for her kittens to arrive. Pins and needles jumped along my legs and down through my feet, but I didn't move, just held on to Jerry, with the cat between us, waiting for yet another birth to begin.

When the alarm went off at 4 A.M., I reached over and slammed the off button with the palm of my hand. Jerry

turned in his sleep, his right arm raised over his head,
revealing a thick patch of blond hair a shocking contrast
to the blue-black spikes jutting from the top of his head.
Bea was sleeping on his chest, one paw resting on his
mouth as if to keep him quiet. I smiled to myself as I
tightened the knot on my terry-cloth robe. This was my
idea of family.

I flipped on the hallway light switch and tiptoed
down the stairs. My head felt strange, full of leftover
dreams. Vaguely I remembered dreaming of Mother
holding me from behind with my arms crossed, the kind
of hold that professional wrestlers were fond of using
before hitting their opponents with flying leaps, elbows
to the canvas. A full nelson. Mother had gone through a
spurt of watching professional wrestling after she'd read
that the royal family enjoyed the tapes sent to them by a
fan from the United States. For weeks she'd done nothing but sit on the sofa, eating apples and watching
championship matches. Her favorites were King Macho,
a man with a giant crown and a black mask, and his
partner, the Jack of All Holds, who wore a velvet cape
and carried a long gold staff. She'd read in the tabloids
that the royal family often watched wrestling in the early
evenings, and insisted we do the same.

In the dream, she and I were a tag team and I
couldn't understand why she'd gotten me into this hold.
The other team, Anita and Dr. Norton, stood in the corner, with their arms clasped together, laughing at us. I
tried to pull my arms down to break free, but Mother
tightened her grip on me from behind and laughed in
my ear.

"Mother," I whispered, "we're supposed to be on the same side."

But she pulled my arms tighter—so tight I could barely breathe. The pain squeezed around my middle just before I woke up, a slow-spreading pain that felt like the beginnings of labor.

As I opened the door of the cattery and went down the stairs, I thought of how strange it was that I should think of Mother's fascination with wrestling now. I hadn't thought of it in years, not since her last slew of personal ads, when she'd begun sleeping with men who looked like professional wrestlers. They all had heaving chests and thick necks, large hands that grabbed Mother by the thighs and pinned them up over her head—counting to three before releasing her. I was about sixteen then and starting to experiment with boys myself, which was why Mother had resumed her sexual activity.

"If you can do it, so can I," she used to say. "Men are only good for one thing, and don't you forget it."

At night I stuffed tiny balls of tissue in my ears to drown out their sounds. Sometimes she emerged from the bedroom late at night to tell me how it felt to be held in a full nelson by an amateur wrestler.

"It's not at all like being with a banjo player," she'd tell me as she sat on the edge of my bed. "That much I can tell you."

I wondered if somehow Middle remembered these things, too, as little as she was. If in her tiny undeveloped brain she dreamed of Mother writing out her personal ads and grappling on the living-room floor with men pumped full of steroids. How much of her memories were also mine? Or if all she knew so far was Mother's face peering into her crib.

I took off my bathrobe and approached the Duchess's cage slowly. She was curled up in the birthing box, resting her weight on her forepaws to dig with her teeth between her legs. This was a sure sign the kittens would be born soon. I had yet to shave her belly and swab her nipples with warm water. Slowly I opened the cage and called to her with kissing noises.

"Come here, Duch," I whispered, reaching for her. "Come let Mama help you."

She looked up at me and blinked, her belly hanging down over her parted legs. Her eyes were dull and half-closed, as if she'd grown tired of giving birth so often. I took her up in my arms and held back the tears, kissing the top of her head. How could I have not seen how tired she'd become? All I'd ever cared about was producing a champion, a bicolor that *Cat Fancy* would proclaim Cat of the Year. How cruel it was for me to keep breeding her when maybe that wasn't something she'd ever wanted for herself.

As I settled her on the grooming table and began shaving her belly with the electric razor, thick clumps of red-and-white fur fell over my feet. I saw out of the corner of my eye a manila envelope on the floor outside the Duchess's cage. At first I thought it was literature from the vet, or something one of the hospital security guards had dropped during the search. Squinting to get a better look at the handwriting on the envelope, I held the Duchess with one hand and extended my leg to drag the envelope toward me with my bare toes. Slowly I slid it closer, the black lettering starting to come clear. When I finally got the envelope inches from the table, the Duchess let out a low moan.

It was nearly time. I grabbed her up in my arms and gently placed her in the birthing box, leaving the door of the cage open so I could reach in and assist. Her belly protruded as she moaned and licked at herself, the nipples swelling. I stroked her head, then reached down to pick up the envelope. When I recognized Mother's swirling script in the light, I felt my chest squeeze.

"For Maxi," it said in bold script, "from the real Mother."

I tore open the envelope as fast as I could, my heart racing. Inside were Polaroids that scattered over the floor when I reached for them in my haste. I gathered them up and spread them across the grooming table, among the shaved tufts of the Duchess's fur.

The first one showed Mother with a backpack, a smiling Middle peering over her shoulder. She was at least nine months old, I could tell from the size of her head and the alertness in her eyes. In the next one Middle stood in a crib, the bars of the crib casting shadows on her dimpled thighs. I was astounded by the prominent birthmark in the shape of a comma over her right eye, and a pink frilly jumpsuit I recognized as my own. In the third one, Mother and the baby wore party hats with a big birthday cake on a Formica table, Middle's feet covered with white frosting, a candle in the shape of a number one in the center of the cake. Frosting lined the tips of both of their noses.

I grabbed the Polaroids on the table and ran up the stairs, two at a time. The Duchess moaned low in her throat, but there was nothing I could do to help her.

"Jerry!" I screamed. "Wake up! Mother's been in the house!"

He jumped out of bed and stood in the doorway, his eyes thick from sleep. I got up and ran for the laminated pictures Mother had sent me before my pregnancy. Jerry trailed close behind me, begging me to calm down as I rummaged through my underwear drawer for the photos. I threw the laminated pictures on the floor and handed him the Polaroids.

"How the hell did she get past the guards?" he asked as we stood there staring at them. The Polaroids replicated my own babyhood exactly. There we were, frozen under plastic with my feet in birthday cake, party hats on our heads. Me, smiling in Mother's backpack, and standing with my dimpled fingers gripping the edge of the crib, slats of light over my fat thighs.

"My god," Jerry said as I collapsed on the bed. "She's living your life all over again."

I buried my head under the blanket and sobbed. Jerry sat stroking my hair as the tears came and came, loud hiccuping sobs that shook the bed. How could she do this? I thought. How could she steal me from myself, steal my own infancy out from under me? What had I done to deserve this betrayal, when all I'd done was what she'd expected of me? I never imagined she'd be capable of this, not only to abandon me for a newer version of myself but to freeze the torment on film.

"It's all right," Jerry said over and over, his fingers stroking my scalp. "We'll find her. We'll get her back."

But I couldn't answer, just kept sobbing into the pillow, even as the Duchess's moans grew louder and more intense. I knew it was time, that she was in distress and needed me, but I couldn't bring myself to move. Bea jumped off the bed and ran down the stairs, Jerry trailing after her.

"I'll take care of everything," he called, but I knew that no matter how hard he tried, there was nothing he could do to help. I pressed one of the laminated photos to my chest and thought of Mother and Middle laughing at us while the Duchess moaned in pain.

I finally dragged myself out of bed when the telephone rang, several hours later. Jerry was still downstairs in the cattery, I assumed, and I said a silent prayer for the Duchess as I picked up the receiver and held it to my ear.

"Hello?" I said, my voice a whisper.

There was a long pause and then Mother's breath in my ear.

"Did you get the pictures?" she asked "I took them just for you."

I stumbled across the floor to the window, hoping that maybe Mother was outside calling me from one of the guards' cellular phones, that at last she'd come to her senses. A dozen reporters were camped across the street, smoking cigarettes and staring at the guards.

"Mother, where are you?" I said. My breath came hard and fast through my open mouth. "What have you done with the baby?"

She laughed and blew into the receiver. Horns blared in the background, the mocking laughter of passersby echoing in the distance. I imagined the two of them curled inside a phone booth, Middle with her ear pressed to the phone, listening in on our conversation. Then again, maybe she knew what I was saying without having to hear it, since she was another form of myself.

"That's not important," she said. "You didn't want the baby, you said so yourself. You wouldn't even hold her when she needed you most. Well, she doesn't need you anymore. I'm her mother now."

Jerry called to me from the cattery, his voice frantic. "Maxi, come quick!" he called. "It's the Duchess! She's in trouble!"

I stood frozen to the floor, lifting one of the Polaroids and staring into Mother's face. The baby laughed from the backpack, drool dangling from her lips. Mother looked younger than she had in years, her cheeks rosy even without stripes of rouge.

"But she's mine," I said, "I mean she's me. Why did you have to go and steal her away?"

I was on the verge of tears now but held them back as best I could. Mother was never very good at comforting an adult in hysterics. Calming a wailing baby was another thing entirely; nothing delighted her more than a colicky baby. She had the touch, she used to say, since she could stop an infant's screaming within thirty seconds or less. But I knew my tears would only irritate her further. Once you got past infancy you were on your own.

An automated operator's voice came on the line.

"Fifty cents, please," the voice said. "Please deposit fifty cents."

The baby hiccuped into the receiver. Several beeps sounded as Mother deposited coins.

"Oh, isn't that cute?" Mother squealed. "That's just what you used to do at her age."

"At my age!" I said, my voice rising now, Jerry's cries for help coming from the cattery. "Of course she does what I did at my age. She's me, for god's sake!"

Mother let out a long sigh, her breath crackling in the receiver. The sound of engines being started reverberated through the phone line. I could almost smell the exhaust.

"Yes, well, she does certainly seem to be like you. Like my own daughter. So if Middle is you, she's my daughter, then, isn't she? She's not really your daughter at all. She's mine."

I sat down on the floor and crossed my legs. How could I argue with this logic?

"But what about me?" I said, my voice quivering. "Where does this leave me? I've got reporters camped outside. I'm a prisoner in my own house."

Mother just sighed and tapped her fingernails on the receiver, a signal she used to show her impatience. The nails clicked in rhythmic spurts, like galloping. I could feel her anger through the phone.

"Why should we care?" she said, her voice low through gritted teeth. "You didn't seem to care about me when they threw me out of the hospital. You didn't care about Middle then. Why should we care about you?"

Jerry called my name again. I jumped up and ran toward the door to the basement, but the cord snapped me back, the telephone cradle crashing to the floor. The Duchess was probably giving birth as we spoke. I paced back and forth, not sure whether to go to her or stay on the phone with Mother—there was no telling when I'd hear from her again. The baby howled into the receiver as if she felt my pain. We both began to wheeze.

"You've upset the baby," Mother said. "She can't breathe!"

I dropped the receiver on the floor and ran to the dresser for my inhaler. With both hands I pressed the device into my mouth and squeezed, sucking the mist down in thick gulps. I crawled back over to the phone and lifted it to my ear.

"Mother?" I wheezed. "Mother, are you there?"

Something banged on the other end of the phone, and then Middle let out a shriek, the same scream I felt welling up in my chest. I'd stifled it since hearing Mother's voice on the phone.

"You come find us if you want us so badly," she said. Someone yelled an obscenity in the background. I pictured Mother cupping the baby's ears to block out the foul language, just as she'd done when I was a little girl. "You turned your back on us, Maxi, not the other way around. And you can tell Norton and the whole lot of them that I'm the one who's had the last laugh."

As I opened my mouth to answer her, Jerry ran into the bedroom with his hands outstretched, palms up, his fingers and forearms lined with blood and afterbirth. His eyes were wide, lips trembling with emotion.

"You've got to come down," he said, panting, his chest heaving beneath his spandex tank top. "Something's happened to the Duchess."

I gripped the receiver and stared at him, my knuckles white. I was frozen, unable to let go of the phone. Mother breathed in my ear.

"Those cats are your babies," she said. "This one's mine."

She slammed her receiver in my ear. For a moment I

sat there stunned. I couldn't remember Mother ever having hung up on me. Even in our worst arguments, she'd always been the one to linger on the telephone, even through long moments of silence.

Before I could tell him what had happened, Jerry pulled me up by the hand and raced me down the stairs to the cattery. Mother's voice rang in my ears. *Middle, Middle, Middle,* I kept hearing her cooing to the infant me. *Don't you know Mother loves you?*

"Maxi," he said, "you've got to hear what I'm saying. You've got to pay attention to me, sweetie."

I nodded. Jerry knew just how to play me. Mother always called me sweetie when she wanted something.

He took my hand and together we shuffled over to the Duchess's cage, where she lay with her back to us in the birthing box. Bits of dried blood caked on her hindquarters, but for the most part Jerry had done a fine job of keeping her clean, which I knew was no easy task. Birth was a messy business.

"How are the kittens?" I asked, half in a daze. Images of Mother and Middle dancing around a birthday cake floated before my eyes. They blew out the candles and ate all the frosted roses without ever saving me one. *Those cats are your babies. This one's mine.*

Jerry bowed his head and reached forward to open the latches of the cage. I leaned forward, on my toes, my chin resting on his shoulder. He smelled of damp skin and afterbirth. Cat hair drifted up my nose. I blew air out my nostrils and held my breath as he reached inside.

"Are there any show quality?" I blurted out, but as soon as I saw the stricken look on his face I knew something had gone wrong.

The kittens lay curled together in the corner of the birthing box away from the Duchess. She refused to look at them. I reached over and gently lifted one with my fingertips, examining the patches of redness on its wet fur. With my other hand I gently rolled it over on its back, the tiny clawlike legs jutting up in the air.

"Oh, Jerry," I said. "Oh, my god."

The kitten's eyes were merely slits, its mouth half open where the jaw hadn't properly formed. I lifted it closer to my face to be sure of what I was seeing, but I knew at first glance: The kitten had no nose. In fact, the nose had receded so far into the skull that all that was left was a tiny slit for air. It didn't matter, though. The kitten wasn't breathing.

"They're all like that," Jerry said, wrapping his arm around my shoulder. "I helped them out one at a time, but not one of them has a nose or eyes, nothing. It was like she knew," he whispered, as if not wanting the Duchess to overhear. "She clamped down so tight I had to reach in to pull them out, like she didn't want to let them go."

It was a feeling I knew all too well. I stroked the Duchess's head to show her that I knew what she was feeling. Even cats must wish that such things were never born.

I set the kitten back inside the box and went to the cabinet for a towel. Jerry ran his hand through the black spikes in his hair and sighed.

"I'm so sorry," he said. "I feel like this is all my fault."

Without a word I set the towel down on the grooming table and wrapped my arms around him, my fingers gripping the flesh of his back, his hands splayed across my shoulder blades. When I released him he wiped away a tear with the back of his hand and touched my cheek. I felt the wetness on his fingertips, the sorrow of all the births that had gone wrong, the kittens and babies that had come into the world through no fault of their own. One by one I lifted each dead kitten and lay it on the towel, wrapping them all in the cloth and tying it up in a knot.

I locked myself in my bedroom and unplugged the phone. Vassy sent a telegram, imploring me to appear with Norton on *Hindsight.*

YOUR MOTHER HAS LEFT NO FORWARDING ADDRESS (STOP) NEIGHBORS SAW HER WITH BABY STROLLER SOMETIME AFTER MIDNIGHT (STOP) BABY AND MOTHER HAVE FLOWN THE COOP (STOP) WE MUST SHOW SOLI-DARITY (STOP) SOPHIE SUSSMAN SENDS REGARDS (STOP)

Jerry tore the telegram into shreds and promised to leave me alone. I didn't want to see any more articles, take any more phone calls. Let the reporters tear the house down if they wanted to, I thought. I drank three bottles of Beaujolais left over from the night of seduction and put on a pair of flannel pajamas, pinned my red curls in a crazy knot at the top of my head.

Jerry buried the dead kittens under a bush in the backyard and chauffeured the Duchess to an appointment at the vet's office. Pictures of Jerry with a bundle of dead kittens would be splashed across the front of the morning papers, no doubt.

At first Jerry was patient with me, tapping at the door to offer me a new bottle of Beaujolais when I'd run dry. He offered to wash my sweaty pajamas and didn't balk when I said I wanted to live in them forever. He fed the Duchess pills, hidden in her soft food, and made steak for Bea as a kind of compensation for having lost her mother. The least he could do was to let me have some peace, he said through the door, though peace was the last thing I felt, lying there among the heavy blankets.

I tried to resist watching television, but by the second day I'd run out of ways to occupy myself. I lay in bed, with a bottle of Beaujolais in one hand and the remote in the other, flipping through the channels.

All the talk-show guests looked the same—women with teased hair and bad teeth, complaining about the men who had left them behind, or worse yet, speculating about Mother's and Middle's whereabouts.

"If I were her mama, I'd drive straight across the country," said one woman with a large overbite and stringy blond hair. "Clone or no clone, I'd go get my baby, sure as shootin'."

One station had offered 1-900 numbers for viewers to vote for whom they thought custody should be awarded to. According to the poll, I was in the lead, with Mother running second and Norton trailing behind in third. Voters could call in until midnight, the announcer said; and in my half daze of drunkenness and little sleep, I was tempted to call in myself, though I couldn't decide whom I would vote for.

On PBS a panel of ethicists and religious leaders were pondering the moral and ethical implications of cloning. Had the whole world gone mad? I wondered, shoving another pretzel into my mouth and washing it down with a swig of Beaujolais. Wasn't there anything else to talk about anymore?

Father George Sinnitt, the priest at my local congregation, said that he remained skeptical that the baby had indeed been cloned.

"We've been offered no evidence to support the idea that this child is anything other than a normal baby," he said. "The church maintains a very conservative stance on matters such as these, especially when, as the hospital suggests, a young woman seems to have split a cell in her womb." He cupped a hand over his mouth and coughed. "The implications border on blasphemy. Maxine Dublin has never been much of a churchgoer, but I can't believe she'd claim to have done something so utterly against the church's teachings."

I blushed at the reference to my failure to go to church, though I knew no one could see me. Several of the ethicists nodded in agreement. When asked what this RGC (as even the media now called her) might mean to the future of medicine, one of the ethicists shook his head and looked wearily at the camera.

"Cloning is the forbidden fruit," one of the men said, eyeing Father Sinnitt, who folded his hands and looked straight at the camera. "The far-reaching ramifications of such a procedure are too great for us to comprehend. The very balance of nature might be altered forever."

He paused and let out a long sigh.

"I shudder to think of what might come next," he said. "Will someone attempt to clone the lamb of God?"

I thought of the last time I'd been in church, for

Candy's and Sandy's First Communion. Together Mother and I had knelt at our pews and watched as the girls hurried down the aisle with their hands pressed together in prayer, their little white veils shimmering in the light. When they opened their mouths in "amen" and the priest slipped the wafer inside, I'd caught Anita's eye from across the church and felt my stomach squeeze. Mother must have felt this twinge, too, because she looked up at the cross, blessed herself, and pressed a hand to my empty womb.

On the third day, I awoke drunk, my head pounding and my throat full of dry air. I heard voices downstairs, and for a minute I thought Jerry had turned on me and sent for Norton to drag me on television, slap me with pancake makeup, and force me to tell my story under hot lights.

I picked up the empty bottle of Beaujolais and opened the bedroom door a crack. The Beaujolais burned in my middle. I almost laughed at the sensation, a fluttering like life inside my stomach. The day I felt the baby move for the first time, I'd gotten into my car and driven straight to Mother's house. I'd never seen her so happy. She'd hugged me as if she'd never let go.

I recognized Anita's voice coming from behind Jerry. Slowly I opened the door wider to have a look at her. Her blond hair was pulled back into a high ponytail, her bangs streaked from the sun. Her nose wrinkled as she leaned in to listen to Jerry intently, shifting her weight from one leg to the other. All the carpooling and Brownie troops had agreed with her, I thought. I'd never seen her look better.

"I'll go talk to her," she told Jerry in a firm voice. "She'll listen to me."

Jerry stepped aside as she moved ahead of him to climb the stairs. I dropped the bottle on the carpet and jumped into bed, pulled the covers up to my chin. The smell of wine and sweaty flannel wafted through the room. I pulled the pins out of my hair and let the wilted curls fall over my face. Part of me didn't want Anita to see me like this after so long, but I was too tired to really care.

She tapped at the door, then swung it open before I had a chance to tell her to come in. Her hand flew to her mouth when she saw me. I tried to smile but felt dirt and sweat sopping under my arms and down the back of my neck.

"Oh, Maxi, look at you," she said, coming toward the bed. She tugged the blanket down below my waist. "You look like hell."

I laughed and tried to run a hand through my hair, but my fingers got caught in a massive knot on the side of my head. I left the hand there and tilted my face toward her as if I were striking a pose.

"Yeah, well," I said, trying to sound casual, "I guess I look better in pictures nowadays. At least that's what all the newspapers say."

She shook her head and sat down at the foot of my bed, clucking her tongue at the empty bottles all over the floor.

"I've been keeping up with all the papers," she said, patting my foot as she spoke, "not to mention the talk shows. Even the people on PBS are talking about you."

She paused, moving her fingers along the edge of the blanket. "I have to say I'm not all that surprised. I'd never put anything past that mother of yours."

She smoothed the blanket with her hands and sighed.

"All she ever wanted was another daughter. I don't know why she never got one of those wrestlers to get her pregnant."

I sank down into the pillows and closed my eyes. Of course Anita wasn't surprised. She'd been there through the personal ads; she'd heard all the birth stories a million times. It was no wonder that once Anita had her own babies, we hadn't seen as much of her. She'd become a mother herself and had her own birth stories to tell; Mother could never tolerate one-upmanship.

"Mother took her away," I whispered, reaching for Anita's hand, under the blanket. "Mother loves her more."

Anita squeezed my hand, then got up from the bed. As she talked she picked up the empty bottles from the floor and gathered up the dirty dishes. She called to Jerry for a garbage bag and some towels for me to have a shower. She was taking charge.

"I can see you're depressed," she said, pulling the blanket away from me and throwing it into the laundry basket in the corner of the room. "But you can't just lie here like nothing's happened. You've had a baby and the whole world wants to know your story. Do you know how lucky you are? Women have babies every day and no one even bats an eye."

When I didn't answer, she kept talking.

"I know just the woman for you to see. A friend of

mine from the PTA recommended her. She's an act-out therapist. Jerry and I have figured a way to get you past the reporters. Besides, you'll like her," she said, smiling. "She's a redhead."

I said nothing as she helped me out of bed and down the hallway to the bathroom. Jerry was waiting at the door, with a clean towel and a bottle of cream rinse for my hair. Without looking at him I took them from him and reached down to open the door, the Beaujolais coming up in my throat. Anita pressed a hand to the small of my back and nudged me forward.

"It will all work out," she said, her ponytail shining under the light. "Even Sophie Sussman thinks so. I read it today in the paper."

I glanced over at Jerry as he held the bathroom door open for me. He gave me a sad smile, his lips pressed tight over his teeth. I thought of that night on the floor of the cattery, the way he'd closed his eyes and thrust against me, the cats' screams filling the air over our heads. The way he'd looked down at me when he saw the new me squirming in the incubator, his blue eyes brimming with tears. If there was anyone to feel sympathy for it was Jerry. We'd used him just like all the others. It was a sorry thing to be a man with Mother around. All the men in our lives could attest to that.

"I'm not a mother," I said softly, just before closing the door behind me. "And I don't think I ever will be."

The first time she saw Fergie on television was a turn-ing point in Mother's life. She'd seen photos of Andrew's other girlfriends, heard the rumors about Randy Andy and the porn stars frolicking on sandy beaches. Having blue blood allowed behavior not acceptable for the rest of us, she said. The pressure of being made to act princely afforded them the luxury of indiscretions. Though she hadn't been able to forgive my own father—whose worst offense seemed to be chain-smoking and preferring the company of other banjo players—she could readily accept indiscretions in royalty.

"Besides," she said, "all the nonsense we were taught when I was young about waiting for your prince to come. I knew even then no prince was coming for me." She'd smile at me then, the corners of her eyes crinkling. "Still," she said, "every woman wants to be queen."

Mother had always said she felt more like an Englishwoman than an American. The closest we had to royalty in the United States were the Kennedys and Johnny Carson, all of whom paled in comparison to the Queen Mum, or even Princess Margaret. But it wasn't until that first interview of Fergie's that her affection turned to deeper love. She'd watched the wedding of Charles and Di, like most of America, laughing uproariously when Di had gotten Charles's name wrong at the altar, at the sweetness of her switching his first name to Philip in her nervousness—an indication of what was to come, she later liked to say. Once they'd divorced, Mother had dismantled her scrapbook, saying that royalty in Britain was not what it once had been. With Di gone, who was there to watch but Camilla Parker Bowles? If it hadn't been for Fergie, Mother might have given up royalty-watching altogether. Fergie, she said, was the real thing.

The three of us—Anita, Mother, and I—were sitting on the sofa together when Sophie Sussman appeared to tell America about the brand-new royal couple.

Though afflicted with a slight lisp—why she hadn't changed her name had been a sticking point for Mother and me—Sophie Sussman could always be counted upon for celebrity coups. Mother adored the way she spoke and masked her age with a soft-focus lens, though she was often the object of comedians' taunts, who, Mother said, had nothing better to do than pick on a woman who outclassed them all. I could do a dead-on impression if coaxed by Anita—"Thith ith Thophie Thuthman with the latetht newth," though Mother forbade me ever to do it in her presence.

As the program began, Sophie Sussman's hair was softly lacquered, her foundation creamy through the filtered lens.

"Here with uth tonight," she began, "ith the royal couple whoth engagement hath riveted the world."

Anita had just become engaged, and we were helping her sort out which champagne glasses to keep, which to return, and which to recycle as gifts for other showers or parties. When the camera panned in for a close-up of Fergie sitting on the couch with her right hand clasped in Andrew's, the three of us gasped.

"My god, Minnie," Anita said. "She looks just like a younger you!"

Mother sat with her mouth open, staring at the television. She took off her glasses and moved toward the TV, reaching out to stroke the face on the screen. I scrambled for a videotape and pressed record, freezing the image of Fergie before Sophie Sussman faded into a commercial.

It was true. The resemblance was uncanny. During a commercial break I ran for Mother's wedding picture, the only photo of her and my chain-smoking–banjo-playing father that remained. In the photo Mother's red hair hung, long and soft, over her shoulders; her cheeks puffed out as she smiled, freckles lining the wrinkles around her nose.

I ran back into the living room and rewound the tape to capture in freeze-frame the image of a smiling Fergie on the twenty-inch screen. With both hands I held the photo up next to the screen so that Fergie's and Mother's cheeks nearly touched.

"Look, Mother," I said, trying to stifle my giggles. "She really does look like you."

Anita laughed and slapped Mother on the back. The list of Anita's unwanted gifts fell on the floor, next to the kernels of popcorn I'd dropped while running for the wedding picture. Mother smiled at Anita and patted her arm. Then she turned to me and gritted her teeth.

"That is not even a good picture of me," she said, putting her glasses back on and switching off the television with the remote. "We look much more alike than that."

I tucked the picture in the bottom of her bureau, where I'd found it hidden under old report cards and baby books that had locks of red hair pasted on every page. Anita glanced at me, rolling her eyes in Mother's direction as she closed the door behind her. She knew how Mother could be when she felt thwarted, even in some small way.

I lay in bed with the lights on that night, my heart pounding with guilt at having forced Mother to look at the man she swore had nothing to do with bringing me into the world. As far as I was concerned, she always said, I had a mother and that was all I ever needed. Still, the image of her apple cheeks under the white veil and the dark-haired man holding her arm often came to me at night when I couldn't sleep. Sometimes I bought a pack of unfiltered Camels and kept them under my nightstand and strummed my fingers over my belly, imagining I was plucking the strings of a banjo.

Later I tiptoed down the stairs and found Mother sitting cross-legged in front of the television set, with an unlit cigarette in her mouth. In her lap was the wedding photograph, images of creamy-skinned Fergie flickering on the screen. Many people say that everyone has a twin somewhere in the world, someone who looks just like you that you've never had the chance to meet. The fact that Mother's twin was royalty was no news to her, she later said. She'd always known that her bright red hair and pale complexion hadn't gone to waste on a banjo player who deserted her. After all, she'd gotten herself a red-haired daughter who looked just like her. Once Fergie came into her life, the desire to produce more red-haired girls for her to love got the better of her. She was too old to do it herself, so now it was up to me. If Fergie could do it, she said, then so could I—prince or no prince.

While she washed dishes, Anita explained that she and Jerry had worked out a plan to get me past the reporters without having my face plastered all over next week's tabloids.

"The last thing you need right now is more exposure," Anita said. "If Minnie finds out we're on to her, we're sunk."

They were taking me to some sort of actress-adviser—the act-out counselor Anita had called her, the one recommended to her by the president of the PTA. Apparently the school had been in dire financial trouble, and this therapist-actress had come to the PTA meeting dressed as the superintendent of schools.

"She looked just like him, right down to the bad mustache," Anita said, shaking her head. "It jarred something in Janet, our president, and the next thing we knew our troubles were solved. Janet came up with an idea to end the austerity budget and we had the most profitable bake sale in the history of Cooper Elementary."

"You may be skeptical at first," Anita continued as

she busied herself with putting the dishes back in the cabinets, "but this woman has a way of handling a crisis. She can literally become someone else if she wants to. Janet swears by her. At least give her a try."

Even though I hadn't seen much of Anita in the past few years, I marveled at the way she was able to set each dish on its proper shelf, never having to open a cabinet door more than once. She hit her mark over and over again.

"She knew what the superintendent looked like without ever seeing so much as a photograph," she whispered, as if saying it too loudly could suddenly make it untrue.

I sat down in the kitchen chair and stared out at the spot where Jerry had buried the eyeless kittens, the earth swelling softly where their tiny bodies pushed upward from beneath the handfuls of dirt.

"Act-out therapy," Anita said, fluffing her ponytail with her fingers. "It's the newest thing."

The cats were crying downstairs. My breasts ached with their sounds. I cupped them in my hands and pressed down in circles, trying to dull the ache. Jerry reached for my hands and pressed them to my sides.

"A shrink who can act," I said, opening my eyes. "Mother would get a kick out of that one."

Anita stepped forward, draped the dish towel over her shoulder, and got down on her haunches to take my hands. She stared up at me, the damp towel smelling faintly of liquid soap and spoiled wine. She pressed her fingers into my palms, hard, until I sat up straight and wouldn't look away.

"This isn't about Minnie," she whispered. "It's about

you." She leaned forward so that our foreheads touched, the way we had sat so many times as children, resting our heads together.

The three of us left the house, with jackets thrown over our heads like criminals. Even if the photographers managed a quick shot of us, our faces were hidden, our bodies blurred by the speed.

The guards held open the door to Anita's blue Grand Caravan as we sprinted across the front lawn.

"Go, go, go!" they shouted, as we piled into the Caravan, Jerry up front with Anita, and myself and the Duchess in the backseat. I insisted on bringing the Duchess, sneaking her out in a pillowcase, under my arm. Since she'd been through so much in the last few days, I'd vowed not to let her out of my sight again. At first Anita refused to let the cat into her car for fear of the dander drifting in the air and becoming trapped in the fibers of her cloth seats. But I wouldn't leave the house until Anita apologized for insulting her.

"Since when did you get so childish?" Anita said, as we sped away from the house. "You're acting just like a little girl."

Jerry stifled his laughter and said that all the excitement of the past few weeks had worn down my nerves. But he knew the truth; since Middle's birth I had become more infantile by the day. One of the psychiatrists on *Dateline* had warned this was possible. The verdict was still out on how similar clones really are, but it seemed only logical that there would be some empathy between us, such as in the case of identical twins. Since Middle was an infant, I might begin to regress.

"It stands to reason that with this RGC in the world, Ms. Dublin, the so-called mother, might be more likely to act out her childish whims," the psychiatrist had said. "With an infantile version of herself as a mirror for her behavior, we're dealing with what might be considered Piaget's theory in reverse."

Already I could see how right he was. Several times I had to stifle the urge to stomp my feet and stick my tongue out at Anita, who gave me the silent treatment through the entire ride.

In the backseat I found drawings made by Candy and Sandy, Anita's twin nine-year-old girls. One was a self-portrait of the two of them, round faces traced in blue crayon with long yellow ponytails jutting from the tops of their asymmetrical heads. Under their faces their names were written in blue Magic Marker and near the top, "For Mom." On another drawing their two stick figures were jumping rope, their big red laughing mouths full of crooked teeth. In still another the girls were reaching out for each other with giant blue hands, their thick bulging fingers locked together. The Duchess squatted over the last one as if she were going to urinate on it, but I pulled it out from under her and passed it up front to Jerry.

Anita glanced over at it from the driver's seat, then flashed Jerry a giant smile.

"Twins," she said, as we pulled into the parking lot of the woman's office. "They do everything together."

"Of course they do," Jerry said as he held the door open for me. I handed him the Duchess. Jerry and Anita looked around for wayward reporters. When they signaled that the coast was clear, I climbed out of the

Caravan and followed them to the office building, glancing over my shoulder in case Mother was lurking, watching my every move.

We all sat in the waiting room in beanbag chairs, the smell of vanilla incense wafting through the room. I held the Duchess in my lap and stared at the paintings on the walls: portraits of Marilyn Monroe, with her famous skirt swirling in the air, and Barbra Streisand, painted on velvet, with a microphone curled between her long fingers. Anita had promised that this was the kind of woman we needed to get Mother and Middle back, though I wasn't at all sure of this by the looks of all the sayings on the walls: "Be all you want to be." "Become someone else." "Wear a black wig and paint your toenails lavender." "Let Streisand show you the way to a better you."

As I sat staring up at these sayings, Anita kept taking my arm and whispering to me in a harsh voice.

"I really think," she said, gritting her teeth and pressing her fingers into my arm, "that you should leave that cat outside. This is not the appropriate place for a cat, Maxi. And I know you know better."

Jerry glanced at me from his beanbag chair and mouthed something I couldn't quite catch. I leaned forward, the Duchess squirming in my lap. "What?" I mouthed back. Anita shushed us both and tried to take the Duchess from my arms. I slapped Anita's hand away and pressed the Duchess to my chest.

"If she doesn't go, I don't go," I said, sticking my chin out at Anita to show her I meant business. Jerry covered his mouth with his hand to stifle his laughter. I twitched in my seat, the beanbag letting out a sound like the expulsion of gas. Jerry and I both burst out laughing, tears streaming down our cheeks; but Anita sat with her arms folded, her face averted. I relaxed my hold on the Duchess; this was the first time I'd laughed in weeks.

We'd calmed down considerably, when the door opened a crack, revealing a hand covered in small brown age spots, freckles around the wrist. I pulled the Duchess close to me and she grunted low in her chest. Jerry stood up and took my hand, helping me to wriggle my way out of the beanbag chair. Before I could say anything, Anita headed straight for the door and took the woman's extended hand.

They whispered for several minutes behind the half-open door while Jerry and I stood shoulder to shoulder, my pulse beating heavily in my throat.

I felt suddenly afraid, the way I always had as a child whenever Mother was angry with me. She never yelled or struck me—that wasn't her style—but there were times when she'd say nothing to me for days if I'd forgotten to do something she'd asked or left her home alone while I was out with Anita or other friends. She could withhold her love at will, turn her back to me and refuse to speak, even after I'd cried and begged her forgiveness. Once, when I was thirteen, I'd forgotten to meet her at Woolworth's to buy mascara and share an ice-cream soda—I had stayed after school to listen to the band rehearse—and she'd locked herself in her bedroom for three days.

Finally in desperation I'd knelt outside her bedroom door and pressed my face against it, tears sliding down my cheeks.

"Please, Mother," I said, "I'll never forget you again."

Only then had she come out and enveloped me in her arms, the two of us weeping there in the hallway. Her blue eyeliner ran down her cheeks and stained my white blouse. For weeks afterward I would take the blouse out of my drawer and look at the stain to remind myself of what I'd done. It was a symbol of the way I'd hurt her, she later said; and the stain never had come out of the blouse, no matter how many times I'd bleached it.

These scenes raced through my head as the door opened and Anita stepped aside to let the woman pass through the doorway. I gasped when I saw her, nearly dropping the Duchess on the floor.

"My god!" Jerry screamed. "It's Minnie!"

The woman laughed and ruffled her red hair. She extended her pale hand and smiled at me, her cheeks puffing, peach rouge caked in the creases of her cheeks. I felt myself swoon. Jerry's arm reached out to steady me.

"I told you," Anita said. "She's incredible."

The woman sauntered over to a corner of the room and pulled a pair of eyeglasses from the pocket of her sweater. I could feel my heart thumping away in my chest, the dull ache of emptiness in my middle spreading. She watched me as she walked from one end of the room to the other, her hands fluttering through her long mane of red hair. She even moved like Mother—the slow swinging of her arms, the careful leaning on her right foot.

"The fact that I look like your mother," she said, looking directly at me as she spoke, "is no accident. I try to look like someone people relate to. It lets them free-associate much more quickly than they might with someone who looks more ordinary, like, say, a Diane Keaton type. With some of my clients, I put on a mousy brown wig, and wear ties and hats. But I knew that wouldn't get through to you. You'd see Diane Keaton, and you'd think: What? Quirky? Woody Allen? Annie Hall?" She moved closer to me and laid a hand on the Duchess's back. "But if I look like your mother," she whispered, "we get straight to the point."

She draped her arm over my shoulder and led me toward the door. I started to cry, long heaving sobs that racked my throat and chest.

"You see," she said, looking back at Jerry and Anita before closing the door, "it saves tons of time."

She led me into her office and settled me into an overstuffed chair. The tears continued to fall, dripping down my cheeks and onto the Duchess's matted fur. The room was filled with costumes: a Barbra Streisand wig and long stick-on nails, feather boas and lacy tights. A long full-length mirror hung on the wall opposite me. I thought of the woman dressing up before her clients arrived, standing in front of the mirror to look like whomever she wanted to.

"Now," she said, slipping off her eyeglasses and wiping them on her sweater, just the way Mother always does, "tell me what you want to tell your mother."

The Duchess growled low in her throat, the hair on her back standing on end. I wiped at my eyes with the back of my hand and tried to stop crying, but the tears came and came, as if they'd never stop.

"Go on," she said, leaning forward in her chair and smiling, "tell your mother you want that clone back. You might as well tell her. It's in all the papers."

When she smiled, her lips parted, revealing small brown coffee stains on the tops of her teeth. Mother was never a coffee drinker. I had nothing to say.

"I can't," I said. "You're not my mother."

The Duchess lifted her head from where it was burrowed under my arm and let out a resounding hiss.

"She doesn't much like being a mother," the woman said, leaning forward in her beanbag chair to get a closer look at me. The red hair sparkled in the overhead light. "And neither do you."

I moved to stand up. This was all some trick Anita had pulled on me, I thought. How cruel it was to dress up as a loved one to break down a patient's defenses. What would Mother say if she could see me now? She and Middle were out there laughing and living my life over again while I sat staring at some bizarre impostor.

The woman stood up, too, and walked over to the window, tossing her hair over one shoulder. Without looking at me she began to hum the opening strains to the wrestling programs Mother liked to watch, raised her arms up over her head and then brought them down again, fists together in a version of "the crab."

I dropped the Duchess on the floor and stepped closer to the door. The woman shuffled toward me, her eyes rolling up in her head. She moved her head from side to side, humming low in her throat as if she'd worked herself into some sort of trance. Before I could move away from her or throw one of the feather boas over her like a trap, she had me. In one swift motion she'd slipped her arms under mine and clasped her hands behind my head in a full nelson. The humming grew louder as she pressed down on my neck. I tried to pull my arms down and set myself free, but she kept pressing down on my neck.

"Mother!" I screamed without thinking. "Let me go!"

I brought my elbows down hard, the way I'd seen wrestlers do when trying to break out of a choke hold. Mother always clapped when anyone escaped from a full nelson. In bed she'd ask the men from the personals to hold her that way only to feel the triumph of lifting her knee and kicking them, backward, in the groin, to set herself free.

The woman lay doubled over on the floor, her red hair spread out over the carpet. The Streisand wig fell off its hook and onto the floor. I grabbed the Duchess, ran for the door, and struggled to open it with one hand while holding the Duchess with the other.

"Wait," the woman called, struggling to her feet. "I can help you find your mother. I can even help you find yourself. But you've got to be willing to trust me."

The Duchess scrambled down from my arms and ran out to the waiting room. I ran after her, stumbled over Jerry's feet, and hit the carpet. For a second I lost track of where I was, felt Anita's and Jerry's arms pulling me to a standing position, heard the Duchess hissing in the corner. Images of Mother in electric blue tights and a cape flooded through my mind. I closed my eyes and imagined Middle running to their corner of the ring to slap Mother's hand, then the two of them heading straight for me, ready to grab me up by the arms and legs, and toss me onto the canvas.

"She got me in a full nelson," I said, burying my face in Jerry's chest. "She knows Mother's turned against me."

Anita tried to calm me down, but I wouldn't hear of it. I picked up the Duchess and ran out to the parking lot. Jerry hurried behind me. I opened the door to Anita's van, shoved the Duchess inside, and stood with my back against it, trying to clear my mind of all that the woman had said.

"I just want to go home," I told Jerry, and he nodded. "I know how you feel, Max," he said, rubbing the underside of my jaw with his thumbs. "But a woman like that who can dress herself up and look like anybody she wants, she's got to be on to something."

I nodded and brushed the hair out of my eyes. At the door to the office Anita and the woman were whispering, peering out at us from behind the glass.

Just as I started to say something, Anita and the woman scurried toward us. The woman had taken off the wig and glasses, and was wearing a long gingham dress, a pair of sneakers with white crew socks. Anita's ponytail swung high in the air. I pulled open the door and climbed into the backseat, pulling Jerry in beside me. Before he could stop me, I hammered down the locks and sat down on the floor, holding the Duchess tightly between my legs.

Anita turned the key in the lock, and the two of them climbed into the front seat. I reached for one of the twins' drawings, crumpled it into a ball, and threw it at the back of Anita's head.

"Hey," she said, turning around in her seat to slap at my hand. "Act your age."

I shoved my face into the Duchess's coat and breathed hair up my nose. Jerry cleared his throat but said nothing. For several minutes we were quiet. The woman leaned her head against the back of the seat and took a deep breath.

"I don't have to be your mother," she whispered, reaching over the seat to touch my hand, "if you don't want me to. But now she has this baby—and the thing is, I know how to use the media to our advantage. I've got the kind of experience you need. Remember, I'm an actress."

The Duchess lifted her head from my lap and stared into my eyes. I stared back at her, thinking of the way she'd turned against Bea and had tried to hold in her dead babies, about all that she'd seen as a mother. I let out a long sigh and sat up in the backseat. Jerry took the Duchess from my lap and gave me a sad smile.

"The thing is," the woman said, taking my hand in hers, her silver rings cooling my flesh, "you've got to be ready to beat her at her own game. You've got to be ready to look for yourself as hard as you're looking for the two of them."

I pulled my hand away, sat back, and leaned my head on Jerry's shoulder. Anita reached over the seat and took my hand, smiling, her eyes brimming with tears.

"You've got to do it, Max," she said, "if you ever want to get that baby back."

For a long time I sat there with my eyes closed, holding on to Anita's hand and thinking of Candy and Sandy drawing furiously in the backseat, their crayons crossing over one another to draw themselves together, their two hands moving simultaneously toward one vision.

When I opened my eyes, they were all staring at me expectantly. If I didn't find Mother and Middle for myself, I knew it wouldn't be long before Norton and his staff would think of new ways to torment me. The newspapers said he'd come out of his trance and had vowed to get the baby back at any cost. Rumors were already circulating that he'd try to prevent my insurance from paying my hospital bills, that he'd gotten the HMOs on his side. With reporters and photographers camped outside my house, there was no telling when I'd be able to sell another Persian.

"OK," I said finally, letting go of Anita's hand and sitting up straight in the backseat. "But I don't want you to be my mother. You can be whoever else you want, but not Mother. There's only one of her, and I want to find her myself."

The three of them clapped, Jerry and Anita reaching across the seat to give each other a high five. I lifted the Duchess onto my lap and stared out the window while the three of them set up plans for where to begin, which costumes to bring, what Mother and Middle might be doing at that very moment.

"By the way," she said, reaching over to shake my hand, "I'm Cecilia."

"Pleased to meet you," I said, and took her hand in mine. I pulled my hand away again when I saw the age spots painted over her knuckles.

Cecilia let herself out of the car and promised to meet us back at my house before we set off together— before Middle grew too much and Mother had a chance to turn her against me.

"We've got to discuss payment," she called as Anita backed the van up and headed out to the road. "A performance like mine doesn't come cheap. The HMOs don't pay for therapy of this kind. It's their loss, I know, but a sad fact of life."

She laughed then and ran toward the office, her red hair streaming behind her in the wind. With her back turned she looked so much like a younger version of Mother that I had to fight the urge to cry out, "Wait, Mother, wait! Don't leave me behind like this!"

But, of course, I knew she wasn't my mother at all and that already it was too late. I'd been left behind long ago, maybe even at the moment of conception when the screaming cats and Mother's face had invaded my life, filling me with some sort of magical seed that wasn't really mine at all. The moment the egg had split itself in my womb, I'd lost myself to this new me. Mother had always said that having a baby was like getting yourself back all over again, but she'd never told me that you lost yourself, too. That was one story I'd never heard. No mother I'd known had ever told me about the loss.

When we got back to the house, Norton and Gus Vassy were parked in my driveway, in a black limousine with tinted windows. Norton's hand dangled out the passenger-side window, a cigarette perched between his thumb and forefinger. Immediately a sense of dread came over me. Flashes of my spinning ova and gloved fingers tweaking my nipples ran through my mind. I reached into my purse for my inhaler and sucked down a preemptive cold stream of air before opening the door to the Caravan.

"I'll get rid of them," Jerry said, puffing up his chest; but I shook my head and picked up the Duchess without looking back.

"It's all right," I said, "I'm willing to talk."

Norton and Vassy sauntered across the front lawn with a team of hospital security guards trailing behind them.

"Over here, Doctor!" the photographers called; and Norton stopped to give them a wide smile. For another shot he reached inside his suit pocket and put on his stethoscope, turning to the side for a profile. Vassy clapped his hands in appreciation.

"Hey, Doc," one of the reporters yelled, "any sign yet of the grandmother and the clone?"

Norton opened his mouth to speak, but the security guards surrounded him and led him toward the door. Before he turned away, Vassy held his immaculately tanned hand in the air and gave them a thumbs-up.

"The doctor will have more to say on this week's *Hindsight* with Sophie Sussman. That's all we have for you boys right now."

One of the security guards waved to Jerry and grinned, his teeth shining. He was one of the men who had searched the house that first day; I recognized him immediately. Jerry must have, too. A fine blush drifted up Jerry's cheeks and down his neck, turning the skin above the neckline of his tank top a soft crimson. I'd never seen him blush before.

"Well, Maxine," Norton said, once we were inside the house, "have you found your mother yet?"

I smirked at him and shook my head. He reached down to press his stethoscope to the Duchess's chest, but she opened her mouth and hissed at him, her ears going flat, the air blowing out over my arms. One of the security guards stepped forward, but I let her drop from my arms before he could grab her.

I looked out the window and saw that Anita had gotten stuck behind a wall of reporters. Only her ponytail was visible above the crowd. Vassy, Norton, and I sat at the kitchen table. Jerry and the security guard were standing by the front door. I forced a smile and tried not to act nervous. There was no telling what Norton might do to get Middle back. The find of his life had been snatched away before he had a chance to claim her as his own. He'd been outdone by Mother, like it or not.

Norton leaned forward on his elbows, the smell of cigarettes and aftershave permeating the air.

"You wouldn't be hiding her in here, now, would you?" he whispered. I felt my stomach tighten, the breath whistling in my chest.

"No, I'm not hiding her," I said, gritting my teeth. "I want my mother back more than you do, I can assure you of that."

"It's all right, Charles." Vassy laughed, patting my arm. "These reporters know every move she makes. The whole world knows what she's up to by now. She couldn't sneak her mother in here if she tried."

Anita came rushing into the front hall, her ponytail bouncing. Norton turned away from me and opened his arms to her. To my amazement, they greeted each other with an embrace, kissed each other's cheeks with loud smacks. I turned around to find Jerry, but he and the security guard were now standing shoulder to shoulder by the stove, leaning close and laughing. I took another blast from the inhaler and tried to catch my breath.

"Maxi," Anita said, grabbing for my arm, "Dr. Norton was my OB! He delivered Candy and Sandy. What a small world, don't you think?"

Norton punched her lightly on the arm and smiled triumphantly at me. The security guards gathered around us and stood with their arms folded, waiting for Norton's next move. He waved his hand to dismiss them, but the blond one lingered, careful to stay as close to Jerry as he could.

"You looked wonderful on television," Anita said, taking the seat opposite Norton. "Actually, at first I wasn't sure it was you, but then I ran for my girls as you started your press conference. They just couldn't believe that the man who brought them into the world was on TV. And frankly," she said, blushing, "neither could I."

Jerry and Ron, the blond security guard, served us coffee and danishes while Norton and Vassy sized up Anita and me. Norton's hair was perfectly gelled, and in the light from the window, I swear there was a hint of eyeliner in the bottom corner of his eye. Vassy just stared down at his manicured nails when Norton began to speak. Even though Vassy was the public-relations adviser, it was clear that Norton was running the show. Whatever setback he'd had by the kidnapping, he was clearly back in form.

"I'm sure by now you realize what the RGC means to the hospital and to me. A birth like this could mean research for sick children, an end to suffering. Women wouldn't even need men to get them pregnant anymore. The divorce rate would drop dramatically. Think of the possibilities for women's liberation. We need you to get that clone back for us, Maxine. And if you don't," he said, exhaling smoke, the gel in his hair thick and lightly flaking away at the scalp, "then certain things can be made difficult for you."

I looked over at Jerry, but he and the blond security guard were standing in the corner sipping herbal tea and comparing bracelets. Anita leaned with her breasts against the table, inching her chair closer to Norton's.

"You mean my insurance," I said, narrowing my eyes. "That's what you mean. I read the papers. I've heard all the rumors."

Norton set his cup down and signaled to Vassy, who reached inside his double-breasted suit for a sheet of paper and a pen.

"Dr. Norton is an extremely influential man, as you well know," Vassy said, handing me the pen. "He could break the HMOs, like that," he said, snapping his fingers. "And they know it. They won't risk losing all the business he brings them, I'm afraid, for one patient like you, clone or no clone."

I took a deep breath and thought of Mother's favorite saying, that you can't fight city hall. If that were true, you certainly couldn't fight the medical establishment. Even Mother would agree with me on this, I thought, which was why she'd run away rather than fight. She knew what we were up against.

"All of this is on one condition," I said finally, and set the pen down on the table. "I will not appear with Thophie—I mean, Sophie—Sussman. That would break my mother's heart."

My voice cracked on the last line. I bit my lip to fight back the tears. Anita reached over and held my hand, and for a minute we stared at each other, her eyes full, as we both seemed to be remembering the first time Mother had seen Fergie. Sophie Sussman had a history with us, and using her against Mother was a betrayal I was unwilling to commit.

Before Norton could answer, Anita let go of my hand and squeezed Norton's arm.

"I could do it, you know," she said, her ponytail

swishing behind her. "I know as much about Minnie as anyone. I've known her all my life. You could say I'm like a second daughter to her." She looked down at her hands for a moment and sighed. "Well, I guess more like a third daughter now, as the case may be. If she saw me on television, I'm sure we'd get a response."

No one said anything for a minute. Jerry moved away from the security guard and glanced at me.

"Actually," Vassy said finally, clearing his throat, "it's not an altogether bad idea. This way we won't appear to be exploiting the mother; and this woman is certainly attractive enough to appear on television. America loves blonds, after all, and I'm sure they'd relish hearing from someone who's been as close as family to these women."

Without looking at anyone I signed my name on the dotted line, promising to hand Middle over to the authorities if I were the one to find her first. I said nothing about the photographs Mother had sent me, just sat sipping at my coffee and watching Jerry and the security guard whispering in the shadows. Then Vassy, Norton, and Anita shook hands across the table. Everything seemed to be in order, they said. They would withdraw their pressure on my insurance company as long as I agreed to cooperate and Anita would appear on *Hindsight* in my place. Given the circumstances, Norton said, it was the least he could do.

"The hospital and I are not unsympathetic to you, Maxine," he said, smoothing his gelled hair back with one hand. "We know what a terrible blow this must be to you, to have your mother pass you over for the new you. But we simply must have that clone before she grows any more."

I said nothing; and Anita walked them out to the front door. Norton was right: It had been a terrible blow. Although I'd begun to feel a kind of distant curiosity about Middle, it was Mother I missed. Mother was my Achilles' heel, and they knew it—and so, it seemed, did the rest of the world.

I didn't bother to watch as Norton and the others pulled away. On the front page of the following day's newspaper a photo appeared of Anita and Norton standing shoulder to shoulder, her long ponytail curved around her shoulder and touching Norton's sleeve. Beneath their faces, the caption read: A FRIEND IN NEED. I tore Norton's picture off the page and lined the Duchess's litter box with the shreds, smiling to myself when she squatted down to relieve herself. *Piss on you,* I thought, as the stream leaked over Norton's face, the urine bleaching his features until all that was left of him was a pattern of crazy dots.

On the day of the *Hindsight* taping, Jerry suggested that Ron, the blond security guard, remain at the house with us for the time being. I didn't exactly see why we needed Ron—we'd be free of reporters for a while, at least, since they'd be following Anita to the television studio, where it was rumored that Norton would also give yet another press conference—but I told Jerry that it was all right with me. After all, we had no romantic attachment; even our night on the cattery floor had turned out to be a blunder.

"We could use another pair of hands," Jerry said, fluffing his perm with his fingers.

"You mean *you* could," I said under my breath; and then we were both quiet for a long time.

Before the taping, Anita called to ask me if I'd mind taking the twins for a time, even if it meant taking them with me to look for Mother.

"These reporters seem to see me as a kind of go-between," she said, her voice breathless with anticipation. "Since Minnie is so angry with you right now, they think it would be best if I did a few more appearances— you know, to try to draw her out. You could take the twins with you. They might even be able to help. You know how your mother's always loved them."

Of course I agreed. Who was I to refuse anyone at this stage of the game, especially since Anita had been the one to pull me out of my depression and force me to take a stand? She'd always dreamed of being on television.

We watched *Hindsight* in the living room—Jerry and Ron on the love seat while I sat in the recliner, with the Duchess in my lap. I'd left Bea downstairs with the others after the Duchess's rejection, in the hope that some time apart might heal whatever had gone wrong between them. Several of my queens were in season, and I needed an experienced cat to keep them calm. Jerry made us a huge bowl of popcorn and real brewed iced tea, but I refused both. Watching Ron and him, squeezed together on the love seat, made my stomach churn.

When the theme music began, a wave of dread washed over me. Hy Brown sat with his hands folded on the desk, his fingers interlaced. Mother had always been a fan of his. She'd often said he was the last distinguished man left in America.

"Hy looks damn good for a man his age," Ron said. He elbowed Jerry and smiled.

"Yes," Jerry said. "Look at that full head of white hair."

I rolled my eyes at Jerry. The Duchess stuck her tail in the air.

Anita and Norton were smiling. They sat side by side in peach cushioned chairs, their arms touching lightly at the elbow. Anita's hair hung down over her shoulders, tiny wisps flipping up at the ends.

"She should have let me do her hair," Jerry whispered. "They've got way too much mousse in her hair."

Sophie Sussman leaned in closer, her face framed in gauzy light.

"If Minnie Dublin could be Fergie for a day," she said after a long pause, "tell us, Anita. What kind of Fergie would she be?"

Norton poked Anita in the ribs, the two of them giggling. Anita's face was flushed under the hot lights, the blond streaks casting a kind of halo over her head.

"She'd be the exact kind of Fergie that Fergie really is," she said, tossing her hair over one shoulder. "Minnie wouldn't change a thing."

I sat there staring at the screen, unable to move for several minutes. Blue lines snaked over Anita's teeth and lips, waves of static warping their faces. Jerry jumped up and ran to the television, banging the set with the palm of his hand until the picture came clear again.

I ran down the stairs to the cattery, two at a time, and let each one of the cats out of the cages. The studs mewed furiously with delight at being released and ran straight for the females, tugging at their necks and pushing them down with their heavy paws.

I heard Jerry calling my name, but I didn't answer; I

just sat cross-legged on the floor, letting the cats have at one another.

All at once Jerry and Ron stood in front of me, their mouths hanging open in horror as the studs began to mount, hips curving, the low growling in their throats.

"My god, Maxi," Jerry screamed, "you'll have kittens till kingdom come!"

I ignored him and ran for the tape player, switching on the tape and turning it up to full volume. Tom Jones's throaty voice drowned out the cats' moans. "What's new, pussycat? Whoa-oh, whoa-oh, whoa..."

The mating went on and on. I sat in the middle of the room, with my fingers in my ears to block out their sounds. By the end of side one of Tom Jones's greatest hits, the studs had triumphed over all twelve of the females—except for the Duchess and Bea, who stayed perched at the top of the stairs, wagging their tails from side to side and hissing furiously if one of the studs attempted to climb even the first step. Jerry and Ron had tried to stop the studs at first, throwing water on their backs and hitting them with newspapers, but it was no use. Finally they'd given up after five of the females had been successfully overtaken. The smell of cat spray hung heavily in the air.

"Do something," Jerry begged, trying to pull me to my feet as the tape player switched itself off. "They're ruining every chance you've ever had for Cat of the Year."

But I just shook my head slowly, an odd smile forming on my lips that I couldn't seem to stop. I mouthed the words to Jerry, leaning forward to whisper in his ear.

" 'What's new, pussycat?' " I sang. " 'Whoa-oh, whoa-oh, whoa...' " When he pulled away I shrugged and smiled sadly. "There's no such thing as the perfect cat, anyway."

The phone rang while I was getting the cats settled back into their cages. We all stared at one another. Ron reached for his gun.

"Do you want me to get it?" Ron asked, but I slammed the cage door and ran, almost tripping over the Duchess on my way up the stairs.

"Hello?" I said breathlessly. No answer, only breath hissing into the receiver. "Anita, is that you? Did you hear anything from Mother?"

A child's laugh rang in my ear, quick hiccuping giggles followed by the sounds of cars whizzing by.

"No, it's not Anita or your precious Dr. Norton," the voice whispered. "It's your mother."

The child's laughter grew louder, the traffic sounds blaring in my ear. With all the background noise, I could scarcely make out the whispers. It had been so long since I'd heard Mother's voice, soft and calm as a dream, that I couldn't be sure if it was really her. Maybe Cecilia could throw her voice, I thought. Maybe her talent for impersonating celebrities and women's mothers wasn't the only crazy thing she could do. Or maybe it was Norton trying to trip me up again.

"Mother?" I whispered back. "Is it really you?"

When she didn't respond, I went on.

"I never meant for this to happen," I said. "You've got to believe me. I did this for you."

There was a long pause and then the sound of muffled whispers. The child had stopped laughing.

"We watched *Hindsight*. We know what you're trying to do. But we're not coming in, not even for Sophie."

When I didn't respond, she let out a long sigh.

"Someone has something to say to you," Mother said. "Someone wants to say hello."

I moved to the edge of the steps and banged on the door to the cattery to signal to Jerry. What could I do to stop her? I'd never stood a chance against Mother on my own; the pregnancy alone was evidence of that. I banged on the door again, but there was no answer, just the collective sounds of exhausted meows drifting up the stairs.

"OK," I said, tightening my grip on the cord. "I'm listening."

I held my breath and closed my eyes, gripping the cord until my knuckles ached. A long slow sigh echoed in my ear.

"Hi," a child's voice said, high-pitched and squeaky. "Hi-hi."

I dropped to my knees and swallowed hard.

"Who is this?" I said, my voice rising. "Who are you?"

Laughter rang in my ear. The voice squealed with delight.

"Me," the voice said. "Me-me-me-me-me!"

I wheezed and choked. Gasping for air, I crawled across the kitchen to the drawer where I kept the extra inhaler. The voice wheezed, too—whistling, ragged gasps of air. The drawer fell to the floor, spilling prenatal vitamins and cat medicine droppers all over the ceramic tile. The inhaler lay next to a snapshot of me in a plaid maternity dress, Mother's arm draped over my shoulder.

I cleared my throat and pressed the receiver to my ear.

"Is it you?" I coughed, struggling to spray the mist down my throat.

"You," the voice said. "Me."

I took a deep breath and held it for as long as I could. Mother came on the line again, her voice quivering as she spoke.

"It's you," she said, sighing heavily. "It's you, all right."

I said nothing for a long time, just sat there on the cold tile, the photo of me in the maternity dress between my legs. My breathing slowed, becoming less labored as I stared down at the snapshot. My face was lit with a soft blush; our red hair shone in the sunlight. *We'd been so happy then,* I thought. Mother and daughter waiting for their new arrival.

Middle started to cry, softly at first, but then louder, and I realized stifled sobs had been welling up in my chest. She could feel my sadness as I stared at that photo, the deep longing from having lost Mother. I wanted to tell Middle that I wouldn't abandon her, that she didn't have to be afraid, that I'd save her from the reporters. But I stopped myself. It was a lie, after all. Even though Mother had stolen her away, I'd let her go. I could have put up a fight, but I simply hadn't been strong enough to stop Mother.

"I'm sorry," I whispered.

The connection was broken before I could say anything else. Gently I laid the receiver back in its cradle and just sat there on the floor for a long time afterward, staring at the photo of myself swollen with pregnancy, Mother's arm draped so casually over my shoulder.

After a time, I heard a knock at the front door, soft at first, then louder and more insistent.

The cattery was quiet. A reporter on TV was recapping the *Hindsight* interview in a monotonous voice. In a daze I walked to the front door and opened it before asking who was there.

Cecilia stood in the doorway, dressed in a red-and-white polka-dot dress and a white picture hat. The style had been a favorite of Fergie's; I recognized it right away from Mother's tabloid magazines. Beside her were Candy and Sandy in their Brownie uniforms, each holding Cecilia by the hand, their eyes brimming with tears.

"Let's go," Cecilia said in a faintly British accent. "Let's go get your mums back for you. And get yourself back, too."

I nodded and got down on my knees. The Duchess and Bea stood in the corner, watching, as Candy and Sandy stepped forward and wrapped their arms around my neck. The cats came over and nuzzled the girls' legs, their red-and-white tails twitching in the air. Without saying anything, Cecilia stood there and stroked our hair, humming "God Save the Queen" low in her throat.

We had packed the Caravan before midnight. Candy and Sandy helped load the Duchess and Bea into the backseat, in their cages, while Cecilia filled the litter boxes with fresh sand. The best plan, we'd decided—after much discussion about childhood and adolescence—was to head south on the interstate and try to find the nearest wrestling match. Using Middle's recent growth spurts as a guide, Cecilia and I estimated that she could feasibly reach puberty within weeks. Mother had taken me to wrestling matches when they were at their peak of popularity, a time which had coincided with my own onset of bodily changes. We'd gone to a slew of matches in Connecticut, and not long afterward, Mother had embarked on a quest for a wrestler of her own. Since Mother seemed to be revisiting the past, it was only logical, Cecilia said, that she would try to recapture some of her own past.

"If this baby is you and you're her and all that lot," Cecilia said in a polished British accent, "then Mum's going to be fixing to have a little spell of fun herself, I dare say, wouldn't you, luv?"

I smiled and said it seemed as fine a plan as any, though the thought of finding myself surrounded by wrestlers with greased bodies and bulging thighs filled me with distaste. I knew that if Mother really was bent on repeating our history, she'd find a way to snatch up a wrestler.

On Cecilia's advice, I gathered photographs of the various stages of Middle's development: the snapshot of me in the plaid maternity dress, the Polaroid of Mother with Middle snuggled in her backpack, and the laminated black-and-whites Mother had sent me.

"Maybe we should watch the Sophie Sussman video," I said, as I stuffed the photos into a cardboard box, then knotted it closed with bakery string. "Anita was there the first time we saw it. It will tie in with *Hindsight*."

Cecilia smiled and squeezed my arm just above the elbow, softly but urgently, just like Mother. I had no choice but to trust her.

Outside, the street was quiet. One of the guards told us the last of the reporters had fled at the first sight of Anita on his portable television.

"The guy just loves blonds," he said with a laugh. "At least now maybe you may get some peace and quiet."

I explained briefly that I'd be going out of town for a time but that Jerry would stay in my place. When he asked if I was going out to look for Mother, I just smiled and looked down at my hands.

"You all have been good to me," I said. "I won't forget you."

While the guards watched Candy and Sandy settle into the backseat with the cats and drawing pads and crayons, I went down into the cattery to look for Jerry. I hadn't seen him since the cats' mating frenzy. As I walked down the stairs, I couldn't help thinking that since the fateful night I'd worn the red teddy and lured him in, we'd come so far and yet hadn't progressed at all.

The cats were asleep in their cages, the studs' mouths open in sheer exhaustion, tongues hanging from their parted lips. I switched on the overhead light and called Jerry's name, but there was no answer. He'd been angry with me for letting the cats mate at will, throwing everything I'd worked for to the wind. Jerry had always hoped we'd travel across the country together when one of my cats won Cat of the Year. He could amass hundreds of clients—Persians, Himalayans, Maine Coons, even some of the shorthaired breeds like the Chartreux. We could show the cat world what a breeder and a groomer could do when they put their heads together, he'd said. Sadly, we knew all too well what the consequences of our togetherness had been.

I was filling one of the cat's water bowls when I heard a shot. The bottle fell from my hands, water rushing over the floor. I ran to the back door and swung it open before I had a chance to think. For a fleeting moment I thought that Norton had come back brandishing a gun and looking for blood. Or that Mother had found herself a militant wrestler to come hunt me down, once and for all, and tie me to a tree in a full nelson and poke at me with his shotgun. But Mother had never liked men with guns or banjos. Any man who would rather pull a trigger or pluck strings was no man in her book. Of course, she knew that Charles and the other royals counted hunting among their favorite pastimes, but she held fast on her stance against guns. The women were the *real* royalty in the family, she liked to say. And when it came to hunting, the dogs did all the work.

I was hiding behind the door, when Jerry came running toward me with Ron trailing behind. They had on army fatigues and black eyeliner smudged under their eyes. I screamed when I saw them.

Jerry pressed his hand over my mouth and stared into my eyes.

"We thought you were Norton," he breathed, then let his hand fall away from my mouth. Beads of sweat glinted in his black spikes. "We saw a van pull up outside and thought it was Norton coming back for ransom. We were staked out in the bushes. Good god, Maxi," he said, taking a deep breath, "We could have shot you."

Ron stepped forward and smiled at me, his heavy blond mustache smudged with black eyeliner.

"Not likely, Miss Maxi," he said, shoving the gun back into its holster. "This gun only holds blanks."

Jerry laughed, slapped Ron on the back, and gave him a playful sucker punch in the stomach. In the moonlight I could see the glow had not yet left Jerry's cheeks.

"Did you hear that?" Jerry asked. "This man shoots blanks."

I stared hard at Jerry, at his glistening biceps and spandex top, the way he hung on Ron's every word. While I was on the telephone being tormented by the sound of my own voice coming from a miniature version of myself and having my life dissected by Sophie Sussman, Jerry and his newfound friend had been outside playing cops and robbers. *Mother was right,* I thought. *Fathers can't be counted on.* Especially those who were never really fathers to begin with.

"He's not the only one," I said.

Jerry stopped laughing. He looked toward the bushes where he'd buried the deformed kittens. I imagined them lying side by side under the earth, their clawlike feet curled up toward their bellies.

He glanced at me and gave me a sad smile, his shoulders sagging. My remark was the kind of thing Mother would have said. She'd always been the sharp-tongued one in the family. Maybe in her absence I was beginning to take on some of her traits.

Ron stuffed his hands into his pockets and headed back toward the bushes.

"I'll be on the lookout if you need me," he called to Jerry over his shoulder.

I'd never before said anything with such cruel intent to Jerry and had to bite my lip to keep from crying. I'd seen the way Jerry had been looking at Ron, how he tried to keep from smiling at him all the time, the fine nervous blush rising in his cheeks. The skittish way he darted his eyes when Ron caught him staring. Jerry had never looked at me that way, not even that night as he lay on top of me in the cattery. I'd caught him unawares, like a seductress, like a wrestler, pinning him down in my teddy with an aching womb and a desperate mother.

Without saying anything more I led him back through the cattery, past the rows of sleeping cats, and up the stairs to the kitchen. My suitcases sat by the door, one of my maternity blouses hanging on the door handle. Cecilia beeped the horn from the driveway. I lifted the blouse, opened the door, and signaled to her that I needed a few minutes.

"You're going, aren't you?" Jerry said, closing the door and leaning toward me. He wiped at his eyes, smearing eyeliner down one side of his face.

"Yes," I said, looking down at the floor. "Anita's going on the TV circuit. Candy and Sandy will want their mommy back. I've got to end this once and for all."

Jerry nodded and reached for my hand.

"And what about you? Don't you want yours back, too?"

One of the suitcases fell over and I reached down to set it right side up again.

"I don't know anymore," I said softly.

As we stood there quietly, I thought of telling him about the phone call, about the excitement I'd heard in Middle's voice at introducing herself. Perhaps Middle could love me, even after I'd cast her off, and maybe I wasn't such a bad person after all. Jerry loved me despite my self-centered ramblings and my fierce attachment to my mother.

An air of impatience hung between us. I looked at Jerry and smiled, reaching up to smooth away some of the smudged eyeliner with my thumb.

"You know I'll come if you want me to," he said. "Ron may have a gun, but it only shoots blanks. The same goes for me. You said so yourself." He took a deep breath and let out a long sigh. "None of this could have happened without you, Maxi."

I dropped my hand to my side and wiped the black eyeliner on my jeans.

"Now I've got to own up," I said, lifting my suitcases

while he opened the door. "But I need someone to stay and watch the cattery. This place will be crawling with reporters when they find out I'm gone. And there will be kittens all over before you know it. I'll have to sell every one to pay Cecilia's bill."

We laughed then and made our way out to the Caravan. Cecilia had stepped down from the driver's seat to open the back door. Her red hair and polka-dot dress blew softly in the breeze. Jerry set the suitcases in the back and then handed me the box of photographs tied together with string.

"We've got to get started on this thing now, mates," Cecilia said. "Your mums await you."

For a minute we stood there in the night air, a cloud of exhaust swirling behind us. In the backyard I saw Ron crouched in the bushes near the kittens' makeshift grave. Jerry shrugged, then caught me in an embrace before I had a chance to catch my breath. We stood there a long time holding on to each other, his warm hands pressed to the small of my back, my cheek scraping the roughness of his five o'clock shadow.

I finally settled into the passenger seat and pulled my seat belt across my lap. Candy and Sandy whimpered in the backseat.

"We want to see Mommy," they said in unison. "Mommy's on TV."

I turned away from Jerry as he closed the passenger door, and signaled Cecilia that I was ready to go. As we pulled away from the curb, I stuck my head out the passenger window and let my curls whip around my face in the wind. The guards stood in line along the yard, their hands raised in salute. I waved to Jerry until he became a shadow on the dark lawn, his arm extended high in the air. The Duchess began to cry then, deep in her chest, the sound reverberating through the car. I turned in my seat to see what was wrong, but Candy and Sandy were already cooing to her through the bars of the cage.

"It's all right, kitty," they said, their heads coming together as they leaned toward the cage. "You just want your mama, don't you? We want our mama, too."

Cecilia reached over and took my hand, her freckled hand clashing with the polka dots in her dress. I looked down at our fingers interlaced on the console, at the thin lines of freckles on my arm and the paler spots on hers. I thought of all the times Mother had held my hand this way, her palm warm in mine, the soft ivory of our skin pressed close together. I wondered if she were holding Middle's hand at that very moment, her strong hand grasping the plumpness of Middle's fingers.

"You don't need your mother to hold your hand, mate," Cecilia whispered as we headed down the road toward Mother's house. "You're a big girl now. You'll see."

I nodded and pulled my hand away, listening to the sounds of Candy and Sandy humming lullabies in the dark. As I laid my head back against the seat, I realized that Cecilia was right. All my life Mother had been holding my hand or I'd been holding hers—through personal ads and high school crushes, in the cattery and in the delivery room. Now that we'd let go, there was a tingling in my arm like the phantom feelings of an amputee.

Winfield, NY (AP)—MacArthur Hospital officials announced today they will begin a na-
tionwide search for the missing human clone.
During his appearance on ABC's *Hindsight*,
with Sophie Sussman, Dr. Charles W. Norton,
the obstetrician who delivered the clone,
claimed that insurance companies have
threatened to withdraw all malpractice insurance if the clone is not recovered. Fur-
thermore, Norton said that doctors could no
longer rely on the support of HMOs if such
kidnappings were allowed to occur.

"It is an outrage against the medical profession that police and federal agents have
not located this clone and remanded her to
our custody," Norton told Sussman in an exclusive interview. "We physicians are the
keepers of the flame. Depriving us of re-
sources such as this and threatening our very
ability to heal mankind is a great blow to our
profession."

"First, Sophie," Norton continued, "do no
harm."

Anita Jones, a childhood friend of Maxine
Dublin, the thirty-four-year-old prize-winning
Persian cat breeder who mothered the clone,
expressed her opinion that Minnie Dublin,
the clone's grandmother, was indeed responsible for the kidnapping. In what Jones said
promises to be but the first of several nation-
ally televised appearances, she appealed di-

rectly to Mrs. Dublin herself, looking straight into the camera at Sussman's behest.

"If you're out there, Minnie, and you can hear me," said Jones, "bring that baby home."

Last night witnesses reported that Maxine Dublin fled her home with a red-haired woman and a pair of twin girls. Neighbors claim to have seen Ms. Dublin leave the home at approximately 12:30 A.M. When asked for a description of her companion, a neighbor had this to say: "I could have sworn she was with Fergie, though I know it couldn't have been really her."

An editorial in the *Journal of American Medicine* expressed the doubts of hundreds of biotechnologists who claim the clone is a fraud perpetrated on the public by Dr. Norton and his publicist, Gus Vassy. Geneticists have decried Norton's reluctance to publish his findings and his increasingly cryptic explanations.

"A clone is produced from a single cell," one geneticist said. "Why won't [Norton] at least disclose the type of cell that was used? The scientific community cannot support the belief that the clone was created by an ovum alone."

Norton will appear in an interview with Mike Wallace on Sunday's *60 Minutes*, reportedly to answer some of his critics. Both Norton and Jones are scheduled to appear on

Live with Gary Tate **this Thursday evening, 9 P.M. EST.**

Sometime before dawn, we had stopped for a newspaper and coffee. Beneath the article was a picture of Mother from several years ago. In the photo she was standing in front of the mantel at her house, which at the time had been covered with snapshots of me from my childhood. I couldn't help but wonder what Mother's house looked like now that Middle had come into her life. Had she hung polka-dot bears from a mobile over the crib like the ones from my baby photos? Would she have cut my face out of family snapshots and glued Middle's face where mine had been? Maybe in her rage she'd turned my old bedroom into a nursery and destroyed everything to show me what she'd done with my past, that she'd sacrificed it for the feel of Desitin on her fingers again and crib sheets stained with drool.

I stole a glance at Candy and Sandy, who were sleeping with their heads together, their hands clasped over a cartoon they'd drawn of Anita trapped inside a TV screen, her ponytail coming out the back like a kind of electric cord. When I turned around in my seat again, Cecilia offered me a teething ring in the shape of a pink pretzel. I had to stop myself from grabbing at it, whisking it out of her hand and into my pocket.

"I believe this is yours, luv," she said, holding out the teething ring. She leaned forward and whispered in my ear, the wisps of her red hair tickling my cheek. "Got to have the right props, now, don't we? Props are a necessity. If you feel like a motherless child, might as well act the part."

I let go of Candy's hand to grab the teething ring. The rubber was worn from all the sucking, tiny holes scattered along the pretzel's loops from the urgent stabbing of a wayward tooth.

"Where did you get this?" I asked. "How did you know this was mine?"

She shrugged and reached inside the lapel of her dress for a pair of eyeglasses exactly like Mother's. Before I could say anything, she put them on.

"It's like I told you, luv," she said in her British accent. "This sort of thing saves tons of time. The way things are headed now with all these HMOs, you're going to need the speediest cure I can deliver."

I stuffed the teething ring into my pocket and turned away. How silly I was to think I could keep secrets from anyone now that I'd given birth to a living, breathing, teething version of myself. Mother had always told me, "I know you better than you know yourself." I'd never really thought it was possible.

Staring out the window, I wondered where Middle might be. If she was still a child, she was now out of synch with my childhood. Mother had not taken me on a long road trip until I was in my teens, to see a wrestling match in Connecticut. Maybe being on the run had caused Mother to rush things. Or maybe Middle wanted to fast-forward to adolescence, past all the "kitchy-cooing" and being held day and night.

I turned around in my seat and offered the teething ring to Candy and Sandy. They rubbed their eyes and reached over the seat to take it from me, both wrapping their fingers around it at the same time.

"I used to have one just like this," Candy said

sleepily. Sandy smiled and leaned her head against Candy's.

"So did I," Sandy said.

I smiled at them and laid my hand over theirs, the three of us touching the teething ring as if it were some lucky charm.

"So did I," I said, and we nodded in unison.

Cecilia shifted her weight in the driver's seat. Beneath the blue-framed glasses, I could see a faint smudging of eyeliner in the corner of her eye. She yanked up the sleeve of her dress and checked her watch. Lifting a pencil from behind her ear, she jotted numbers down on a pad of white paper.

"We're off the clock now," she said, dropping the British accent. She smeared her freckles with a tissue. "No more Fergie today. This session's over."

I didn't respond. *She can certainly be abrupt,* I thought as I watched her scrubbing at her face with a tissue dampened with saliva. I'd always thought that therapists asked all kinds of questions about how things made you feel, whether you dreamed in color or black and white, what animal you might be if ever given the choice to transform yourself. It was a relief not to answer such questions. Apparently being Fergie was enough.

Several hours later Cecilia said we were back on the clock again. She had put on her red wig and painted on her freckles, though I insisted she not wear the eyeglasses. As she drove I told Cecilia (who insisted I address her as Fergie for authenticity) what I remembered of Mother's days with the wrestlers. There had been quite a few different men, I said, but none of them stood out in my memory. In fact, the more I thought of them, their faces all seemed to meld into one, veins bulging from their foreheads at the sound of my birth story being repeated to them like a mantra.

"Was she trying to get pregnant?" Cecilia asked, and I laughed at first, but then stopped myself as I realized that that might have been what she was after all along. "They can give you a baby," she'd said, "that's the only thing men are good for." Why else would she have told the story of my birth so many times? She must have been desperate for another daughter.

"I'd never thought of that," I said; and Cecilia grunted low in her throat. "Besides, the wrestlers disappeared once Fergie—I mean you—came along."

Cecilia turned toward me and laughed. I had to give her credit for precision. Each freckle was carefully delineated, the wig the exact same shade as Fergie's.

"Do I really look like your mum?" she asked in her lilting British accent.

"Well, when she was younger, at least," I said. "Not so much anymore, of course. But when she was young, she was a dead ringer. I've got the wedding picture to prove it."

I dug it out of my overnight bag and handed it to her, holding the wheel while she propped the photo against the steering wheel and smiled.

"I'll say, there is quite a resemblance, luv," she said. "Sounds like Mum's got one big bloody ego."

I didn't answer, just slid the photo back inside my overnight bag, my signal that our session was over. Cecilia didn't seem to mind. She scribbled some numbers on her little white pad, but this time she left the freckles alone, checking herself periodically in the rearview mirror. She really seemed to enjoy being Fergie.

The twins had slept most of the trip with the Duchess and Bea sprawled across their laps. I looked back at them from time to time and thought about what a wonderful job Anita had done as a mother. The girls were no trouble at all, content to draw together and pet the cats without whining about having to stop for the bathroom or crying for their mother. For the most part they seemed happy just to be together, holding hands and smoothing each other's hair with contented smiles on their faces.

"I don't get it," I whispered to Cecilia when we stopped at a doughnut shop for coffee and a newspaper. "They seem to be fine without their mother."

"That's because they have each other, luv," she said. "They've always got each other."

Cecilia smiled as I paid for the doughnuts, coffee, and paper, then we hurried back to the car. I couldn't help noticing that her British accent had not begun to fade as the hours passed. She bit into a doughnut as I buckled myself into the driver's seat. The girls asked politely for chocolate doughnuts and licked at the frosting. Cecilia took a large bite of a jelly doughnut, smearing white powder over her nose and mouth. She wiped her mouth with the back of her sleeve, powder clinging to the wool of her dark green sweater. Although her physical resemblance to Fergie was undeniable, she had a long way to go in learning royal manners. If Mother had seen her doing such a thing, she'd have known right away that this Fergie was a fake. I slipped Cecilia a napkin from my paper bag as I pulled onto the ramp of the interstate.

"I can only keep up the Fergie routine for so long," she said, patting her lips with the napkin. "It takes too much energy to be regal."

She smiled and rubbed under her eyes, smearing the freckles. The dots widened into round circles over her cheeks and along her chin. I reached over and poked at one on her arm.

"Hell," she said, yawning and tossing the napkin over her shoulder, "I've got to save some energy for the showdown. God knows what your mother might do when she sees me. She might wrestle me to the ground out of pure shock."

I said nothing and continued to drive south while Cecilia slept in the passenger seat. Candy and Sandy woke up sometime later, and leaned forward in their seats. The smell of cat urine had grown intense. We had to stop and find a place to freshen up.

"Are we almost there, Aunt Maxi?" Sandy asked.

"When is Mommy going to be on TV again?" Candy asked.

I promised that we would stop in time to watch their mother on *Live with Gary Tate* and asked them to draw me a picture of Cecilia while I drove. They were happy with that suggestion and went straight to work, scribbling with their crayons as the sun came up. I glanced over at Cecilia, who was sleeping heavily, her mouth open, a thin line of drool hanging down from her lip and dripping onto the front of her green sweater.

With just the road ahead of me and the sound of the twins rubbing their crayons against the manila paper, I thought of what Mother and I might say to each other when we finally met again. There would be no script this time, no rehearsals. No time for getting it right. Whatever we said to each other could not be attributed to a flubbed line, a careless slip of the tongue. What we would say to each other when we met again could only be new.

I stopped for gas sometime later. The twins and I got out and stretched our legs and took turns using the ladies' room. The Duchess and Bea relieved themselves in their litter boxes; I replenished the boxes with fresh sand and filled plastic bowls with water and tunafish. Cecilia primped in the rearview mirror. Carefully she let down the long red hair and shook it over her shoulders, squinting in the mirror while she retouched her freckles with an eyebrow pencil.

I went inside to pay for the gas, keeping an eye on the twins through the plate glass window. Cecilia had no mothering instincts as far as I could tell. She hadn't once bothered to ask the girls if they needed to stop for the bathroom or to offer comfort where Anita was concerned—maybe seeing their mother on TV would only make them feel worse. Granted, Cecilia was hired as my actress-therapist, but at the very least, I'd expected she might show some concern for the girls. She'd barely glanced at the Duchess or Bea, who had several times purred in her direction, rubbing their faces over the back of her seat once we'd let them out of their cages. Even I felt a tightness in my throat at the sight of Candy and Sandy coloring in portraits of their mother with a long yellow ponytail and a skirt swirling with psychedelic polka dots. Without so much as a glance in their direction, Cecilia went about the business of perfecting her Fergie look, oblivious to anyone around her. All of her attention focused on me, a fact which, *unsettling* as it was, I had to admit I found flattering.

I watched from the counter as the twins offered drawings of Anita to various passersby. When the clerk handed me my change I tiptoed out to the parking lot so as not to startle them.

"This is my mother," they said as they handed out the pictures. "She's been on TV."

"That's nice," said one middle-aged woman, who stopped by the Caravan to peer in at Cecilia. She patted Sandy on the head and tapped at the window.

"Hey," she said, crumpling the drawing in her fist, "did anyone ever tell you how much you look like Fergie?"

Cecilia leaned out the passenger-side window and flashed the woman a smile smeared with pink lipstick. The woman dropped the drawing on the ground by the twins' feet.

"Someone's got to look like Fergie," Cecilia said with a sigh, her British accent returning suddenly, "It might as well be me."

Without looking at each other the twins knelt down on the pavement and picked up the crumpled ball of paper. I hurried across the parking lot and handed Cecilia a wad of napkins through the window to blot her lipstick. Sandy pressed the drawing against the side of the Caravan and spread her palm across Anita's face, her fingers smoothing the ponytail, flattening the creases in the polka-dot skirt. I handed each of the twins candy bars that I'd bought inside.

Candy took hers and nibbled at it thoughtfully for a moment before taking the drawing from her sister and pressing it over her chest.

"Maybe we won't need a TV to see Mommy," Candy said as I held the door open to the van. "Maybe Mommy will find us instead."

None of us said anything as Cecilia blotted her lipstick over and over until it was the exact same shade as Fergie's in one of Mother's tabloids. Then Cecilia mumbled under her breath that therapy was not free, that she was not about to counsel a pair of abandoned twins.

"It's you I'm here for, luv," she whispered. "One bloody set of twins at a time."

I smiled to myself and turned the key in the ignition. The cats began to howl when the van started, deep growls that rumbled in their chests.

As I pulled out of the driveway I noticed the middle-aged woman staring at Cecilia. She ran for the pay phone on the corner as I pulled out onto the street, waving her arms when we drove by.

"Fergie," she called, over the whine of the traffic, "is it really you?"

Without a word Cecilia rolled down the window and tossed out the wad of paper napkins. The white balls flew toward the woman, pink lipstick blots spinning in the air. The woman ran after them, hands outstretched, fists opening and closing as she fought to catch the napkins in her hands.

"What the world won't do for a piece of Fergie." Cecilia sighed.

I nodded, not looking at her. For a moment I glanced at the rearview mirror and caught a glimpse of the woman dancing in circles on the street corner, lipstick-stained napkins clutched in her fists. That could have been Mother, I thought with a sad smile as I turned onto the interstate. She would have held on to those napkins for dear life, never bothering to realize that Fergie's kiss would never smear so cheaply; Fergie's kiss would be permanent. If it looked like Fergie's kiss, then it might as well have been, no matter how cheap or false it actually was.

Later, we stopped at a diner, planning to ask directions to the nearest wrestling match. For the past few hours we had been off the clock, and Cecilia had had little to say, only commenting occasionally on the landscape or doing vocal exercises designed to strengthen her British accent. She mustn't sound like a commoner, she'd said, with bad cockney or the wrong lilt. Besides no one had ever said therapy was easy, she continued as we pulled into the parking lot. Often all you had to go on was the fuzziness of memory and the belief that what lurked inside your head was worth examining.

I let the Duchess and Bea out of their cages to roam free in the Caravan while we went inside for a bite to eat. Candy and Sandy were silent as we headed to the ladies' room while Cecilia settled into a booth.

A few hours earlier Cecilia had put on a blond wig with a ponytail that hung down her back. She had asked the girls if they wanted her to bake some brownies. The girls had started to cry immediately and begged her to remove the wig. She was not their mother, they'd said. They might be young but they weren't stupid.

"Our mommy bakes brownies from scratch," Candy had said through her tears. "You could never be her."

It had taken me some time to calm them down, playing tic-tac-toe and hangman in the backseat. I promised them that Cecilia would not impersonate their mother again.

As we stood in line waiting for an open stall in the rest room, the three of us huddled together. The girls' ponytails drooped down their backs, snarls of hair tucked around the rubber bands.

"Why don't you let me fix your hair?" I asked.

They nodded and smiled up at me, their faces lined with sleep, eyes moist from missing their mother. *At nine,* I thought, *it is so easy to be forgiving.*

I knelt down on the floor and positioned them in front of me. By now I could see how different they really were, and I wondered why it had taken me all these years to notice. Perhaps I'd never taken the time to really look at them. Sandy's chin was slightly longer, her smile more crooked and easy. Candy's eyes were deep set and smoky blue, her shoulders broader and more pronounced. Slowly I eased the rubber bands out of each of their ponytails and lifted the silky hair between my fingers. Carefully I tugged the brush through the knots. When I was almost through I leaned forward and pressed my nose to their scalps, breathing in the sweetness of baby powder and innocence. An ache settled in my chest and held there. *This is what it is like to have a daughter,* I thought, imagining Anita with the twins' newborn scalps pressed against her, tufts of hair tickling her nose and mouth.

When we were finished they each took one of my

hands without saying a word. Together we walked across the room to the booth where Cecilia sat smudging freckles on her arms with a tissue. We sat on one side of the booth, Cecilia on the other.

"Hey, lady," a trucker said as we slid into our seats, "did anyone ever tell you how much you look like Fergie?"

When I realized he was looking at me, I thought he might have recognized me from the news. My heart pounded at the thought of a reporter on our tail. I nodded toward Cecilia, but he shook his head and gave me a big smile full of crooked teeth.

"No, not her," he said. "You."

I laughed and tossed my hair over one shoulder. "Oh, sure," I said, trying to disguise the tremor in my voice. "People tell me that all the time."

We said little to one another as we ate. Cecilia nibbled heartily at an English muffin and slurped tea, and the girls shoveled down french fries while I sipped coffee and nursed a baked potato.

I'd bought the *New York Post,* and I shuffled past yet another headline, complete with a photo of Norton and Anita, their shoulders touching. What more could anyone want, the editorial suggested, than a committed doctor and a devoted best friend? I folded the newspaper in half in case the sight of their mother on the front page might upset the twins. Seeing Mother in the news was disconcerting enough for me; since this was the very same paper she'd used for her personal ads, I couldn't imagine how it would have felt at nine.

Luckily the truckers had turned their papers to the sports pages. I scanned the sports section for wrestling matches, but there were only listings of televised matches and times, the latest in the NBA.

Cecilia hummed softly to herself, her lips glistening with butter. I stared at her as she ate, her lips pursed, tongue dabbing at the corners of her mouth to catch the dripping butter.

"You've got to have faith in me as a therapist, luv," Cecilia said, her British accent growing fainter as she spoke. She shrugged and crunched at her muffin. "If I'm going to help find your mother and your clone, we must be a team, you see. But you're not even sure if you want to find them—or yourself, for that matter."

The twins spit out their fries and burst into tears.

"What does she mean?" Candy asked, pulling at my sleeve.

"You don't want to find your baby?" Sandy said, her voice rising.

I hugged each of them to me and glared at Cecilia. She raised her teacup and smiled, her lipstick leaving a heavy blotch on the rim.

"Don't be silly," I said, gritting my teeth. "Of course I want to find her."

The girls clung to me as I soothed them. Cecilia sipped at her tea and stared out the window. I sent the girls off to the ladies' room to wash their faces and blow their noses, assuring them that I wanted to find my baby as much as they wanted their mommy back. Yet the truth of Cecilia's words stung me, even as I sat there sifting through the *Post*, the ink staining my fingertips.

I blotted my lips with a napkin and turned to the personal ads. Cecilia excused herself to paint on a new set of freckles out in the van. I just nodded as she walked away, too upset to trust my voice enough to respond to her. Maybe she wasn't such a fraud after all. At the very least, she knew how to get the better of me, just as Mother always had. When we met the wrestlers from the personal ads for coffee and bagels, Mother would inevitably tell them the sad story of my father's departure.

"Maxi's father took off before ever getting to know her," she would say between sips of her decaf, her eyes fluttering at the sight of the muscles bunching at the sides of their thick necks. "I guess he cared more about that banjo than he cared about her."

Although I never completely accepted this explanation of my father's exit, I couldn't help feeling sorry for myself at the prospect of being loved less than a five-string, even by a man I could hardly remember anymore.

When the twins returned from the ladies' room, I gave them a handful of bills to pay for the check at the register. Cecilia hadn't bothered to chip in, and I supposed that meals were included in her overall fee. While I waited for the change I scanned the ads, remembering all the men who had passed through our lives while Mother told the story of my birth over and over again like a seduction. I was about to close the paper and toss it away, when an ad in the upper right-hand corner caught my eye.

> *You—Seeking me. Me seeking you.*
> *You + Me = You. Signed, Me.*

Coffee spewed out of my mouth, spraying all over the newspaper. My heart pounded in my chest as I squinted to read the ad again. "Me seeking you." "You—

Seeking me." It was *her!* Even in her primitive baby-speak, her words sent the chill of recognition straight through me. I grabbed the newspaper and ran from the booth, my breath coming hard and fast as I pulled the twins by their arms and raced out to the van.

"It's her!" I screamed to Cecilia, who was sitting in the driver's seat, buckled in and ready to go. "Middle's put an ad in the paper!"

The cats yowled as the girls hurried into the backseat. Without a word I pressed the paper right up under Cecilia's nose—the way I would if one of my cats had urinated on it, I thought frantically, to prove to them what they had done. She pushed the paper away and lifted Mother's glasses to her face, peering at the words. Her face drained of color.

"Good lord, luv," she said, throwing the car into reverse, "she's gone out looking for you! We're on the clock again!"

I clutched the newspaper to my chest and buckled myself into the passenger seat, my head snapping back as Cecilia hit the gas. "Just drive, just drive!" I shouted. A spray of gravel ricocheted through the lot as we screeched toward the highway.

Sandy leaned forward from the backseat and pressed a hand on my shoulder.

"Your baby's looking for you?" she asked, her voice soft in my ear.

I just nodded and felt Cecilia reach over and take my hand, our fingers interlocking as we sped down the dark road.

The twins squealed with delight.

"Faster, faster!" they called. "Your baby wants you!"

I laughed giddily and threw my head back, the wind from the open window whipping the curls around my face, the cool air rushing in my open mouth. I hadn't felt this giddy since the night on the floor with Jerry, the cats' howls echoing through the cattery as we clutched at each other, so eager to produce a new me. "Do it for Mother," I had said in the heat of the moment, as if willing my own egg to split in two. And now the other half was coming for me, eager to welcome me back after the terrible way I'd rejected her. "Me seeking you," she'd said, her words there in black and white despite all that Mother had done to try to keep us apart.

Of course my elation lasted only a short time. When I turned on the overhead light, I realized there was no address or box number where the new me could be reached. I grabbed Cecilia by the arm and begged her to pull over.

"It's a tease," I said. "I still don't know where they are."

Cecilia tried to hold me back, but I bolted out the door and ran to a phone booth across the street. I dialed the number to Mother's house, pausing at the sound of her voice singing on the answering machine. I knew she had remote access to her machine and would have left another message for me by now. If there was one thing I knew about Mother, she was fastidious when it came to punishments.

Her voice came on after the third ring, as bold and as sharp as I'd ever heard it.

"Middle and Maxi sitting in a tree," she sang. "C-l-o-n-i-n-g. First comes love. Then comes Mother. Then before you know it, you've got another!"

Laughter rang through the receiver. Mother had teased me when I was beginning to like boys. The school-yard song had mocked my juvenile infatuations— only the original version ended with a baby carriage, just as she'd always dreamed it would. I gripped the receiver with both hands and waited for the beep.

"Hello, Mother," I said, taking a deep breath and straightening my shoulders. "I know you'll hear this wherever you are. Well, I got the message and I'm going to find out where you are. Maybe Middle will leave you, too, if you're not careful. Maybe she'll say you're unfit and that it's me she really wants. After all," I said, pausing to let my words sink in, "I'm her real mother."

I slammed the phone down and paced around the parking lot, trying to catch my breath. My chest felt tight. Cecilia called to me from the Caravan, her white arm waving out the window like a flag of surrender. Slowly I made my way across the street and felt air surge into my lungs. The attack had passed as suddenly as it had come.

Cecilia got out of the Caravan, her dress fluttering in the breeze, a bright Fergie-like smile painted on her lips.

"An act of defiance," she said, reaching to pat me awkwardly on the back. "It's about time."

I nodded and reached into the backseat for the Duchess and Bea. The twins relinquished them, passing them gingerly over the seat back. The cats settled in my lap, lying with their heads together, their throats humming in a resounding purr.

I had defied Mother only once before, when I was a teenager. One of her personal ads had been answered by a man named Marty, who was not a wrestler per se but was quite a fan of the sport. More important, he had a deep affection for royalty, he said. She showed me the letter he'd sent, and told me to meet her after school the next day, at the coffee shop where they'd set up their rendezvous. I'd told her that I was unable to make it, that I was staying late after school to watch band practice— even thinking of joining to be closer to Pete, the clarinetist who had serenaded me in the hall on my birthday.

"You're an old pro at this," I'd said teasingly, poking her in the arm. "You don't need me."

She'd stepped away from me, her face drained of color. Then with both hands, she reached out and grabbed me by the wrists and shook me there in the kitchen, her blue eyes burning beneath her glasses.

"Don't you ever say such a thing again," she whispered, pulling me to her and pressing her face in my hair. "I will always need you. You're my girl."

The look on her face had frightened me so intensely that I promised to meet her that day or any other. "I'll be there, Mother," I'd whispered back. "I'll do anything you say."

The next day I could not forget the desperation in her voice, the way she'd gripped me to her, her hot breath on my scalp. Nevertheless, I stayed to watch the band and got home after dark to find her sitting in the kitchen with the lights out, a candle flickering on the table. I'd gone straight to my room and closed the door. We'd never mentioned the incident, but neither of us had forgotten it, and shortly afterward she'd stopped watching wrestling for good.

I thought about all of this as the Duchess and Bea

sat languidly in my lap with their tails curled together, breathing in unison.

"It won't be long now," I said, stroking the cats' heads as Cecilia pulled out of the parking lot. "Mother does not respond well to threats."

Cecilia threw her head back and laughed. Candy and Sandy began to giggle, too, softly at first, then louder and louder as we approached the ramp to the highway. Before I knew it, I was laughing, too, though I wasn't sure why. I imagined all the times Mother must have laughed at me—after leaving the Polaroids in the cattery or making her terrorizing phone calls—and I kept on laughing, even after the others were quiet. Finally, the only sounds in the car were the cats purring in my lap and my laughter, which emanated from my throat even after I tried to stop it.

We checked into a motel that night, signing ourselves in under the name Ferguson for added assurance in our plan. It was only a matter of time before the media homed in on us again. If Mother and Middle were lurking anywhere in the vicinity, I reasoned, they'd be sure to come calling if the name Ferguson were somehow leaked around town. There was no point in driving aimlessly down the highway in search of some phantom wrestling match; we'd just set up camp and wait for Mother to make the next move. She'd listen to her messages and find a way to get back to me. Mother was always the one to have the last word.

The desk clerk asked how many were in our party, and I rattled off the names without a second thought.

"My twins, Candy and Sandy, and my aunt, Sarah
Ferguson. I, of course, am Maxine Ferguson. We are also
accompanied by two bicolor Persian cats, who are both
registered in the *Cat Fancy*. This one's a grand champion," I said, lifting the Duchess onto the counter so that
the woman could see. "Her name is Red Duchess."

The woman leaned forward and stroked the
Duchess's back as the cat twirled her tail in the air and
sauntered across the desk to show herself off. Even
though Jerry hadn't groomed the Duchess in days, she
was still a beautiful specimen.

"Ain't she a beauty?" the woman said, clucking her
tongue. "I'd like to have one of them myself."

I recalled the last night at the cattery, imagining the
swarms of kittens that would be arriving in a matter of
weeks.

"Well, there will be plenty of them soon," I said, "Perhaps we could barter, make some kind of arrangement."

While the woman and I were talking, Cecilia came
through the door with Candy and Sandy trailing behind her. The girls' faces were flushed from lack of sleep.
Cecilia lead the way with her head held high, the brim of
her white hat casting a shadow over her eyes. She turned
and winked at the desk clerk, her perfect freckles twitching as she squinched up her nose.

The desk clerk grabbed my arm and shook it.

"Your aunt," she said, motioning toward Cecilia as
she headed for the elevator. "Is that who I think it is?"

I nodded and signed my assumed name in the ledger.
Without looking at the clerk, I lifted the Duchess into my
arms, leaned over, and whispered in the woman's ear.

"Sarah Ferguson," I said, "but we'd like to keep it quiet if we could." I passed her a crumpled ten-dollar bill. The Duchess brushed her tail across the woman's face. "She's going through a rough spot with the royal divorce and all. She's come to the States for some peace and quiet, to get away from the press. If word gets out that she's here, there's no telling what might happen."

The woman stuffed the crumpled bill down her blouse and winked at me.

"Of course," she said, reaching over the counter to press a hand on my arm. "We understand the need to be left alone."

I smiled at her and sauntered down the hall without looking back. If only Jerry had been there to see the way I'd handled myself, how far I'd come in standing up to Mother, how coolly I'd tossed off the notion that Cecilia was really Fergie.

The twins were waiting for me at the door, their faces glowing with expectation. I set the Duchess down on the carpet and hugged each of them in turn. They looked up at me and forced themselves to smile.

"We thought it might be Mommy when we heard you at the door," Sandy said.

"We knew it was you," Candy said, twirling her ponytail around one finger, "but for a second, we hoped."

I just nodded and smoothed their hair. How could I tell them that this was what it was like to be a daughter, that those feelings of expectation never really disappeared? Here I was at thirty-four, knowing Mother had abandoned me, and yet, despite all logic, every time I saw a middle-aged redhead I felt my heart flip over in my chest, hoping against hope that Mother had forgotten all this nonsense and just wanted to be my mother again.

"Don't worry," I said, though I could feel how forced it sounded, "we'll see her on TV tonight."

Cecilia emerged from the bathroom with her hair wrapped in a towel, her pale face stripped of all freckles. She smiled at us and lit a cigarette, stretched out on the double bed and crossed her legs. After several long puffs, she patted the space beside her. The Duchess and Bea hurried to her side, sniffing at her robe and growling low in their throats.

"They don't recognize me," she said, laughing, clouds of smoke swirling over the twins' heads. "They must really think I'm Fergie."

I walked over to the bed and stroked the cats' backs. "They're not the only ones," I said, and we both burst out laughing. I then told the cats in a soft voice that there was nothing to fear, that Mama was with them.

Because Cecilia and I had agreed her fee was contingent on time "on the clock," we decided she should reserve her performances only for those times when it was necessary. She said she'd gotten used to being Fergie, though, and rather liked the idea of being in on this quest.

"Don't worry so much about the money, luv," she said in a faintly British accent. "What's important here is that we help you to find yourself."

It was only a matter of time, I explained to Cecilia, before the desk clerk spread the news that Fergie was staying at this motel. In order to perfect the charade, Cecilia would dress in full Fergie regalia, careful to pass by the window, allowing passersby to catch periodic glimpses of her from the street below. Given the Fergie impersonation, Middle's personal ad, and the defiant message I'd left on Mother's answering machine, meeting Mother could not be far away.

When I finished outlining the plan, Cecilia leaned forward and shook her wet hair out of the towel. Long, mousy brown strands dripped over her pale blotchy face. No one would ever believe she was Fergie if they saw her at that moment, but once she got into costume, the transformation was as complete as any I'd ever seen.

"Splendid idea, luv," she said, as she jumped from the bed and gathered up her makeup case. "Your mum will come running for sure."

I smiled and took out the ad from the *Post* that I'd folded into my pocket. The twins sat on the floor, drawing pictures of Anita, as I read the ad over and over again, the words seeming to swim over the page. "You— Seeking me. Me seeking you." The Duchess and Bea leaped onto the windowsill and peered outside as if on the lookout. I watched the cats sitting there so peacefully, the twins drawing frantically on the floor, and I closed my eyes and imagined Middle sitting alone with a newspaper open on her lap, I wondered if she felt the yearning that lingered inside of me from when she'd struggled to grow right before Mother kidnapped her. It seemed so long ago that we'd lain side by side in the hospital, weeping in unison, the birthmark shaped like a comma curving over our right eyes. Now that Mother and I were estranged, I felt a profound curiosity to know Middle—not at all sure it was possible, given that she was essentially me—to see her again, at the very least, to look into her blue eyes and find out whether I had indeed seen myself.

Before settling in to watch *Live with Gary Tate,* the twins kept watch for reporters by standing out on the balcony outside our third-floor window. Cecilia had gathered up all the magazine articles she could find and was pasting them into a scrapbook she'd brought along with her, taping the covers of *Newsweek* and *Time* to the stiff pages.

"That's what therapists are for, luv," she said when I asked her what she was doing. "We preserve your memories for you, like it or not."

When it was time for the program to begin, the four of us settled onto the floor in front of the small-screen television. The twins laid several paper airplanes on the carpet, noses pointed toward the screen.

"Is Mommy going to find your baby?" Candy asked.

"When is Mommy coming home?" asked Sandy.

I was about to answer them as best as I could when the theme music to Gary Tate's show filled the room. The twins sat up straight and clasped each other's hands.

"Tonight we have with us Dr. Charles Norton, who, as most people know by now, recently delivered the first human clone, only to have the clone kidnapped by her grandmother. Also joining Dr. Norton is Anita Jones, childhood friend of Maxine Dublin, the clone's mother. And with us via satellite are Dr. Robert Frasier, from the National Institutes of Health, and Dr. Kenneth Coleman, Harvard Professor of Bioethics and Genetic Engineering."

Anita sat at the desk with her hands folded, Norton

by her side with his hair slicked back dramatically and a stethoscope around his neck. The twins shrieked when they saw Anita, rushing up to the TV screen to touch her glowing face.

"I just have to say this, Gary. This is the man who delivered my girls," Anita said, twirling her ponytail around her finger. "And if you're watching, girls, remember Mommy loves you."

They started to cry softly, leaning against me with the cats in their laps. Cecilia sat in a lotus position.

It was clear that Gary Tate was smitten with Anita. He brushed his elbow against hers and glared at Norton, who held his stethoscope out at him as a kind of rebuke.

"Well, well," Cecilia said under her breath. "A bloody star is born."

I watched in amazement as Anita and Norton bantered back and forth. The twins now held their paper airplanes in their fists, their eyes wide. The cats shifted in their laps, tails curled around themselves. I held my breath.

"Charles," Gary Tate said, adjusting his glasses. "May I call you Charles? Have you any indication of where the clone might be at this time? The whole country seems to be out looking for this clone, so why has she been so hard to find?"

Norton patted Anita's hand and looked directly at the camera.

"Well, Gary," Norton said, "the problem is that we are dealing not only with a crazed grandmother, but with a clone who is growing at an alarming rate. No one knows exactly what she might look like at this point, though our best medical hypotheses put her somewhere in the nine- to ten-year range."

"About the same age as my girls," Anita cut in, smoothing her ponytail to one side. "Candy and Sandy," she said. "Not clones," she added, brightening. "Identical twins."

The girls said nothing, just reached over and gripped each other's hands. The sound of their names was a shock, even to Cecilia, who continued pasting articles in the scrapbook and clucking her tongue.

I sat there with one hand rubbing each of the twins' backs in slow circles as Anita chattered on about her relationship with Mother, how she and I had been inseparable as kids, Mother always along for the ride. When asked where she thought Mother might be now, Anita shrugged and smiled coyly at Norton.

"God knows," she said. "Minnie's always been able to get her own way."

I felt my attention drifting, as had so often been the case since finding my life thrust into the limelight. The two doctors argued about Norton's credentials, one of them even going so far as to call Norton a fraud. They threatened that if Norton didn't publish his findings in a reputable medical journal he'd see himself become the laughingstock of his profession.

"We have got to put a stop to this now before all science as we know it is inexorably smirched by such scandals," one doctor said. "I urge Congress and the American people to issue a moratorium on cloning as of this very moment."

"Here, here," I said, louder than I should have. "I'll drink to that."

During the commercial break the twins fashioned their remaining drawings of Anita into paper airplanes and sent them sailing off the balcony and into the wind. The ends of Anita's blond ponytail curved over the wings as each paper airplane softly floated down and disappeared into the dark street below. Cecilia and I stood in the doorway watching as the twins sent each one into the air, the wind flipping them on end and sending them nose-diving off the edge of the balcony. I was about to call them in again, but Cecilia shook her head.

"Let them alone, luv," she said. "Seeing their mum on TV may have been too bloody much for them."

I nodded and went back inside. Gary Tate and the others were speculating about Mother and her motives, the chaos that had ensued because of the clone. Norton held a photo of Mother between his manicured fingers for a close-up. He adjusted his stethoscope and sucked at his teeth.

"If you're out there, Minnie," Norton said, "you know what to do. Let us have her where she can do some good for mankind. Let that clone go."

The twins and Cecilia appeared in the doorway just as the phone call came in.

"From Sioux City, Iowa—no, from Taos, New Mexico—no, from Dayton, Ohio—I'm afraid we're having trouble with the location here," Gary said, looking offstage and signaling to his producer as the twins lay down on the carpet. "We have Millicent on the line. Are you there, Millicent? Hello," Gary Tate said.

There was a long pause, then labored breathing on the line. I dumped the Duchess off my lap and moved forward on my knees.

"Millicent, are you there? Same name as the RGC, Charles; a coincidence, don't you think?" He playfully punched Norton on the arm. "Let's go to Jim from Kansas City. Hello."

The camera cut to a close-up of Norton, who was staring intently at Anita, his lips wet. The telephone line crashed with static. A series of giggles rang through the phone.

"It's me," she said, her voice clearer and more defined than it had been the day Mother had offered her the phone. "Middle."

Norton's face went white with shock, blue veins bulging in his forehead. The camera veered crazily, the satellite pictures of the other doctors hissing with static. Gary Tate fought to keep control of the show, bellowing at the cameraman to keep the camera steady, not to lose the signal.

"Millicent—Middle," Gary Tate said, his voice booming, "is that really you? What do you have to say to America?"

The twins wrapped their arms around my neck and held me tightly. Cecilia jumped to her feet and turned up the sound full blast. I squeezed the twins and tried to keep from screaming.

"It's me," she said, laughing. "Looking for—"

Her voice broke off as the sounds of Mother's shouts suddenly flooded the line. "Stop, please, stop," Mother pleaded, her voice hoarse with the strain.

Anita stood up and reached over the desk as if for an imaginary phone and called Mother's name.

"For god's sake, Minnie, let her speak!" Anita cried;

but before Middle could say anything more, the line went dead.

Every major news station carried the story. Cecilia flipped through the channels: "Clone calls Gary Tate, film at eleven," one reporter announced. "Gary Tate to clone: phone home," another said.

"In a bizarre development in the increasingly mysterious story of the missing clone," one anchorman said, "Millicent Dublin, the Rapidly Growing Clone who was kidnapped by her grandmother last week, and who now seems to prefer the nickname 'Middle,' called *Live with Gary Tate* on the air tonight, resulting in ten seconds of dead air." The anchorman sifted through the pages on his desk. "No one knows what the clone was trying to communicate since she was apparently cut off before she could finish a sentence. She managed to say only, 'It's me,' and indicate she was looking for someone or something, though neither Gary Tate nor his producers could determine who or what this was. Surely this latest turn of events sheds light on recent reports that the clone is now suspected to be preadolescent. According to Charles Norton, the doctor who claims to have delivered her, she is now roughly eight or nine years old."

"Was that your baby on the phone?" Candy asked, when I finally shut off the television out of sheer exhaustion. "Was that your baby everyone's talking about?" She sat beside me on the bed with Sandy beside her, their faces flushed from all the excitement.

"Yes and no," I said, trying to smile. "I don't really know who that was on the phone. I'm afraid I don't really know who she is," I added, which was the most truthful thing I could think of to say.

I helped the girls to bed, smoothing the covers over their bellies and across their chests. They were too young to understand what was happening, of course, but I could see by the way they looked at me that they felt a certain pity for me—or perhaps not pity, exactly, but empathy. They smiled up at me and patted my arms. I kissed their foreheads and wished them a good night.

"Sweet dreams, luvs," Cecilia said, as she reached over the bedside table and unplugged the phone.

We weren't expecting calls, of course, since no one knew where we were, not even Anita. But she trusted me with her daughters, and that was what mattered.

"Once your mum sees me as Fergie, she'll let the little one go," she whispered in the dark, reminding me we were on the clock again. "Or at least, that's what we bloody well hope. This session's over for tonight."

I lay in bed next to the twins and stared across the room at the television set where Middle's voice had been transmitted. Over and over I thought of Mother's pleading, the desperation in her voice. If Middle didn't find me, I would have to find her, I realized as the Duchess and Bea curled themselves together beside my pillow. I owed her at least that much after letting Mother take her away. Later, when everyone was asleep, I reached behind the bedside table and plugged the phone back in, just in case.

The next day, while Cecilia meticulously painted her freckles on and the girls took baths, I called Jerry from the pay phone downstairs in case the phones in the cattery had been tapped. This was the longest I'd ever gone without speaking to Jerry since I'd met him, and by far the longest I'd ever been separated from my cats. I felt strange inside, jumpy, like I didn't know who I was anymore. If not Minnie's daughter or a champion cat breeder, then who had I become?

Jerry answered on the first ring, like he'd been sitting there beside the phone, his hand on the receiver, waiting for it to ring.

"Hello?"

"Jerry," I said, my voice breaking, "it's me."

"Maxi?" he cried. "My god, Maxi, is that really you?"

Sirens wailed in the background. The receiver crackled with static.

"Jerry," I said, poking a finger in my other ear, "what in the world is going on?"

The desk clerk stared at me from the lobby. I waved to her and tried to smile, but she turned away and headed for the front desk. I saw her grab the telephone and frantically dial.

For a minute I could hear nothing but sirens. Then Jerry's voice rose above the commotion.

"They've got the place surrounded," Jerry shouted. Megaphones blasted in the background. "Hospital security, the police, FBI, you name it. It's a standoff. They think we've got Middle stashed away in here, since she called Gary Tate. Ron's tried to hold them back, but he's only one man, after all. A hell of a man, at that, but only one. We don't know how much longer we can hold out."

A crowd of women gathered around the registration desk as I was trying to think of what to do next. What would the FBI do to Jerry if they got their hands on

him? Would they arrest him at Norton's behest? I'd
seen the rage in Norton's face, the blood rushing to his
cheeks—even through all that pancake makeup—as he
struggled to keep his composure in front of Gary Tate. I
couldn't allow anything to happen to Jerry, or to all my
pregnant cats lying there helpless in their cages. I took a
deep breath and turned away from the women, who
were whispering to one another and waving at me from
the front desk.

"Maxi." Jerry's voice was hoarse with strain. "I don't
know how much more we can take."

I thought of the twins upstairs in their bubble bath,
their long blond hair glistening, their drawings of Anita
with her ponytail snaking out the back of a television set.

"Anita wants the girls back," Jerry said, as if he'd
read my mind. "She doesn't think it's safe for them.
You've got to tell us where you are."

I felt the breath constricting in my chest. For a moment I heard nothing but the whispers of the women at
the front desk, the terrible pounding of my heart. I
gripped the telephone cord and closed my eyes.

"Maxi," Jerry said, his voice clearer now, "think of
the twins. These reporters will be out for blood."

I leaned against the phone booth and felt my shoulders sag as if all the wind had been knocked out of me.
Being in the middle of a scandal like this was no place
for little girls. Middle must have been scared to death.

For a minute I considered refusing to give in, I
wanted to pack up the twins and move on. Maybe
Norton and his FBI agents would give up and we'd find
Middle and Mother before they had the chance.

"OK," I said, and bit my lower lip to fight back the

tears. "We'll send the twins back. We don't want anything to happen to the twins."

I could hear men shouting in the background, and I imagined Jerry and Ron enveloped in thick clouds of tear gas while they slowly danced to Tom Jones songs, a SWAT team busting down the cattery door, scaring my cats to death.

"You tell Norton no more interviews, Jerry," I said, my voice louder and more firm. "You tell him he keeps his mouth shut or the deal is off. I'll find Middle myself and pack her on the next plane to Guatemala. Tell him that is not negotiable."

Jerry dropped the phone before I could say anything else. In the sudden quiet I stood there thinking of Norton coming to sabotage our plans. Mother would never surface if she knew Norton was in the area. Middle might be scared off, too, if she thought that I'd sold her out to a doctor who wanted to take her back to his lab and study her under bright lights.

I turned around and saw the desk clerk lay down the receiver just as Norton's voice blasted in my ear.

"All right, Maxine," he said, "you find that clone and I won't talk to the press. I can't promise anything where Anita's concerned. The heart has a mind of its own. Send back those twins I delivered, but I'm coming for you and your clone now. I've got a grant riding on this, years of genetic research in the making. A phone call from a clone on national television is more than this hospital will stand for. We'll put an end to this once and for all."

I said nothing to this, promising that Mother and Middle would not be far behind. *He has no choice but to trust me*, I thought, to believe I would lead her home.

Still, it would be only a matter of time before he realized he'd been duped. I was just stalling for time now. We would send the twins back, I told him, if he kept his face out of the papers.

"Miss Ferguson, about your aunt!" the desk clerk called, but I didn't turn back. I ran down the hall and up the stairs, hoping that Cecilia would be there waiting at the door and would tell me everything was going to be all right, just like Mother had always done.

Cecilia was not waiting for me as I'd hoped, but as luck would have it, she'd showered and was back in full Fergie regalia. Although I knew all of this "treatment" was going to cost me a fortune, I realized that Cecilia was right: I had to hope that it would all be worth it.

Without saying a word I started to pack up the few belongings the twins had brought with them. Cecilia just nodded at me and winked as if she understood. Never in my life had I been so thankful to have someone anticipating my next move, even reading my very thoughts. I'd always felt somehow Mother was omniscient, that she could see things in me I didn't want to reveal. I felt that with Cecilia now, too.

"Come on now, girls," I said, hustling the girls around the room, helping them pick up a stray sock or ponytail holder, "Mommy's waiting for you now. You mustn't keep Mommy waiting."

The Duchess hopped up next to me as I collapsed on the bed. I buried my face in her side to keep from having to watch the twins getting ready to leave. She nuzzled my hair in sympathy, her sandpaper tongue scraping tentatively at my scalp. I snuffed, and a wad of fur went up my nose. Tears welled in my eyes but I stifled the urge to cough.

After a few minutes the girls came over and sat beside me on the bed. Candy reached out and nudged my shoulder until I sat up and spit a clump of the Duchess's hair onto the floor.

"We have to go now, Aunt Maxi," Candy whispered, reaching her arm around my waist.

I nodded and hugged each of them to me, feeling their shoulders pressing heavily against my breasts, their ponytails tickling my nose. Sandy reached up and hugged me around the neck, her warm lips grazing my cheek.

"Mommy's waiting," Candy said. "You said so."

I kissed the tops of their heads and closed my eyes for a long moment, letting myself feel their warmth against me so that I would remember it in the long days and nights that followed.

Cecilia sat down on the bed opposite us and clapped her hands.

"Now, now, girls," she said, "no time for messy good-byes. We've got a mum waiting for you two and another who may be on her way. We've got to hold it together. Remember, big girls don't cry."

I thought this last comment was uncalled for, given the fact that she was a therapist and trained in helping people to release their emotions. What if the girls wanted to cry? They'd lost their mother to the bright lights of cameras and TV monitors, for heaven's sake. I shot her an angry look as she reached across and took both my hands in hers, pulling me forward, her cubic zirconia rings pressed hard against my fingers.

"Maxi," she said, "you've got to get hold of yourself now. Your mum tried to steal Anita away, too, didn't she? She tried to make her into a bloody friend of her own." She squeezed my hands and lowered her voice. "But she didn't succeed at taking Anita away. She can't take you or Middle—or whoever she might be—unless you let her get away with it. This time you won't let her get away with it, now, will you?"

Cecilia gripped my hands even tighter and held on to them, squeezing until I felt rage burn in the pit of my stomach. For a second I wanted to ask her if we were on the clock, but I thought better of it. I had to hand it to Cecilia. In the short time that she'd known me, she'd pieced together an accurate picture of my relationship with Mother. Everything Mother had ever taken from me, every need she'd ever foisted on me, every demand she'd ever made rang through my head all at once. I saw her standing in the corner of the hospital room while I lay drugged on the bed, unable to move as she stole my baby from her incubator and disappeared into the night.

"You see, luv," Cecilia said, "it's there now and we'll use it when we can. But right now we've got the doctor on our tail and we've got to be strong. We need to send these girls back to their mum. And we've got to hurry before he finds us. It won't be long before the whole world knows where we are."

Candy and Sandy reached for me and helped me to my feet. They looked up at me and smiled sadly, as if somehow they knew what I was feeling, or at least tried to imagine it in their nine-year-old minds. I smiled weakly at Cecilia and tried to steady myself.

"OK," I said, "I know you're right."

Images of Mother flashed through my mind, her head thrown back, laughing at me.

She's laughed for the last time, I thought.

As I moved toward the window, a brilliant light flashed from the street below. For a minute I thought they were police lights, that somehow Norton had sent the FBI after us for running off and leaving him without his precious clone. But as I stepped closer to the window I realized they were flashbulbs. I inched toward the window and hid my face behind the curtain to peer down at the street. A dozen flashbulbs popped as I eased the curtain open with my fingertips.

"Fergie!" the crowd called from the street below. "Fergie, we love you!"

Cecilia ran toward the window and crouched down beside me. The twins gathered at our sides; the Duchess and Bea leaped onto the windowsill. The Duchess's tail parted the curtains as she wagged it back and forth, a low growl coming from deep in her chest.

"She doesn't like crowds," I whispered. "Never has."

Before I could say anything else Cecilia crawled over to the closet where she'd hidden her supply of wigs and hats in case the need for costume changes arose. I imagined what Mother would say if she were standing below, being elbowed by the crowd, her heart in her throat as she waited for a glimpse of her beloved Fergie. I could almost feel her excitement as I watched Cecilia fumble through the closet, tossing wigs and wide-brimmed hats over her shoulder. I imagined Mother holding me by the hand, her palm sweating in mine, as we stood in anticipation, the flashbulbs leaving orange spots in our eyes.

"All right, folks, it's show time," Cecilia said, pulling me out of my reverie.

Without looking at her, I crawled over to the lamp and snapped it off, leaving on only the bathroom light, which cast a soft glow. Slowly Cecilia approached the window, the shadow of her tiara growing larger as she moved closer to the window.

"Ready, girls?" she said, and Candy and Sandy nodded, taking their places at each end of the drapes, their ponytails bobbing with excitement, waiting for Cecilia's cue.

"Now," she whispered. "Now."

I fell back on my haunches as the girls tugged the drapes open all at once. Cecilia stood in front of the window, her face turned in profile, her plastic tiara throwing baubles of color on the walls. The window flashed with light from the street below, the cheers echoing through the room. In one long movement, Cecilia lifted a gloved hand in the air and waved to the crowd below, then pressed the glove to her lips and blew them a triumphant kiss. She winked at the girls and stepped away from the window as the twins pulled the drapes closed and collapsed on the floor in a fit of giggles.

"They think you're her!" the girls laughed, half screaming, as Cecilia tossed the plastic tiara to the floor and caught them both in an embrace. "They really think you're Fergie!"

I sat on the floor for a long time with the plastic tiara in my lap while Cecilia peeled herself out of her costume and the girls finished packing up their belongings. The Duchess and Bea tried to climb onto my lap, but I just sat there on the carpet with the tiara resting on my knees, thinking this should have been one of my finest moments, a triumph in my quest to draw Mother out of hiding and send her running back to me.

Instead of triumph I felt only sadness as I sat there on the floor. Motherhood, I thought, was a cruel hoax that drew women in with the illusion of unconditional love and moments of joy when in reality it was filled with loss, a slow breaking apart of our souls the minute we sent new lives out into the world. How unfair it seemed to feel so secure in pregnancy when we'd have to spend the rest of our lives fighting off the emptiness that came with the infant's inevitable exit, that final push that expelled the child forever. We spend our whole lives trying to recover from the shock.

Sometime later the crowd dispersed, and it became quiet enough for us to deliver the twins to the bus terminal without being photographed. At first Cecilia said that she should be the one to take the twins, since Mother and Middle—or Norton—might not be far at this point. If any of them showed their faces at the motel, I should be the one to greet them. But if Mother had come looking for Fergie, she'd want to see her before attempting to make her way up to the third floor for a face-to-face encounter. Cecilia needed to stay in costume and make periodic appearances at the window per our original plan.

"You take the little ones," Cecilia said. "If your mum shows up here, I'll find a way to hold her for you."

With the plan settled, the twins and I headed down the fire escape behind the motel and out to the dark parking lot across the street. I tied a kerchief around my head and walked with my head down, the twins' hands clasped in mine. A small group of photographers were smoking cigarettes at the curb outside our window, leaning against a car and laughing. I'd decided it was best to walk in case the license plates to the Caravan had been traced. We headed away from the reporters, their laughter echoing in the distance. The girls squeezed my hands as we broke into a slow trot. When we turned the corner onto the main street, they both collapsed into giggles.

"We fooled them, didn't we, Aunt Maxi?" Candy said.

I just nodded and tried to keep the pace. The last bus was in twenty minutes, and I had to be sure they were on it. Sandy looked up at me and smiled.

"We're used to fooling people," Sandy said. "We're twins."

The three of us burst out laughing. I recalled when the twins were born, how Anita drew their first initials on their Pampers with a Magic Marker to tell them apart. She'd felt terribly guilty about doing this, thought that a good mother would be able to tell her twins apart without the aid of Magic Markers on diapers or color-coded onesies. Of course, she'd learned to recognize all of their subtle differences as they'd grown—the tiny dimple on Candy's left knee, the slightly longer third toe of Sandy's right foot—but at times they fooled even her. When they started preschool they often played tricks on their teachers, surreptitiously switching hair ribbons or knapsacks during nap time. I remembered how I loved hearing these stories, how I'd envied their ability to switch in and out of character, to pretend to inhabit the other's skin. I wondered if Middle and I would ever have such an ease with each other.

When we reached the bus station I bought the girls their tickets and asked a woman in a long blue coat if she would mind keeping an eye on them during the bus ride.

"They'll probably sleep most of the trip," I told her,

looking over my shoulder at the other passengers who were lining up, "but if you could just sort of watch over them, I'd appreciate it."

She smiled at me and pressed a hand on my wrist.

"I'd be glad to, dear," she said, flashing her dentured smile. "I have twins myself. Grown girls now with children of their own; but oh, what fun they were growing up. Identical, too, just like these little ones. Sometimes they even had me fooled."

She smiled at me again, this time leaning forward to have a closer look at me, her blue eyes searching. I smiled back and turned away, but she caught me by the shoulder, her hand gently nudging me back to face her. The twins held their tickets as they made their way toward the waiting bus.

"Excuse me, dear," the woman said, walking with me as I followed the twins, "did anyone ever tell you how much you look like Sarah Ferguson, the Duchess of York?"

I smiled and knelt down in front of the twins as they stopped at the door of the bus to say our good-byes.

"Of course, I can't tell if you're a redhead under that kerchief, but really," the woman said, hunching over to whisper in my ear, "you know, you could be her clone."

I tightened the kerchief around my chin and stood up to face the woman. If we were really trying to draw Mother out, I thought, then the least I could do was play along.

"Yes," I said, smiling modestly, "people tell me that all the time."

The other passengers lined up at the door of the bus. Sandy tugged my arm and pulled me toward the door.

"Come on, Aunt Maxi, we have to go now."

I just nodded and hurried toward the steps of the bus, the woman in the blue coat trailing behind us. She hovered over us as I checked to make sure each of the girls had their brushes and socks, that they knew their mother would be waiting for them when they got home. The driver took their tickets and patted their blond heads. He gave me a wink as I leaned down to hug them one last time.

Together they wrapped their arms around my neck and sighed heavily. Our arms encircled one another, the rumbling of the bus vibrating in our chests. I kissed their cheeks and whispered to them to not be afraid, that neither Dr. Norton nor the reporters would hurt them, reminding them that Mommy was waiting for them back home. They held me tightly until the woman was upon us again, leaning over us to direct the girls to their seats.

"Everyone says that grandmother who stole the clone looks just like Fergie," the woman whispered to me as she handed her ticket to the bus driver. She placed her hands on the twins' shoulders and directed them up the steps. "But you look much more like her than she does. That woman is much too old."

Heat rushed to my face in embarrassment on Mother's behalf. I wanted to tell the woman that she was wrong, that she should have seen Mother when she was young, when she was still fresh-faced and lovely, before age had gotten the better of her. Before I could answer, she herded Candy and Sandy up the steps and into adjoining seats at the back of the bus. I ran toward the back of the bus and stood staring up at them, their eyes drooping from fatigue at having been without a mother for so long. Slowly I brought my hand up to my lips and kissed it, then pressed my hand against the window. They smiled down at me and pressed each of their small hands against mine, the outline of our fingers touching through glass.

As they were about to turn the corner, Sandy took a deep breath and called, "Good-bye, Aunt Maxi! Good-bye!"

I waved until long after they could see me any-more—until my arm grew heavy. Without looking back I walked back to the hotel with my head down and my hands shoved inside my pockets, shoulders hunched. Even during my pregnancy in the last months when I spent hours alone at the kitchen table coaxing the baby with my fingers to turn this way and that, giggling at the quick stab of an elbow or pulsing of a knee—it had never felt like this.

When I could see the motel at the end of the street, I breathed a deep sigh of relief. As I stood at the curb waiting for the cars to pass by, I could hear the reporters laughing in the distance and could see the ends of their cigarettes glowing in the dark. They were leaning against a car, their ties loosened, heads thrown back with their laughter. I waited until I was sure they were absorbed in conversation before I tucked my hair into the back of my collar and ran across the street as fast as I could. All I needed now, after all this time, was to have some frantic reporter snap my picture on my way back to my motel room.

Just as I reached the curb I saw a flash of red hair from the corner of my eye. At first I thought it was my own hair blowing out the sides of the kerchief. But as I stood at the door, I saw it again, bright and bouncing, across the street. I turned slowly toward the reporters, who were still smoking their cigarettes and laughing loudly. Slowly I turned my body again, shifting my weight from one foot to the other. My heart pounded and I opened my eyes wide, forcing myself to look.

A figure galloped across the street, long red hair flying behind. I stepped closer to the curb, air caught in my lungs. She ran fast, defiantly, her arms pumping back and forth, sneakers pounding the pavement. I wanted to call out her name, to take a deep breath and feel the air sailing out of my lungs, but no sound would come. Just as I was about to try again, I saw Mother chasing behind her, arms flailing.

Before I knew what I was doing, I stepped off the curb to chase after them and screamed Mother's name at the top of my lungs, my breath ragged.

"Wait!" I screamed. "Mother, wait!"

For a minute all three of us froze. I stopped in the middle of the street, straddling the double yellow line. Mother's glasses had flown off her face and landed at her feet. My kerchief had fallen from my head. Mother squinted at me, then reached down to pick up her glasses, shoving them back onto her face with both hands. Middle now looked to be about twelve years old, her hair hanging down to her waist.

We stood there staring at one another, each of us standing firmly where we were, not daring to move.

"Mother?" I said again, softer this time, afraid she might run away.

She took a tentative step forward, a smile coming briefly over her face. Before she could say anything, Middle screamed.

"Mama!" She reached her arms out as she stepped off the curb and ran toward me. "It's you! It's you!"

Everything seemed to happen in slow motion then: Mother lunged forward and grabbed Middle, pinning Middle's arms above her head in a full nelson. Middle screamed as Mother wrestled her to the ground. Lights flashed all around us as the photographers came running.

"Look!" one of them shouted, pointing toward the window where Cecilia was standing, her plastic tiara casting a shadow over the drapes. "It's Fergie!"

One reporter knocked me over as he ran back across the street below our window. The camera bag smacked me in the eye, sending me down onto the pavement, my hands scraping asphalt. I lay there stunned for a minute, but then I heard Middle's voice again piercing the darkness. I struggled to my feet to run to her, but by the time I'd gotten up and stumbled forward a few steps, Middle and Mother were gone.

I ran behind the building for the fire escape, climbing all three flights as fast as I could. When I reached the top I stood there gripping the railing while Cecilia gently tried to coax me inside.

"Mother!" I screamed, as loud as I possibly could, "it's Fergie! Just for you, Mother! It's the real thing!"

The photographers all began snapping photos of me at once, the flashes leaving purple and yellow spots in my eyes. I covered my face with my hands to shield myself, but they kept shooting me from below. Finally

Cecilia pulled me inside. The tiara fell off her head and landed on the floor. Neither of us bothered to pick it up.

Together we sat quietly on the edge of the bed, our knees touching. I wanted to describe Middle and how she'd called out to me, her long hair flowing, her coltish legs springing forward, nearly out of Mother's grip. As soon as she'd seen me, she'd bolted forward and come running for me, arms open, mouth set tight with determination, before Mother pulled at her from behind, locking her arms in a full nelson.

And then there had been Mother's fleeting smile, the flash of her teeth when she'd seen me there. She'd let go of Middle and seemed to be turning toward me. Without thinking, I'd smiled at her, too, and for the briefest of moments, started to run toward her.

I considered telling these things to Cecilia but was too exhausted to speak. *Besides,* I thought, *I don't want to have to pay to utter them.* More important, I didn't see how saying these things out loud would make me feel any better. Saying that I missed my mother could not stop the ache of missing her. If anything, it would only underline my need.

"So, what do we do now?" I finally asked, when the silence in the room grew too thick to bear.

Cecilia shrugged her shoulders and picked up the tiara, slipping the red wig from her head, letting her mousy hair fall softly over her shoulders. She stood to face me, her powdered skin stark against the brown curls. Freckles still dotted her face.

She took one of my hands and patted it, her cubic zirconias lightly tapping my knuckles. The Duchess and Bea slept side by side against the drapes, oblivious to all the turmoil around them. Cecilia reached down and stroked each of them on the head, her long fingers pushing through the thick fur.

"We wait," she said. "We have no choice now but to wait."

As she stood up, the Duchess's fur clung to her fingers. Slowly Cecilia opened her hand and then closed it again, sending the fur flying in a puff. If only it were that easy to throw off our failings, I thought, as I watched the clump of fur float down and land on the carpet. Instead they cling to us—or we cling to them, as it were; sometimes it is difficult to tell who is holding on to what.

A news flash came on later. A reporter in a minidress, her hair blowing straight back, stood among the Fergie followers outside the building.

"They're out there, luv," Cecilia said, adjusting her wig and pinning on her tiara. "This world can't seem to get enough of Fergie."

Together we closed the drapes and switched off the light, the television casting an eerie glow in the room.

"We're here live at the Hamilton Motel where sources claim to have spotted Sarah Ferguson, the Duchess of York, blowing kisses from the third-floor balcony. The desk clerk at this motel, Gertrude Kennedy, claims that the duchess checked in here two nights ago with an entourage—a pair of blond twins, her niece, and two Persian cats."

The camera cut to a woman with a banner over her chest, Fergie's face emblazoned on the front.

"Ms. Kennedy claims that the duchess came to the

United States for a much needed rest, and that the motel was more than happy to admit the two Persians despite its strict policy against housing animals. Isn't that right, Gertrude?"

The desk clerk smiled and leaned in toward the camera.

"Oh, we made an exception in her case," she said, looking down at her feet, women waving wildly behind her. "It's not every day that we get royalty in these parts."

The reporter thanked the clerk and pulled her microphone closer to her mouth.

"Many are speculating that there is some connection between the duchess's arrival and Minnie Dublin's kidnapping of the world's first RGC, though officials have declined any specific comment," the reporter said. "Only time will tell if the arrival of Persian cats and the Duchess of York will bring about the return of the missing clone." She smiled at the crowd behind her. "Now back to the studio for your regularly scheduled programming."

The cats jumped onto Cecilia's lap suddenly, as if sensing the danger that might be lurking below us, and Cecilia stroked their backs. They lifted their tails in the air and stared at me, their copper eyes wide. I walked to the window and peered down at the crowd below, the women holding candles and humming to themselves.

"I know that song," I said, as the strains of it filtered up toward the window. Before I could say anything more, Cecilia had begun humming, too, the cats closing their eyes and curling together on her lap.

" 'What's new, pussycat?' " we sang softly in the dark,

the television throwing blue light on our faces and hands. "Whoa-oh, whoa-oh, whoa," came the words from the crowd below. How odd it seemed that strange women from all over the country should be playing my song.

After the crowd finally dwindled, we tried to stay awake as long as possible in case Mother should return, even resorting to playing Go Fish at around 3 A.M. Neither of us knew much about cards, but the twins had left a deck behind. It seemed fitting that we play a child's game, Cecilia said, because my child was out there somewhere trying to break free of Mother's grip while I lay in wait for her to come to me. Matching pairs seemed the most natural thing in the world.

"Do you have a seven?" Cecilia asked. "Do you have a queen?"

At this we both laughed and slapped our knees.

"No," I said, "but I have a duchess. In fact, I have two."

Once Cecilia got the hang of the game, she took nearly every card in the deck. One by one I handed over the cards she requested. After three consecutive wins in which Cecilia had collected nearly every pair in the deck and I had been repeatedly told to go fish—to no avail— we decided to get some sleep. The photographers had finally cleared out and the motel was quiet except for the incessant running of the toilet next-door. In the morning we would decide what to do in light of the recent turn of events, but for now we simply had to get some sleep.

"It's just a matter of time now," Cecilia said, as she pulled on her red wig in case Mother came to us as we slept, "as long as that bloody doctor doesn't get to us first."

I just nodded and settled the Duchess and Bea next to me on the bed. The Duchess fell asleep on the pillow next to mine, her soft breath hissing in my ear. Bea burrowed under the blankets and purred against my knee. I lay for a long time staring up at the ceiling, listening to the rhythm of Cecilia's breathing, smoothing the blanket over and over again with my hands. A nervous churning started in the pit of my stomach and held there, squeezing the muscles down around my lower back. If I didn't know better, I mused sadly, I'd have thought these were the beginnings of labor pains—the tightening around the abdomen and long, slow stretching through the back, the fluttering mixture of anticipation and fear. I couldn't help but think of how I'd been lying in bed, after giving the cats their protein supplements, when the cramping began, and how I'd rushed to the phone to call Mother, who had anticipated my every breath and was already on her way. The relief I felt when she got to the house was intense; and we met at the door, reaching for each other without a word.

"You're going to be a mother," she'd whispered. She'd smoothed my hair and then held her hands on both sides of my face. "It's like I always dreamed it would be."

I turned over on my side and lay watching Cecilia. Taking deep breaths through my nose, I blew the air out my rounded mouth like I'd been taught to do in Lamaze training. Bea shifted her head under the blanket, her cool nose tickling my shin. I reached over to stroke the Duchess, thinking guiltily about what she'd had to go through without me there to help her. At the time, I'd been so absorbed in my own loss that I hadn't been able to help her through hers the way any good breeder would have.

I dreamed that Mother baked me a cake for my birthday, a large sheet cake in the shape of a cat, with orange frosting for the body and tail, light brown M&M's for the eyes. Anita and I wore bright pink dresses and party hats. Anita's hat was multicolored with a strip of elastic under her chin; mine was shaped like a crown, with silver rhinestones that glittered when I walked.

"How old am I today?" I whispered to Anita when Mother couldn't hear me.

"I don't know," Anita said, pulling at the elastic strap under her chin. "But I think you're still a kid."

Mother came out of her bedroom wearing a long white robe. She smoked an unfiltered Camel cigarette and dragged a wrestler by the hand.

"Who invited him?" I said, stomping my feet. "This is my party. No boys allowed."

Mother laughed and slapped the wrestler across the face.

"That's how men are," she said, "always spoiling a party."

The wrestler lay down in the middle of the carpet. The three of us joined hands and played ring-around-a-rosy, singing the refrain at the top of our lungs. When we got to the part where we were to all fall down, I saw that the wrestler had left the circle and had Mother by the throat. I dropped my crown onto the floor and smashed it into pieces.

"My princess!" Mother screamed. "Princess, come and save me!"

The wrestler tightened his grip around Mother's throat; her eyes bulged.

"What should I do?" I cried to Anita, who was now eating the cat cake in fistfuls, orange icing smeared over her cheeks and lips.

The elastic snapped beneath her chin and the hat fell to the floor. I shrieked as her head grew larger and larger, her ponytail growing down her back like a weed. I tried to pick up the tiara but the pieces were stuck to the rug.

"You're not a kid anymore," Anita said through a mouthful of cake. "Do what grown-ups do. Save yourself."

When I woke, the sheets were drenched with sweat. I sat up and wiped my face with the front of my nightgown and reached over to see if the Duchess was still there. She mewed a bit when I touched her but laid her head down again. Bea was asleep beside her, their backs touching, tails intertwined. Maybe cats were the only ones who truly knew what it meant to be mothers. They suckled their litters until the milk ran dry and let their young ones out of the box and into the world as soon as the desire struck them. The queens didn't live or die according to what became of their kittens. With cats their lives were always their own, no matter who had given birth to them or how many litters they'd had.

It was still dark outside when I tiptoed across the room to the bathroom. Cecilia slept heavily, her mouth open, wig pressing down on her forehead. Even in sleep she looked remarkably like Fergie. With the hair mussed and freckles smeared, she still could have easily fooled Mother.

I was about to get back into bed, when I saw a pink envelope jutting out from under the door. I glanced over at Cecilia. I considered waking her but thought I could handle this on my own. I'd come to see that most of the progress we'd made had been because of me. The plan to appear at the window had been mine. I was the one who spotted the personal ad and had seen Mother and Middle on the street. Still, I knew Cecilia would have wanted me to consult her before I opened the envelope. In therapy, patient and client are a team, she would say, and teams stuck together, especially in times of crisis.

I got down on my hands and knees and crawled toward the door so I wouldn't wake Cecilia. As I moved past my bed, the Duchess and Bea lifted their heads in the air and sniffed. I raised a finger to my lips to quiet them, but the Duchess bounded off the bed and ran ahead of me toward the envelope.

"What is it, Duchy?" I whispered. She rubbed the sides of her head back and forth against my arm and crawled between my legs.

I grabbed the envelope and lifted the Duchess in one arm, then reached over to scoop up Bea with the other. Quietly I made my way back to the bathroom and closed the door behind us. I sat on the lid of the toilet and set the envelope on my lap. The Duchess and Bea sat on the floor, fanning their tails out behind them and staring up expectantly at me. I patted each of them on the head and tore the envelope open in one swift motion.

Dear Mama/Maxi/Me,

I have been waiting for you to come and take me away. Mother will not let me go. She says that I am hers, but I say no. I am only me. And you are me, too. You—me—we—two.

If you won't come for me, then I will have to come to you. I know how to set myself free. I know how to give Mother the slip. Even her full nelsons can't keep me. I have tried to tell her this, but she won't listen. That's how it is with mothers, I guess. I hope that's not how it is with you.

I will meet you on the fire escape tomorrow at midnight. When Mother comes to see the lady dressed as Fergie, I will find you. This is the only way. Everyone must grow up. Believe me. I know. Even Gary Tate can't help us now.

You must be alone when I come. The Fergie lady is not invited. If she's there, then you may never find me.

Remember: You + Me = You.

XXXOOO,
Middle

I turned the paper over and found a message scrawled in blue ink at the bottom of the page. "PS," it said in fine block letters, "I like Tom Jones. I want to play the banjo. How about you?"

I sat reading the letter over and over again, turning it this way and that, even sniffing at the ink. Bea scratched at my leg as if she sensed my inner torment, her claws drawing thin lines of blood down my shin. I pressed a hand over my mouth to keep from crying out, then dabbed at the blood with squares of toilet paper from the roll hanging on the wall beside me. After I'd wiped away all traces of blood, I lay down on the cold tile and held the letter up to the light.

My first instinct was to wake Cecilia, to sit with her on the bed while we read the letter—written in my own hand—but Middle's instructions were specific. I recognized my handwriting, from letters I'd written in junior high to Pete, the lanky clarinetist who serenaded me in front of my locker. What a shock it was to revisit my own handwriting, to see the way I'd once dotted my *i*'s with open circles and rounded my *s*'s, the way the tail of my *y*'s swooped down to the line below as if waiting to catch the other letters in their wake. Every letter smacked of hope, I thought as I studied the *X*s and *O*s she'd drawn for signs of affection above her name. I found a pencil inside the sink drawer and signed my name below Middle's to compare the two. Now my writing was cramped and tight, words trailing off at the end, a hurried mixture of print and script. I tried to copy the roundedness of her name, but the pencil point broke off when I pressed too hard, the wood splintering over the page.

Together the cats and I lay down on the cold floor. I lay on my side with my knees drawn up to my chest, the Duchess and Bea curled into the crook of my body. With my right hand I clutched the letter to my breast and let the tiles press into my cheek, assuring myself this wasn't a dream. After all we'd been through, Middle had come to find me.

I shuddered to think of Mother's rage when she discovered Cecilia was a fraud. While Mother and Cecilia got acquainted, Middle and I would be alone together for the first time. After her birth, we'd been constantly surrounded. We'd hadn't had the chance to meet face-to-face.

I wondered how our first meeting would go. Would we immediately embrace? Shake hands? Stand several feet apart with our arms folded? I then wondered if Candy and Sandy had made it home safely, if Anita had gathered them into her arms like she'd never let go. What joy Anita must have felt to have her children back. But how do you welcome yourself home again, I wondered, when you hadn't even realized until it was too late that you were actually gone?

I closed my eyes and kissed each one of the cats, letting my lips brush against their fur. What would Mother do if we both abandoned her? The thought made me shudder. If she lost both of us, what would she have left? I shook my head to chase away the thoughts and pressed my face into the cold tile until there was nothing but the smell of disinfectant and cat breath drifting up my nose.

In the morning, I tried my best to keep Cecilia from becoming suspicious. For the most part she seemed to think I was agitated because I'd had to send the twins back home to Anita. We had a brief session, because Cecilia said it would do me some good to talk with Fergie about my feelings.

"It's no wonder you're feeling blue, luv," Cecilia said, as she peeked from behind the drapes to have a look at the photographers camped below. "You had to give your babies back last night even though they were never yours. I've got two sweet girls of my own, you know, Beatrice and Eugenie. I know how it feels."

I felt foolish pretending that I was telling my innermost thoughts to Fergie, but I went along with it just the same.

"Of course," I said, imagining Candy's and Sandy's faces pressed up against the windows of the bus as the clouds of exhaust washed over me. "You're right. Sometimes I forget in the excitement of all this that you're both a duchess and a mother."

Cecilia smiled and adjusted her wig in the mirror,

rubbing her fingers under her eyes to wipe away excess makeup.

"But that's what you hired me for, wasn't it, luv?" she said, still staring at herself in the mirror, at her pursed lips and perfect freckles. "We mustn't lose sight of that. You needed a spot of help to find yourself. Righto. You hired me and found yourself and Fergie all at once. And I'll say it's been a bloody bargain so far."

We still hadn't discussed payment for her services; I'd not forgotten that. But the fact that she brought up the subject of money when I was on the verge of meeting Middle—that she was so cavalier when talking about my life—filled me with disdain. I thought of saying that all she'd done was dress up like Fergie and that there were plenty of impersonators who could have done that. With my red hair and freckles, I could have pulled it off with ease. I wouldn't have even needed a wig.

Still, this was no time for a confrontation. I just laughed off the comment and tried to appear distracted, tripping over the tiara on the carpet and combing out the Duchess's matted fur. The last thing I needed was a blowout with Cecilia when Middle's arrival at the hotel was imminent. I suggested we make the most of whatever time we had left, until Mother or Norton or Middle came calling for us, putting an end to all this mystery. Cecilia agreed wholeheartedly, plopping down in a cushioned chair while I went to the door to see about breakfast.

The desk clerk had sent up a complimentary breakfast cart complete with champagne and plastic roses, which the bellhop had left outside the door. We had to be careful not to be seen by any of the other guests or employees, who might have recognized us as frauds if they got a close enough look. Already the palace had issued a formal statement denying Fergie's presence in the States. We couldn't afford to push our luck. I opened the door a crack to be sure no one lay in wait for us in the hall, and rolled the cart across the room. In the middle of the tray sat a note edged in purple hearts.

"Dear Duchess," it said in a fine, even print. "We don't care what the queen says about you. We believe you should be queen. What do you people normally eat? Hope you like pancakes. With Love and Loyalty, the Staff."

"Good lord, luv," she said, eyeing the piles of pancakes and sweet butter, the long red tapered candles and the champagne nestled in a brown plastic bucket from the ice machine down the hall. "It's a breakfast fit for a queen."

We laughed, then sat down across from each other with paper napkins tucked inside our collars. The drapes were drawn in case an ambitious photographer or a zealous fan decided to try to scale the wall for a closer look at their precious Fergie. The candles flickered, casting shadows on the walls, which the Duchess and Bea swatted with their paws as if the shadows were living things. We ate in silence, swabbing at the syrup with bits of pancake, pricking strawberries with our forks and sliding them into our mouths. We poured orange juice and champagne together to fashion mimosas, sipping at them from straws with crowns embossed on the sides. I couldn't remember when I'd enjoyed a meal so much, when I'd felt such delight at the feel of soft fruit swirling in my mouth. It took all I had to keep from humming to myself the way I had when I was a little girl, when eating had brought me the simplest joy.

I'm going to be a mother tonight, I thought, but then I swallowed hard and caught myself.

When we were finished eating, Cecilia lay down on the bed. She'd have to rehearse at some point, she said, and needed her strength to gear up for the final performance.

"We're at the midnight hour now, luv," she said, spreading the sides of her wig out on the pillow like a pair of wings. "Now we cross our fingers and pray."

I worried that she'd somehow seen the letter written in my handwriting. Maybe she'd planned to be waiting for us out back on the fire escape at midnight—waiting for a final session.

"Things might get ugly if Mother shows up," I said, biting at my lower lip. "After all, you've never seen Mother in action."

"True," she said, covering her mouth to stifle a yawn, "but I have seen her type. Of course your case is a bit more complicated with your double floating around somewhere; but you're not alone, my dear. Believe me, you're not alone."

She let her eyes close. Her head lolled from side to side, her mouth hanging open and her eyes moving back and forth beneath their lids.

I rolled the breakfast cart across the room and out into the hall, checking first to make sure no one was waiting outside. By the time I crossed the room again, Cecilia was snoring, mouth hanging open. The bobby pin slid from her hair, leaving the red wig in a pile behind her head.

For a while I paced back and forth in the room, tip-toeing from the door to the window. With one finger I peeled back the drapes a quarter of an inch, just enough to get a glimpse. Several photographers were camped out on the street, and a small crowd of women had gathered around them, their necks craned as they stared up at the window. I scanned the crowd for Mother, but there were no redheads, just a bunch of middle-aged brunets with sagging faces and bad dye jobs. I could see the gray roots even from three stories up. Jerry would have had a field day with women like these, I thought, laughing a little to myself as I let go of the drapes and paced back to where the cats were sprawled across my bed. I sat beside them for a minute but I couldn't stay still, so got up again and went on pacing until it felt as if I'd crawl right out of my skin.

I had to call Jerry. I simply couldn't stand keeping this secret to myself, pacing the floor for hours while waiting for my other self to meet me out on the fire escape. If there was anyone who could understand what I was going through, it would be Jerry. As a bisexual, he must have known what it felt like to be split in two, to feel the two halves of yourself as separate and to desperately yearn for them to come together, no matter how frightening that idea might seem. Or at the very least to have one half win and the other half bow out of the game and call it a day—to either melt in the arms of his security guard or spend all of his days with me in the cattery, our version of domestic bliss.

I tiptoed past Cecilia and made my way to the closet to have a look at the costume choices. I couldn't call Jerry and risk waking Cecilia in the middle of telling him about my secret rendezvous. Middle's directions had been explicit: "The Fergie lady is not invited." If I went against her now, then all bets were off. "Then you may never find me."

Cecilia had wigs in every color of the rainbow: black shags, curly blonds, the mousy brown Annie Hall bob she'd mentioned the first day we'd met, even a magenta punk-rocker look with spikes jutting out from the scalp. Red wigs in all different shades hung from hooks— strawberry blonds and dark russets, light auburns with streaks of gold, and a pure flame red. I chose a Barbra Streisand wig—straight blond with a dip in the sides— and a pair of tinted amber sunglasses to match. To complete the look, I wrapped a silky green scarf around my neck and shaded my freckles with Cecilia's eyebrow pencil. Before leaving the room I stared at myself in the mirror, throwing the scarf over one shoulder like a starlet. I fluffed the wig with my fingers and slipped on the sunglasses. *If Mother could see me now,* I thought, *she would not believe her eyes.*

The hallway was clear when I went out, except for a maid at the end of the hall—but her back was turned and she was folding towels when I slipped past her and down the stairs. There was a different desk clerk on duty, so I relaxed a bit while I dialed, trying to hold myself together while I waited for Jerry to pick up the phone. The things that had happened to me in the last few weeks happened to *other* people, I thought, not sensible cat breeders who spent their days acquiring compatible studs and cleaning litter boxes and trimming feline fur with baby scissors.

"Hello," a voice boomed after the third ring. The

opening bars of "She's a Lady" echoed in the background. "Jerry's Grooming Service. You breed 'em, we brush 'em."

I couldn't believe what I was hearing. Was this some sort of cruel joke? I'd left Jerry in charge, but that didn't give him the right to take over the cattery and turn it into his own pet salon.

"Hello," the voice said again. "Is your pet in distress? Matted fur? Flyaway dander? Litter cling? How can we help?"

I took a deep breath and adjusted the sunglasses on my face.

"You can start by telling me where the hell Jerry is," I said; and as much as I'd tried to sound strong, my voice cracked as soon as I said Jerry's name.

"Miss Maxi," the voice whispered. I realized it was Ron, the security guard. I'd known Jerry's new flame was around but honestly hadn't expected him to have moved into my house, let alone answer the cattery phone. "Good lord, is it you?"

"Who else would it be?" I snapped. A tear slid from the corner of my eye and got trapped under the weight of the bulky sunglasses.

"Oh, Miss Maxi," Ron said, "we've been answering that way to throw off the reporters. The phone's been ringing day and night. We hardly get any sleep. Sometimes when we answer all we hear is somebody breathing, real harsh and slow, like a heavy smoker, you know? He never says a word, but we know it's Norton. It was Jerry's idea to answer like this is a sort of grooming place, so Norton'd think we couldn't care less where you were—you or your mama and that RGC of yours. But of course that's not the truth. Me and Jerry, and the cats even—well, Miss Maxi, we've just been sick about you."

The tenderness in Ron's voice got the better of me, and I started to cry thick tears that pooled in the frames of the sunglasses. My scalp was sweating under the heaviness of the Streisand wig. I felt so terribly foolish about feeling jealous of a man who wasn't really mine, of being thirty-four years old and still needing my mother, at standing there in a blond wig and sunglasses because I'd convinced the world I was Fergie's niece. I tried to speak, but the tears just kept coming. I was afraid if I opened my mouth I would sob.

Ron's voice continued, even softer this time. "I'll go get him for you, Miss Maxi," he said. "Don't hang up."

I nodded—though Ron couldn't see me of course—and wiped my face with the green scarf. The freckles I'd outlined on my cheeks left brown smudges all over the silky green material. I rubbed the edges of the scarf together to try to scrub them away, but the smears grew darker and more pronounced.

"Maxi!" Jerry shouted in my ear. I was so startled, I dropped my sunglasses on the floor. "For god's sake, Maxi, I've been worried sick."

For several minutes I couldn't speak. I felt a squeezing in my chest and dug in my purse for my inhaler. The bottle was nearly empty; all that came out was a puff of air. I closed my eyes and tried to calm myself. The last thing I needed was an asthma attack.

"Maxi, honey. Jesus," Jerry went on, his voice sounding harsh and strained, "you don't know all the hell we've been through. Day and night the phone rings with somebody new begging for a quote, the cats are swelling by

the day. We've got thirteen queens pregnant all at once—
and please, God, let them at least be pet quality after
what happened that night. Then Anita went to pick up
the twins and Norton took off, she's been crying all the
time, the poor thing. The twins keep asking for you; and
frankly, I think Norton has a thing for her."

Jerry let out a long sigh, his breath pulsing softly
through the receiver.

"I haven't dyed my hair in weeks," he whispered,
"and I miss you like hell. When are you coming home?"

I blew my nose into the scarf and felt the air expand
in my lungs. I wanted to throw off the wig and smash
the sunglasses right there on the carpet and scream out
to the world that Jerry missed me.

"Oh, Jerry," I said. "I miss you, too."

We laughed then, deep laughs from our diaphragms.
For a minute it was like none of this had happened. I
wasn't a mother, Jerry wasn't in love with a security
guard, and we could dance barefoot to Tom Jones songs
in the living room. Mother still lived in the same town
and called me four times a day. Anita carpooled to 4-H
while I took Persians out on the campaign trail for Cat
of the Year and prayed for the perfect cat to appear one
day after all my frantic crossings and recrossings, chart-
ing out possibilities with every inbreeding combination I
could conceive of.

"Jerry," I said, when I was finally able to catch my
breath, "tonight is the night. She's coming for me tonight."

Jerry let out a long sigh. "Well," he said. "I guess
she's come to her senses."

For a minute I wasn't sure what he meant, then I laughed a little at his mistake.

"No, not Mother," I said. "She knows where I am, but she won't come for me. Not anymore. She's coming for Fergie—I mean Cecilia. Middle's coming for me."

"Are you sure?" Jerry said. "Minnie was screaming at her on the phone. She couldn't even finish a sentence. Gary Tate lost control of the show."

I realized how bizarre all of this seemed, even to Jerry, who had been there since the moment of conception.

"Things have changed," I said. "Middle sent me a note. I don't know what to make of it, actually. She says she knows how to give Mother the slip once and for all, like the two of us will be together and leave Mother behind. I don't know what I'll say to her, Jerry. What if I can't bring myself to leave Mother?"

For the first time since I'd known him, he raised his voice.

"For god's sake, Maxi, you're thirty-four years old. It's about time, don't you think?"

I stood there for a long while without saying anything, staring at my reflection in the metal base of the pay phone. Dark pencil smudged my cheeks, collecting in the corners of my eyes where crow's-feet had begun to appear. The wig hung sadly on my head, the scarf wilting as if it, too, felt ashamed at not being able to let go.

"Maxi," Jerry said after a minute, "are you still there?"

I cleared my throat and adjusted the wig, then pushed the sunglasses up the bridge of my nose.

"I'm here," I said. "I've got to go."

We didn't say anything for several minutes. I held on to the receiver with both hands, thinking of all the times Mother and I had been reluctant to end a conversation, neither of us wanting to be the one to break the connection.

"OK," Jerry said. "OK."

"OK," I said back, and before he could say anything else, I hung up the phone and held it there on the cradle, bracing myself against the pain. As hard as it was to let go, I had realized something as I hung up that phone. Everyone I knew had someone to turn to, someone to comfort them in times of sorrow. Jerry had Ron, Anita had her twins, and Mother had Middle. Even the Duchess and Bea had each other. Of course, Cecilia would probably have said that I had her and a cattery full of near-perfect Persians to see me through, but I finally realized the truth: All I had was myself.

On the way back up to the room I stopped at the second-floor balcony and looked out at the crowd below. Women holding poster boards stenciled with hearts framing pictures of Fergie filed past the photographers, who kept their lenses aimed at our window. This fake Fergie was finally getting the kind of attention the real Fergie deserved. Looking down at the scene, I realized that this was just as Mother had always dreamed Fergie would be treated—not as the breast-baring adulteress or trashy fly-by-night the media often painted but as genuine royalty.

When I got back to the room, Cecilia was still sprawled out on the bed, only now her wig was in place and her freckles had been carefully stenciled on and then covered over with a fine pale base. I tiptoed past her and was about to return the wig and scarf, when she sat up suddenly and threw her arms open.

"I'll say, you've done it, luv!" she shouted, her British accent thicker than I'd ever heard it. "You've gone and become someone else."

Without looking at her I threw the wig and sunglasses into the closet, then forced a smile and turned to face her. With the back of my hand, I wiped at the smudged freckles and let the scarf fall to the floor.

"I just went out to make a phone call," I said, moving over to the bed and pulling the Duchess and Bea onto my lap. "There's a big crowd out there. I didn't want to attract any more attention."

She laughed and got to her feet. She stood beside my bed, her hands on her hips. The cubic zirconias sparkled. When I looked closely, I could see she'd even painted freckles across her knuckles and down the length of her index fingers.

She sat down beside me. Her eyes seemed bluer now, her cheekbones edged in a soft peachy glow. If I closed my eyes, I could see Mother's face staring at me from her wedding picture, the briefest of smiles lingering. Cecilia leaned in closer, her wig stabbing at my cheek.

"How much do you think it would be worth to your mum," she said, "to have a full-fledged Fergie as her own all the time? She could certainly use the bloody therapy, no question about that."

At first I was quiet, but then I felt anger burning in my chest. Cecilia kept staring at me through those blue contacts. It seemed this was all I meant to her: a paycheck, the price of admission. What had she done that I hadn't suggested? Whatever therapy she prescribed came in the form of costumes and wigs, a painted-on face—not empathy or concern or even friendship.

She laid a hand on my arm and held it there, her rings cold against my skin.

"I know it's not easy to pay for therapy," she said, dropping the British accent, her voice high and somewhat nasal. "It's painful to have to ask a stranger to help you find yourself." She pressed her fingers into my wrist and smiled, her caked-on freckles crinkling. "But we're running out of time; and frankly, I've just got to bring this up. With all those cats you've got brewing at home, you will certainly be flush. Now is as good a time as any to settle up."

I got up from the bed—the Duchess and Bea tumbling from my lap—and ran across the room to find my purse. Inside I found the checkbook I used for emergencies—feline C-sections when I could no longer help a delivery, or purchasing an extraordinary stud I happened upon. I scribbled on the check the amount of the balance in the account and signed my name in bold letters on the signature line.

"Here," I said, tossing her the check. She smiled at me and tucked it inside the pocket of her long gingham dress. "When Mother comes, you put on a good show," I said, feeling the tears welling up in my eyes. "You make sure she gets the Fergie of a lifetime, no matter what the cost."

With that I scooped up the Duchess and Bea and headed for the door. As I ran down the stairs, the cats bouncing at my hips, I heard Cecilia call my name in her British accent, her voice echoing down the halls. I ran past the desk clerk and out into the crowd, elbowing my way through the throngs of people chanting Fergie's name. At the time all I could think was that I had to get out of that room, away from the face that so resembled Mother's wedding picture, away from the falseness of costumes and horsehair wigs. I ran straight through the blinding flashes and across to the parking lot, fumbling in my purse for the keys to the Caravan. I opened the door and pushed the cats inside, the Duchess hissing at me as she jumped into the backseat.

I switched on the ignition and revved the engine, not sure where I was going or how I would get there. I'd promised myself I'd meet Middle at midnight, but I couldn't stay in that room any longer. All I wanted to do was go back to my cats and Jerry and the life I'd known before. I pulled the car into reverse, when I felt a hand reach over the backseat and squeeze my shoulder.

"Maxi?" said a sheepish voice.

Of course I knew it was Mother before I turned around. A woman never forgets the sound of her mother's voice. After all she'd done to drive me away, her voice still struck a chord in me the way it had when I was seven years old. I turned my head and stared at her. Her lower lip quivered and her whole face crumpled up, fell in on itself, as if it had taken everything she had to hold herself together but she had suddenly run out of strength.

"I've lost her," she whispered.

Before I could say anything, she wrapped her arms

around my neck from behind and hung there. Later I realized that I hadn't cried but had simply held still for a long time, feeling the weight of her pulling me from behind, her arms tight around my neck. Her whole body shook with the effort to hold on, to keep me from pulling away, from letting her go.

When Mother finally stopped crying, I started to drive. Her arms were still draped around my neck and her glasses had fallen over my shoulder, landing directly above my left breast. Without a word I handed them back to her and made my way out of the parking lot. The van bottomed out as I raced out of the driveway.

I just kept looking straight ahead as Mother sniffled against my shoulder. She was back, I told myself over and over again as I breathed in the smell of her hairspray, feeling a lightness in my head from her grip around my neck. In the rearview mirror, I caught a glimpse of the crowd in front of the motel, the banners with Fergie's name emblazoned on them growing smaller in the distance. In her distress over losing Middle, Mother didn't even seem to notice the Fergie lovers. The loss of Middle, it seemed, had taken away even Mother's greatest pleasures.

After my view of the motel had disappeared, Mother finally raised her head and spoke.

"You've got to help me get her back," she said, her

voice low and earnest. She leaned farther forward in her seat and pressed her face against the back of my head. "You've just got to."

I nodded, and her lips pressed against my hair in a kiss that lingered, one hand reaching up to stroke my hair. Over and over again her hand smoothed my hair as I drove from street to street, turning left at one corner as Mother suggested, right at the next. I held my head as straight as I possibly could, staring ahead. I felt no anger then, only numbness, a dulling of my senses, like seeing the world through a tunnel of water.

"It's been so long already since she was a baby," she said, almost cooing to herself. "I tried to keep her from growing."

I thought of Middle's note tucked inside my purse, the brazen loops of her teenage script meant only for my eyes. "I know how to give Mother the slip," she'd written.

It had taken me several weeks to even admit to my curiosity about Middle, let alone hope for some sort of reunion. I thought of telling Mother this, that she'd been the one I'd longed for from the start. The words moved through my head in slow motion—all of the things I wanted to say—but my throat was blocked by sorrow.

"You can still give birth," she said as she led me through the streets where Middle had last been seen. "You can try again. But me, what chance do I have? I've got nothing else."

I could have said that she was wrong, that all this had been dramatics, that she was selfish and uncaring to think she had nothing else. I could have said that her life could still be full. I could have said simply, "But you still have me, Mother. You'll always have me."

But I didn't say these things. Instead I forced myself to meet her gaze in the rearview mirror and stare right into those cool blue eyes.

"You're right, Mother," I said. "You're right."

We drove around for hours, up and down side streets, back through the center of town. Mother rolled down the back window and stuck her head out, her hair flying back as she screamed Middle's name over and over again.

"Come to Mother, darling," she called, as we passed a group of girls on bicycles with flowered baskets on the handlebars, their long ponytails blowing in the wind. "Mother wants you back."

The girls pedaled beside us on the sidewalk, their legs pumping hard to keep up. When we reached the end of the block to turn down a residential street, one of the girls stuck her tongue out at Mother and raised her fist in the air.

"Hey, lady," the girl screamed, her voice ringing through the street, "why don't you leave her alone?"

Mother stuck her head out to scream back, but just as she did we saw a flash of red hair and pale legs dart out from behind a row of hedges, then across a manicured lawn.

"That's her!" Mother yelled, and before I could stop her she had opened the door of the van and tumbled out. Her glasses flew off her face and were smashed in the road. I cut the wheel hard and slammed the van into park, grabbed the keys and my purse, and took off after her. Bits of glass crunched as my foot landed directly on what was left of the frames.

In the distance I saw red hair flying, arms pumping, then heard someone falling to the ground. *Oh no,* I thought, as I hopped over a row of petunias in someone's front yard, *she's caught her. Now we'll never get away.* Guilt stabbed in my chest at even thinking such a thing. What had become of me? My heart pounded as I jumped over hedges and a tangled garden hose, my pulse thumping in my jaw. This was how my whole life had been— chasing Mother.

"Middle!" she screamed. "Middle, come back!"

I jumped over another row of hedges, caught my shoe on a branch, and landed flat on the ground. For a minute I lay there stunned.

A screen door slammed shut.

Slowly I pushed myself up from the ground and got to my feet. With both hands, I wiped mud off the front of my pants and stumbled toward the backyard fence. Mother lay beside it in a heap. A woman in a robe and curlers was hunched over her.

"Are you her daughter?" the woman asked, looking up at me.

I didn't answer, just stared down at Mother's rumpled coat and dirty knees. Mother sat up and leaned forward, rocking back and forth, and moaning. She clutched a white sneaker to her breast, mud smeared over the heel and toe.

"I almost had her," she sobbed, her whole body shaking. "I almost had her this time."

The woman tried to help Mother to her feet, but Mother just sat there, cradling the sneaker and weeping. Before she could say anything more, I turned away and hurried across the yard. Middle may be injured, I thought, feeling a sharp pain in my right foot and imagining Middle hobbling through the streets with one bare foot. I broke into a sprint and was almost at the van when I heard the woman shout.

"Hey, I know you! You're the one with the clone! Are you just going to leave your mother like this?"

I turned and saw the woman running toward me, her robe shifting in the wind. She stopped beside the van and clutched at her breast to catch her breath. I threw my pocketbook inside. The Duchess and Bea peered up at me expectantly from the floor.

Perhaps I shouldn't have left Mother there with only a sneaker to hold on to. Perhaps I should have gathered her up and helped her to the van, taken her to the motel and let her bond with her precious Fergie. Or perhaps I should have driven her through the streets until she finally found Middle, and let her have her once and for all.

I smiled at the woman and placed a hand on her arm, as if to tell her how hard I'd tried, that I was too small a person to fill Mother's needs. I was about to say this when Mother came flying toward me. Her rouge flaming up her cheeks.

"Don't you take her from me!" she screamed.

The woman turned and stepped between Mother and me, leaving me just enough time to climb into the van and slam the door. I pressed my foot to the gas and left them behind in a cloud of exhaust. The cats moaned low in their throats as I floored the accelerator.

"You won't get away from me," I heard Mother shout. "I know where you live."

I gripped the wheel with both hands and careened down the street, opening up all the windows and letting my hair fly wildly in the wind. As I drove through town, I remembered my father smiling down at me as he said good-bye, holding his banjo out to me, his dark eyes shining.

"You keep this one, Maxi," he whispered, then pressed his lips to my cheek. "When I come back we'll play something special, just you and me."

I nodded and smiled as he closed the door, holding in my tears while Mother ran from room to room slamming doors and screaming. Then she'd come to me and tried to grab the banjo, but I'd held on with my little-girl grip.

"Daddy said this is mine," I cried. But Mother wrested it from me and opened the case. She marched me by the hand into the kitchen and set the banjo on the table. With a hammer from the kitchen drawer she smashed that banjo to pieces. The plucky wires hung crazily from the base, shards of plastic flying across the kitchen.

When she was finished she knelt in front of me and held me to her, her grip so fierce I choked.

"There is no more Daddy anymore," she sobbed. "There's just you and me. From now on that is all there is. You and me."

How strange that I should remember this now after so many years. Since Middle's birth I'd felt fragments of myself returning, snippets of memory long forgotten. No wonder Mother had kept me so close to her all my life. I was all she'd ever had.

FERGIE SPOTTED AT HOTEL
CLONE'S GRANDMOTHER ON THE LOOSE

An anonymous source from the Hamilton Motel in downtown Hartford, Connecticut, claims to have seen Minnie Dublin, the grandmother of the first human clone, among the fans gathered around this motel, where it is rumored Sarah Ferguson, the Duchess of York, has been staying for a much needed vacation.

Motel guests reported hearing an old Tom Jones song being sung through the night, though no connection can be found between the Welsh singer and the Duchess's alleged presence at the motel.

Although palace officials have vehemently denied the Duchess's presence in the States, women from all over the country have gathered beneath her balcony window for sightings. It was at such a vigil that an onlooker claims to have seen Minnie Dublin, who reportedly made an appearance through the media several nights ago by phoning *Live with Gary Tate*. Though Ms. Dublin was apparently not accompanied by the clone, authorities have expressed hope that the clone will be returned to the hospital where she was born so she can be examined by leading genetic researchers.

When asked what he plans to do once the clone is returned, Dr. Charles Norton, the

**obstetrician who delivered the clone, refused
to comment, though his spokesperson, Gus
Vassy, said he believed Norton would "win the
Nobel Prize."**

I found Middle sometime after midnight, huddled on the
back fire escape. Her right foot was bloody and pitted.

Photographers were everywhere out front as Cecilia
had been giving quite a show for some time out on the
balcony, her tiara gleaming softly. The paycheck must
have inspired her, spurring her on to greater performances, I thought wryly.

Middle sat on the fire escape staring out with a big
smile on her face, all of her teeth showing, the comma
over her right eye twitching with mischief. She didn't see
me at first, so I stood just watching her, my heart pounding at the sight of her bony knees and freckled skin. To
think she'd come out of me, conceived on the cattery
floor and emerging in the delivery room, a squirming
pasty body. She'd wailed louder than any infant I'd ever
heard, as if she'd known the minute she was free—just
as I had—that we were one and the same. It was enough
to make anyone scream.

I stepped forward and cleared my throat. She lifted
her head and smiled up at me but made no move to
stand.

"Where's Mother?" Middle asked, and my heart sank
to think the first thing she should say to me was about
Mother.

I shrugged, not trusting my voice to answer. She
stared straight at me and got to her feet, hopping forward on one foot until she stood directly in front of me.

Her eyes still had a milky sheen, I noticed with a shock, as if she hadn't yet been able to shake off her infancy, despite her rapidly growing body. She had small breasts and narrow hips, long slender legs, and tons of flaming red hair. Her lips turned up at the edges, as if she were smiling to herself about some secret, a sexy joke she thought no one would get. Despite all the accoutrements of adulthood, she was heavy-lidded and smelled faintly of baby powder. Her eyes wrinkled in the corners as if she'd just awakened from a nap.

As I stared at her, I suddenly had a flashback of chasing one of Mother's wrestlers around the living room. The wrestler had stolen one of my sneakers and was taunting me with it, waving it in the air over his head. I kept jumping up to pull it out of his hands, but each time, he lifted it higher, just out of reach. His veiny arms bulged as he strained to keep me from grabbing the sneaker out of his hands. His breath reeked of body oil as he laughed in my face.

"Give it back!" I screamed, repulsed by the sight of his twitching arms, the long blue veins dancing under his skin. I started to cry and lashed out at him. "Give it back to me; it's mine!"

When Mother came in and found him, she chased him out of the house, pulling the sneaker from his hands and slapping him on the back with it. When he was gone, she held me in her arms and we both cried as I pressed the sneaker to my chest.

"You see," she'd said through her tears, "men come and go, but mothers are forever."

I stared down into Middle's pale face, at the tiny freckles scattered over the bridge of her nose, the birthmark sloped over her right brow. She blinked her milky eyes at me and smiled, a sad sort of smile, one that lingered but brought no light to her pale porcelain face. She reached up with one hand and touched the birthmark over my eye. Her fingers traced it slowly, edging over the curve of my brow. With her head tilted back, I could see the pulse beat in her throat. Her filmy eyes looked straight into my own.

"Do you know what happened to my sneaker?" she asked. Her breath smelled sweet, like powdered milk.

I just nodded and knelt to have a look at her foot. She sat down beside me and untied my right sneaker and removed it, then peeled off my sock, my foot bracing against the cold night air. To have her touch my foot felt as natural as anything I'd ever known. We lay back on the fire escape side by side, our freckled feet pale in the moonlight. There was so much I wanted to ask her, yet at the same time I felt doing so would be redundant.

"Where will we go now?" I whispered, as the crowd's cheers echoed from the front of the motel.

Suddenly Middle sat upright and clutched her knees to her chest. She took a long deep breath and then let it out slowly.

"I hate wrestling," she said. "And I want to play the banjo. I want to smoke cigarettes and listen to the clarinet and eat cupcakes." She stood up and twirled around, wincing as her damaged foot touched the metal floor of the fire escape. "I don't like hospitals. I don't like doctors." She paused and stared at me, a smile playing at the corners of her lips. "And I hate Mother."

As soon as she said it, I felt myself stiffen. A chill ran down my back.

"Don't say that," I said softly, reaching for my sock and sneaker. Slowly I pulled them on, leaving the shoelaces untied. I turned to her but could not look into those milky eyes. "You don't mean it," I said. "You shouldn't say things you don't mean."

Middle reached up to grab the railing, using both hands to pull herself up, and I joined her. We both stood there for a moment, staring down at our feet. Blood was caked along her heel and down around her toes.

"Yes, I do," she said, moving toward the steps. "I do mean it. You know that I do."

I didn't want our first meeting to be colored by an argument, so I took a deep breath and pressed a hand on her shoulder. The bones there were so thin, so tiny, that I nearly pulled my hand away in surprise. Had I ever been so young, so delicate and fragile? Had the theft of my sneaker really left such a profound mark on me? I hadn't thought of that incident in years. A little surge of fear ran through me, squeezing in my stomach and farther down, as I wondered if Middle would bring back other unpleasant memories I'd chosen to forget. I wondered if I had ever truly hated Mother, as Middle now swore she did. *Hate* was such a strong word.

"I want to go home," I said, and as soon as the words came out of my mouth, I felt a lump rise up in my throat and catch there. I tried hard to swallow it down. "I've got to go home now. We can't stay here anymore."

Middle smiled at me, running a hand through her hair. Her eyes crinkled at the edges. She took my arm

and leaned on me as we made our way down the steps.
She was not at all what I'd imagined she'd be, I thought.
Yet at the same time, I couldn't imagine how she might
have been any different.

To get to the Caravan we had to move to the front of the
building past the crowd that had grown in the hours
since I'd left the motel. Hundreds of women swayed together, arm in arm, screaming their love of Fergie to
Cecilia, who stood in the shadows, blowing kisses in her
long white gloves. Middle and I hid behind police cars
waiting for the right time to cross to the parking lot. It
seemed we might never make it.

"Who is this Fergie lady?" Middle asked as we peered
around the corner. "Why does Mother love her so much?
She doesn't even look like Mother. She looks like you."

I laughed a little in my throat and scanned the crowd
for signs of Mother. Middle hadn't lived long enough to
know Fergie or understand Mother's obsession.

"Don't tell that to Mother," I said. "She thinks she's a
dead ringer for Fergie."

At this Middle snorted and wiped the sides of her
eyes. She laughed and laughed, slapping at her knee, her
foot coming down hard on the pavement. With the back
of her hand she continued wiping at her eyes, as if trying
to clear them of the milky film, trying to see more
clearly.

"What's so funny?" I asked. Suddenly she stopped
laughing. When I said her name, she just narrowed her
eyes and pointed up at the balcony outside Cecilia's window.

I turned around slowly and looked up. Middle leaned

against me from behind, her small hands gripping my shoulders. As I took a deep breath I felt her inhale with me and hold the air in, her chest pressed up against my back, heart pounding against my spine.

I gasped when I saw what she was pointing to. Cecilia burst forward from the shadows, to the edge of the balcony, and leaned over to grab at a figure hanging from the ledge.

"Oh, my god!" I screamed, and before Middle could stop me I ran toward the crowd, tripping over my shoelaces. I pushed my way to the front, not stopping to see if she'd come with me or not.

"Mother!" I screamed at the top of my lungs. "Mother, don't!"

She hung by her fingertips from the edge of the balcony, her red hair flying in the wind, bits of glass falling from her clothing and sprinkling the crowd. Her coat was open at the waist, a sneaker hanging from her neck by the laces. Cecilia had her by both arms and was hunched down on the ground, struggling with all her might to pull Mother up. Her plastic tiara tumbled from her head and smashed on the ground. The crowd surged forward, women crawling under the police barricade to grab up the rhinestones, stuffing them into their pockets and laughing.

"Fergie, Fergie!" the women sang. "I've got a piece of Fergie!"

I scrambled under the barricade and stood on the curb staring up at Cecilia and Mother struggling three flights up. A policeman jabbed me in the ribs with his nightstick. I doubled over.

"That's my mother," I gasped.

I heard the voice in unison—my own voice saying the words, and another echoing them at the same moment. When I straightened up, Middle wrapped her arm over my shoulder and held me there, her nose nuzzling my neck.

"What do you mean, that's your mother?" the policeman said, slapping the nightstick in his palm. I tried to catch my breath as he gave Middle the once-over. His eyes lingering at the points of her breasts, and he leaned down to have a closer look at those milky eyes. I sucked in my breath, relief pouring over me as I realized he didn't know who we were.

"Just what she said," Middle said, poking the policeman with her finger. "That's our mother up there!"

The policeman tried to grab me by the arm to take me to the officer in charge, he said, but I simply couldn't move. I leaned on Middle as she dragged me forward, my feet hanging slack and my sneakers scraping the pavement.

"Come on, Mama, come on," she said.

I tried to will myself to scream, to throw myself on Mother's mercy and beg her forgiveness. But the air in my lungs held tight, and I collapsed at the curb, Middle's arm falling away from my waist.

I watched Mother swinging from side to side, Cecilia's hands clawing at Mother's, a torrent of British epithets spewing from her lips. Middle's face hung over mine, and I strained to see past her—to see whether it was Middle's hair in my face or Mother's or Cecilia's wig dangling precariously from the edges of her scalp. I felt all four of us meld into one—one squirming body hanging on by a thread, a smashed tiara at our bloody feet, one mass of snarled and matted red hair.

"I can't hang on, for the love of god!" Cecilia screamed. "For god's sake, luv, save yourself!"

Middle's mouth moved slowly as she said my name over and over.

The last thing I remembered was the sight of Mother's body floating through the air—her overcoat pushing out from her sides like wings, Cecilia's red wig clutched in her fists—and my reflection in the depth of Middle's eyes as together we screamed over and over: "Mother, Mother, Mother."

13

Of course they caught her. A team of policemen and security guards had formed a circle in the crowd and held their arms together. There wasn't time to call for a full-fledged rescue complete with a net and a high cushion of air. The men had simply huddled together and used their bodies to break Mother's fall. Her overcoat covered them like a fierce blanket, and the muddy sneaker pelted one of them on the head. All told, the casualties were only a dislocated shoulder and a welt above one of the men's eyes.

"I never saw anything like it," one of the rescuers told a reporter in an interview I read later in a newspaper Jerry saved for me. "She didn't even seem to care that Fergie was a fake. As soon as she hit the ground, she said she had to find her daughters—that her daughters had run away. What she thought Fergie had to do with her daughters," he said, "I couldn't figure out for the life of me."

Mother was dazed but unhurt. She refused medical treatment at the scene and acknowledged the crowd's applause. With a brilliant flash of her dentures and a kiss blown through her scratched hands, she gave her first statement to the press.

"That girl is mine," she said. "I've got to have that little girl."

Middle had hidden in the crowd while I was reviving, and she had listened to the onlookers expressing shock when they realized Cecilia was a fake. After I came to, she helped me back to the van and settled me inside. Then she taped a bag of ice cubes she'd gathered from the ice machine to my head and rubbed my neck. I'd missed seeing Mother, but it felt so good to have someone comfort me, to rub my hair and comfort me in a soft voice.

The Duchess and Bea sat quietly in the corner while Middle rattled on about her adventures from infancy to adolescence. They sniffed at her from time to time, moving from one of us to the other as if not sure who was who anymore.

"We went to playgrounds and ate ice cream. She sang me songs and told me how much she loved me. 'There's only you and me in the whole world, Middle,' she said. 'You're my girl.'"

I said nothing, content to just let her talk. It seemed the only thing to do.

"She knew I was growing. She cried about it. 'Not you, too,' she said, 'not another one.' I said I didn't want to leave her. At first I really didn't. But when I asked her for a banjo and said I wanted to find you, she got crazy and wouldn't let me go. I couldn't be with her all the time, you know. I had to have some things for myself."

She took a deep breath and let out a long sigh, as if she'd already seen too much in her short little life.

"First she loved me and then she turned against me,"

Middle said, as she stroked the cats' backs and rubbed her eyes. "She loved me so much it hurt."

I nodded and adjusted the bag of ice on my head, smiling to myself at the simplicity of her phrasing. Judging by the way she looked and the content of her memory, she was me at fourteen or fifteen, long and lithe, a hint of melancholy lurking behind those filmy blue eyes. Unlike me, she was so sure of herself, had no doubt that life and everything in it was exactly the way she saw it.

Some things about Middle were uniquely hers. She liked to chew gum and crack it in the sides of her mouth, something I couldn't remember ever doing. And she couldn't wait to see Anita again—the Anita from my childhood, not the sensible Anita of today with her severe blond ponytail and sturdy legs, and a Caravan filled with little girls carpooling to 4-H. Middle dreamed of being closer to Anita than I could remember being, the two of them dancing to old records and smoking cigarettes on the sly. More than anything else, she wanted to get as far away from Mother as possible—on a cross-country trip in a pickup truck, the two of us strumming a pair of banjos for spare change. Middle swore she remembered several songs her father—our father—had taught her before making off with the Mummers, but I didn't see how this was possible.

"He used to sing 'O Susanna,'" she said, shaking her head at the memory, "and bounce me on his knee. We used to play it together. I can teach it to you if you want."

I said that would be fun but doubted the reliability of

her memory. Besides, I couldn't remember ever having wanted to get away from Mother when I was fifteen; if anything, the thought would have terrified me.

"You should have seen the way she flew," Middle said, clapping a hand over her mouth to keep from laughing. "Like a crazy old bird trying to keep her chicks from leaving the nest."

I gripped the steering wheel with both hands. It amazed me that she could be so insightful at fifteen, so full of yearning and desperation to make her own way. Her eyes glowed as she talked about what life would be like without Mother in it, how we could play the banjo until dawn and smoke cartons of cigarettes. We wouldn't need Jerry or Anita or even Candy and Sandy anymore, none of the people from my former life. We could set Mother's pictures of Fergie on fire and laugh as they turned to piles of ash.

"Do you remember what I said back there while Mother was hanging from the balcony—what I said the exact same time as you?" she whispered, as I turned onto the highway that would lead us home. "You know what I meant when I said that?"

I turned to her for a minute and softened at the sight—the rows of freckles over her nose, the corners of her eyes forever etched in sleep. I reached over and pressed the back of my hand to her cheek.

"Do you mean when you said that that was your mother hanging from the balcony?" I whispered. "Is that what you mean?"

She closed her eyes and turned her head toward the windshield, headlights reflecting over her face.

"Yeah," she said softly, her breath catching in her throat. "But I didn't mean her. I meant you."

As we made our way down the interstate toward home, I tried not to think about what might lie ahead for us, what life might be like with another me to share it with. The thought was disconcerting to say the least, but I'd always felt a little bit lonely, even when the best-quality Persians were born and in the few moments of my life when I'd been truly held—by Mother or Jerry or even Candy and Sandy. Surely Mother and Cecilia were not far behind; I was not so naive as to think that Mother would give up so easily. She was not one to admit defeat.

Middle lay with her head against the window, her eyes closed. Freckles were scattered around the soft turn of her mouth. She shifted in her seat as I tried chasing away my visions. The comma above her right eye did a knowing dance as she raised her eyebrows.

"You've got to stop thinking about her," she said sleepily, reaching across to lay a hand on my lap. The Duchess and Bea raised their heads for a moment, then settled happily into her lap again. "It's the only way."

I nodded and smiled, though I knew she couldn't see me, and took a wide turn onto the entrance ramp. As I accelerated, I switched on my blinker to signal to the cars behind me and reached down to hold Middle's hand in mine. A van in the right lane sped up, as if trying to keep me from merging in, but I pressed the accelerator even harder and cut in front of the van, our bumpers nearly touching. The driver raised his fist in my rearview mirror, but I just laughed. Ordinarily I would have waited patiently for the man to pass, lifting my foot off the accelerator to slow down, but now I wanted to rush ahead. No one was going to stop me from going where I had to go anymore, now that I knew where I was headed.

We stopped at an all-night drugstore when Middle's foot wouldn't stop bleeding. At first she said she didn't mind the blood, that the sight of the crusty scabs reminded her Mother would stop at nothing to get her back, which was just what we needed to keep us on course. By midnight the foot had swelled and turned a soft green-ish color. Purple and yellow veins appeared under her translucent skin.

"I think my foot's in trouble," she said abruptly, sitting up straight in the passenger seat and squeezing the cats at the scruffs of their necks. "Mother really hurt my foot."

My own foot ached as well, but I hadn't thought much of it, figuring the trauma of the past few days had finally taken its toll on my body. Chasing Mother and running like a teenager, what did I expect? I glanced over at Middle's foot and gasped. The toenails had turned black. Blood was encrusted between her toes and down the fine slope of her arch. All the time we'd been driving she hadn't once mentioned her foot. I turned off at the next exit and pulled into the nearest drugstore parking lot. Without a word I tore off my socks and sneakers and slid one white sock over her foot, wrapping the other sock around her ankle like a tourniquet.

"I've got to go in and get some first-aid supplies," I

said, reaching over and touching her softly on the shoulder. "We've got to fix up that foot before it gets infected, get some peroxide and bandages at the very least."

I grabbed my purse and opened the door, but she reached over and grasped me by the shoulder, hard. When I turned to face her, there were tears streaming down her face.

"What if she comes for me while you're gone?" she said, trying to move forward and across to the driver's seat. She winced with pain. "I can't run away."

The Duchess suddenly scrambled off Middle's lap and leaped into my arms, burrowing her face in my armpit, her whole body shaking. She hadn't acted this way since she was a kitten. Duchess was the bravest Persian I'd ever raised. Bea meowed loudly and got down on the floor, cowering in the corner next to Middle's injured foot.

"What is it, Duchy?" I said, scratching the scruff of her neck. But she just gripped my shirt with her claws and shivered. I hadn't seen her this nervous since the first time she'd given birth.

"OK," I said, both to the Duchess and to Middle, "you'd better come on inside with me. It's probably not the smartest thing to leave you out here alone."

I locked the driver's door and walked around the van to help Middle out. I thought it best to leave Middle in the van, but how could I leave her there in pain, especially after having abandoned her in the beginning? Already there was so much I had to make up to her.

As I held the door open for her, she hooked one arm around my neck and held on. "It's OK," I whispered, holding the Duchess with one hand while helping

Middle balance her weight. I bent my head down to her level. She pressed her face into my hair, keeping her arm wound tightly around my neck. With a little hop she leaned forward out of the way of the passenger door so that I could close it.

"What about you, Bea?" I cooed, but her head was buried under the seat, her tail quivering in the air.

"She wants to stay," Middle said. "She doesn't have to go everywhere her mother goes."

I used my hip to slam the door shut, then we hobbled across the parking lot to the drugstore. While Middle pulled the door open, I looked fearfully over my shoulder to see if Mother and Cecilia were already in our wake. The lot was empty except for a battered old Volkswagen, a group of teenagers leaning against its hood and smoking cigarettes. One of them took a long look at Middle and whistled under his breath, but neither of us turned around. When we made it inside the store, I noticed we were both blushing.

The store was nearly empty, so we took our time choosing peroxide and bacitracin, a roll of adhesive bandages, and a box of dry cat food, which my Persians normally despised but would have to do until I got them home to the gourmet cat food they were used to in the cattery. Maybe that was why the Duchess trembled so, I thought, as I piled our purchases on the counter, leaving room for Middle to add the six packs of chewing gum she needed for that endless cracking she did. She chose a candy bar, too, one with chocolate and layers of nuts and other goo, and I had to stop myself from warning her that eating candy might cause her to break out.

"It will give you zits just like it did to me," a high

rasping voice said inside my head. I held my breath to keep quiet.

When we were finished we made our way back out to the van, Middle's arm still around my neck and the Duchess and the paper bag held tightly to my chest. One of the boys smoking near the Volkswagen hurried across the parking lot and opened the passenger door for Middle.

"What did you do to your foot?" he said softly, holding the door as she pressed her fingers to my neck and pushed herself up into the seat. What if she looked up at him with those infant eyes and he laughed in her face? What if he realized she was me?

"She's all right," I said, stepping between them to hand Middle the paper bag full of supplies. I dumped the Duchess on the floor, and she whirled around and hissed at me.

"Hey," the boy said, raising his hands in a gesture of peace, "I just thought she looked like she needed some help. All that pretty red hair and all, and hobbling around on one foot."

I was about to slam the door, but Middle reached out and held it open, her arm taut. She glared at me, the comma over her eye raised high above her brow.

"I had a little accident," she said to the boy, cracking her gum and twirling a long red curl behind her ear. "I lost my sneaker while I was running, you know. Slipped and fell trying to run away."

I stepped away from the van and felt tears well up in my eyes, but why, I didn't know. The boy leaned closer and looked in at her foot, clucking his tongue and shaking his head with sympathy. He was tall and lanky with blondish hair that swooped down over his eyes.

"Where are you headed now?" the boy asked, his head now inside the door. I walked over to the driver's side and buckled myself in, then started the ignition and revved the engine a few times. "Are you still running away?"

Before she could answer him he leaned forward and hummed a few bars of "What's New, Pussycat?" in her ear. Middle giggled, pressing a hand over her mouth. She glared at me as I raced the engine over and over, sending clouds of exhaust pouring over the boy. She turned away from me as the boy edged away from the van, holding his hand over his mouth to keep from coughing.

"Hey," the boy said, cupping a hand over his mouth, "what's your mother's problem?"

With that, I put the van in reverse and poked Middle in the ribs, a clear signal it was time to go.

"She's not my mother," Middle called as we started to back away. She raised a hand and waved to him, a smile spreading across her face.

"Thank god for that!" the boy called, and I slammed the car into drive, causing the bag filled with medicines and bandages to spill all over the floor. Middle didn't even look at me, just folded her arms over her chest and snapped her gum, pushing the rolls of bandages away with the bloody side of her foot.

We didn't speak for hours. I drove the speed limit and took no more chances when changing lanes, slowing down considerably to let others pass, rather than run the

risk of being honked at or otherwise embarrassed.
Middle sat with her arms folded over her chest. She
chewed stick after stick of gum, cracking it loudly with
her back teeth, her purplish foot poised defiantly on the
dashboard. By now her toes had swollen to nearly twice
their normal size, and thin lines of blood dripped from
the heel. She wiped at the blood absently with a tissue.
My own foot throbbed in sympathy. I glanced at her
from time to time, out of the corner of my eye. I also
kept an eye on the rearview mirror in case Mother's
Taurus suddenly appeared behind us—though part of
me felt calm just then, as if we'd been given a temporary
respite from pursuit.

It was no wonder motherhood hadn't worked out for
me. When other women spoke of the thrill of nursing despite their cracked and swollen nipples, I winced. After
Anita gave birth to Candy and Sandy, I'd been with her
the day she brought them home—two little balls of
downy flesh, their bald heads with pale blue veins, so
fragile with new life. Sure, I felt a warmth in my chest
when I held them, smelled the sweetness of baby lotion
and breast milk on their breaths. But when their faces
contorted and their mouths turned gummy with pain, I
recoiled. It was a fact I couldn't deny. Mother had seen
this from its very beginning, which was why she thought
raising Persians would help get me over that hurdle, lure
me into motherhood. A new litter to look forward to
every few months, balls of fur wrapped in their sacs like
gifts waiting to be opened, one closer to perfection than
the next.

When we were nearly home I turned to Middle and

cleared my throat. What a sight we would be, not speaking to one another. How would I explain this? "I'd introduce you to the new me, Jerry," I'd say, "but frankly I'm not speaking to myself at the moment." Even though we were essentially one person, it was clear we needed time to get to know one another.

"Penny for your thoughts," I said, almost laughing to myself at the stupidity of the statement. It reminded me of Cecilia and the way she'd faked caring for me, how all along she was just after a fat paycheck at the end, my psyche split in two.

Middle turned to me then and stared straight at me.

"I liked that boy," she said. A film covering the darkness of her pupil made the blueness of her eye appear to be one great circle of color. "I liked that boy and you sent him away."

She leaned over and snapped her gum in my ear. My hands shook at the sudden noise.

"I'm not like Mother," I said suddenly, swerving into the next lane, nearly missing our exit. "I'm not like Mother at all."

Middle leaned back in her seat and slid her injured foot across my lap. I looked down at it and wrapped my hand around her swollen toes. Her foot was cold, but it grew warmer as I held on, dried blood sticking to my fingers as we sped down the exit ramp and through town.

After we drove past Mother's house, Middle wrapped her foot in a bandage. She narrowed her eyes and straightened her shoulders.

"Don't let her take me," she said, but I didn't answer, just turned to her and smiled. At moments like this, with her soft translucent skin and milky breath, she truly seemed to be a baby; and I, in my heart of hearts, felt like a mother.

We decided to go in through the cattery door to avoid waking Jerry. It was late and the yard was dark. There wasn't a reporter in sight. For a moment I forgot that Middle didn't know her way around and I left her behind. She bumped into the elm tree near the door, then gripped me by the elbow and hobbled along, her bandage coming loose around the edges. Bea ran ahead of us and scratched at the screen door while the Duchess lingered near the rosebushes where we'd buried the eyeless kittens. It all seemed like another life, I thought as I turned the key in the lock, the whines of cats hanging in the air.

"Come on, Duchy, we're home," I called softly as I switched on the overhead light and held the door open for Middle. The Duchess had sniffed in the dirt for a moment as if saying her final good-byes. Now she bounded into the cattery ahead of us.

"Well," I said, laying a hand on Middle's arm, "here we are."

At first she stood there with her foot poised in the air. Blood had soaked through the bandage. I was about to kneel down to inspect it when she suddenly moved toward the cages, peering in at each one, rubbing at her eyes. The cats were blinking, trying to adjust to the light. When they spotted me in the corner, they began to howl, sticking their paws through the cages at me. Middle opened her mouth wide, and the two of us stood there staring at all the pregnant cats for what seemed an eternity. On the wall hung the chart I'd made years ago, with recessive and dominant genes carefully mapped out, a series of piebald genes crossed to form what would become the perfect bicolor. Now they'd all been matched chaotically. These beautiful females housing any kind of haphazard litters.

"So this is where you live," Middle said sleepily, sitting down beside me on the floor and crossing her bandaged foot over the other. She smiled, wrinkles forming in the corners of her eyes. "It's not at all like I pictured it."

I laughed a little and gathered the Duchess in my arms, closed my eyes, and breathed in all the familiar smells—cleaning fluid and fresh litter, the malty smell of hairball remedy, and dry shampoos—all the things I'd been missing.

After a time I helped Middle to her feet and up the stairs, taking them one step at a time. Her brows were knit, a mixture of pain and confusion on her face. I helped her into the bathroom and was about to lean down to unwrap her bandage, when someone shoved something cold in my back.

"Stop right there, miss, or I'm afraid I'll have to shoot."

I held my hands in the air and whirled around, my breath catching in my throat. Ron stood there in his boxer shorts, brandishing a gun, his mustache wilted at the ends. We both started to laugh and Middle grabbed hold of me, burying her face against my breast.

"It's OK," I said, but she held on tighter, gripping me with both hands, her nails digging into my back.

Ron laughed and dropped the gun on the floor. Jerry

came running up behind him. His hair had grown and had turned a soft golden brown, the spikes now hanging low on his brow like bangs. We stared at each other for a while, and then he laid a hand over his chest.

"Oh, Maxi, honey, I'm so glad you're home."

Without thinking, I let go of Middle and lurched forward, throwing myself into Jerry's arms and burying my face in his neck. I cried and cried, as he held me there in the doorway, his biceps curving around my back.

"Jerry," I said finally, prying myself out of his arms, "I'd like you to meet Middle." But when I turned around she was gone.

"Where the hell did she go?" I shouted at Ron, panic rising in my chest. "Didn't you see her go?"

He just shrugged and wiped sheepishly at his mustache as if he hadn't even noticed her. Then he and Jerry ran down the hall to look for her. *Not again,* I thought. *Not again.*

But she was gone, the only trace of her a wad of bloody bandage and a piece of chewed gum stuck defiantly to the bathroom counter.

14

We spread out through the house to look for her. Jerry and Ron headed down to the cattery while I checked the rooms upstairs. The house was not very big, I told myself, heart pounding, as I followed the traces of blood she'd left on the carpet. She couldn't have gone far. Perhaps all the excitement had been too much for her and she'd fled, as children are sometimes known to do—except, of course, she wasn't really a child. Or was she?

I was just about to search under the bed when I heard Jerry yell for me.

"Maxi!" he called. "Come quick!"

I ran down the stairs, two at a time, slid across the kitchen floor, and twisted my ankle on the cattery stairs. What if Mother had gotten to her through the basement? It wouldn't have been the first time. I thought of the day in the hospital when Mother had stolen her from the nursery. The resident's words echoed in my brain. *Hell hath no fury like a mother scorned.*

When I reached the last step, I felt the air squeezing in my chest. Jerry and Ron were standing in front of me, shoulder to shoulder, their bodies blocking my view. I held on to the banister and tried to scream, but could only wheeze.

"Oh, good lord," Ron said, "they *both* can't breathe."

I felt my knees go out from under me, a terrible pain in my right foot, the air squeaking in my throat. Jerry and Ron ran up the stairs and back down again—and suddenly I felt a blast of air moving down my throat. Ron squeezed the inhaler again for me, but I struggled to get away, crawling across the floor to where Middle sat wheezing, too. She lifted my inhaler to her lips and squeezed, her milky eyes rolling up in her head. Jerry stood several feet away from her, as if he were afraid. The cats howled.

When I could finally breathe normally again, I reached over and touched her shoulder.

"Why did you run away?" I whispered; but she pulled away from me and narrowed her eyes. On her lap were the Polaroids Mother had sent. Middle smiling in Mother's arms, a wayward tooth sprouting up from her gums; Middle with her feet covered in frosting; Mother and me with party hats on our heads. If not for the obvious difference in Mother's age, it would have been difficult to tell who was who.

She turned to me and held up the last one, a photo of me when I was pregnant, my body turned in profile, Jerry's hand resting playfully on my belly. Mother had taken this one right before our last rehearsal. "What harm could it do to have the father in the photograph?" she'd said—only then we hadn't realized there would be no father at all.

"He's not my father," she said, tearing the photo to shreds and stomping her injured foot on the floor. She pointed at Jerry and threw the pieces at his feet. "My father smokes cigarettes! He plays the banjo! He doesn't live here, he lives far away!"

She reached down and tore the bandage off her foot, lifting her purple toes in the air and squeezing, causing blood to seep down her leg.

"I'm going to bed" she said through gritted teeth, then she stormed up the stairs.

I knelt down on the floor and picked up the pieces of my favorite photo, the only one I had of Jerry and me when I was pregnant, the only photo that showed there was something normal and pure about the pregnancy.

"Maybe I should have let Mother have her," I said softly. "Maybe that would be the best thing after all."

Jerry signaled to Ron to give us some time alone, and he sauntered away, up the stairs, in his boxer shorts. Together Jerry and I placed each piece of the photo on the floor as if putting together the pieces of a puzzle.

"You don't really mean that," Jerry said, reaching over to stroke my hair as I fit the last piece of the photo in the corner. "You've got to give yourself some time. You've only just found yourself," he said softly, then brushed his lips against my forehead. "It takes some of us years to get that far."

After all I'd gone through to chase after Middle and get her back, I couldn't help feel the same sense of dread I'd felt that day in the delivery room when she'd first opened her eyes.

"Maybe if we'd just put her back," I whispered, but Jerry shushed me and took my hand. We had to come up with a plan, he said on the way up the stairs. Now was not the time for self-pity. Mother would not be far behind.

"Don't kid yourself into thinking she's letting you go," he warned, as we said good night in the hall. "You've got to think about changing your life. Do the things you've always wanted to do."

He leaned forward and pressed his mouth to my forehead, his warm lips lingering over the comma curving above my right eye. With a hand on each side of my face, he whispered, "She does look a lot like you. I've always wished I'd known you at that age. I wonder if you were like her."

I just smiled.

Then he and Ron went arm in arm to the guest room, pausing to smile back at me before closing the door behind them.

It was too soon to tell how much Middle really was like me. Jerry was right, of course, as he always was. I had more than just myself to think about now—or at the very least, more of myself to think about.

When I slipped in bed beside Middle, she slid her foot out from under the blanket and turned toward me. It had nearly doubled in size, the blood dry but the toes and heel ever more swollen. I gasped and reached out to touch it, but she pushed my hand away and bit her lower lip.

"She hurt us," she said in a low voice, her eyes seeming to thicken with sleep. "You can't forget about that."

I promised that I wouldn't, but she didn't seem to believe me. She turned over on her side, her back curving against me. I didn't know what she meant exactly by "being hurt"—whether she meant being stolen or keeping my father from us or tearing away her sneaker in a strange backyard. Stealing her away from me. I wanted to tell her that it would do neither of us any good to hold on to such hate, but I knew without questioning it that Middle was not one to forgive.

We watched television while Middle soaked her foot in a basin. The peroxide hissed even over the sounds of the reporters' voices. Gary Tate devoted an entire week to celebrity interviews about the question of cloning, while Sophie Sussman tried in vain to coax Mother on to her program with ads in *Variety* and telegrams delivered to my house. She even promised to interview her with Fergie if Mother would agree to appear.

DEAR MINNIE (STOP) NO TRICKS THIS TIME (STOP) NO MORE FALSE FERGIES (STOP) YOU'LL HAVE THE REAL THING (STOP) A DUCHESS TO CALL YOUR OWN (STOP) LOVE (STOP) SOPHIE SUSSMAN (STOP)

Reporters for all the major networks broadcast live every night from outside the hospital, where Norton had locked himself in an operating room in a last-ditch attempt to save himself further embarrassment in the press. Tom Brokaw and Dan Rather interviewed dozens of geneticists who denied any knowledge of a human clone being produced at MacArthur General.

"Each human cell is like a note in a major symphony," one specialist said. "Charles Norton would have had to not only isolate the correct cell from the living host—Maxine Dublin—but get that one cell to play every note in the right key with the right pitch. With all due respect, it would be like asking a second-grader in music class to play Mahler's Ninth."

Another report focused on the dramatic rise in sales of Tom Jones records, which the media attributed to the groups of women who had sung "What's New, Pussycat?" as a means of luring the duchess out to the balcony.

We laughed from time to time at the reporters and lay on the couch with our heads together, not moving except to change the peroxide in Middle's basin. We didn't answer the telephone, leaving the answering machine to record our messages. There were three from Candy and Sandy and one from Anita, all asking when they could come over and see us. I dispatched Jerry to return the calls, said we weren't ready yet to see anyone but each other.

Ron and Jerry took turns keeping a twenty-four-hour guard at the door, guns shoved inside the waistband of their matching spandex shorts. They would keep the reporters away for as long as they could, they said, but they didn't know how long they could hold out. Ron carried the answering machine into the hallway and motioned for me to join him. I left Middle with the remote, then Ron pressed the play button and shook his head.

"We want the baby!" a reporter shouted. "Not some lanky teenager! The whole world is expecting a baby!"

When I didn't say anything, Ron shook his head and switched off the machine.

"Maybe they'll leave you be, Miss Maxi," he said as I headed back toward the living room. "After all, that's no baby in there. She sure isn't what *we* expected her to be."

Later Anita snuck in the back door with Candy and Sandy, carrying a present.

"Aunt Maxi!" the girls called, running toward me with their arms open. I knelt down on the kitchen floor and gathered them into my arms, ran my fingers through their long silky ponytails, kissed their warm flushed cheeks.

When the twins finally let go, I stood up and turned to Anita. The large box she held had frilly pink bows all over it, long curly ribbons hanging from the sides. She set the box on the table and took a few hesitant steps toward me. There were dark circles under her eyes, and her hair hung flat against her head.

We laughed and hugged. The twins looked up at us and grinned.

"Where's your little girl, Aunt Maxi?" Sandy asked, reaching for my hand.

"We want to see her," Candy said.

I crouched down on the floor and touched their faces. How could I explain to them that I'd given birth to myself, that part of *me* had come out like a newborn but now languished in her pajamas watching bad television, pining for the boy with the Volkswagen, and begging for a banjo? That one day I had a baby and the next she was a teenager who wanted to go out on her own despite the hazards of the world.

I was about to concoct some kind of story when Middle appeared in the doorway, her right foot dragging behind her as she limped toward us.

"Maxi?" Anita said, reaching to grab my arm. "Is that who I think it is?"

Middle hobbled over to the table and tore open the gift. I wanted to tell her to stop, to wait to have the gift handed to her, but the shock of seeing her with Anita and the twins—parts of my childhood and adult life all mixed into one—kept me silent. She tossed the tissue from inside the box over her shoulder and picked up the clothes Anita had bought her; a frilly pink dress and matching hair ribbons, a Brownie uniform with her name stenciled on the sleeve.

"I thought she was only eight or nine," Anita whispered; and I just closed my eyes.

Middle threw the clothes down and stomped her swollen foot.

"I thought you were my friend," she screamed at Anita, and ran up the stairs in tears. Her sobs echoed down the hallway, and drops of blood were left in her wake. The twins scurried after her, carrying the uniform in their arms like a peace offering.

"She's not a little girl," I said, picking up the clothes and setting them back inside the box. "She thinks everyone should know that by now."

Anita was silent for several minutes, staring at me and then at the trail of blood Middle had left behind.

"I haven't been able to watch TV since *Live with Gary Tate*," she said. "Norton's been calling me day and night. I just couldn't watch TV after that night, not after seeing my own face on the screen." She covered her face with her hands.

We sat there for a long time, then I reached across the table and took her hand. Her palm was warm and soft in mine.

"I know what you mean," I said finally. "My childhood has come back to haunt me," I whispered, in case Middle was listening, "and I don't know what to do."

Sometime later I heard footsteps on the stairs, the sounds of Candy's and Sandy's voices talking to Middle in hushed tones.

"If you didn't get to be a baby very long," one of them said, "then why were you born?"

Anita and I just stared at each other. I held my breath waiting for the answer.

"Because I had to come out," Middle said in a flat voice. "I couldn't stay inside anymore. I just had to come out."

When Anita and the girls were gone I went upstairs to find Middle. She lay curled up on the floor, with photographs strewn all around her, the Brownie uniform Anita had given her folded against her belly. I stood in the door watching her sleep, her red hair spread over the carpet, her pale freckled hands reaching for the photographs. How difficult it must have been for her to piece her life back together, a life that wasn't really hers, a life I was sure she was beginning to sense, but I was not willing to relive.

Norton appeared on television promising to present the facts of the cloning if Middle was returned. The hospital posted a $500,000 reward for her return within twenty-four hours. He and Vassy stood shoulder to shoulder on the hospital steps, Norton's teeth coming down over his chapped bottom lip.

"We have secured the cooperation of the president in this matter," Norton said, raising his stethoscope high in the air. "We will call out the National Guard if we have to. If you can hear us out there, Maxine, don't let it come to this."

Ron got word from an informant in security that Norton and a team of geneticists were prepared to do whatever was necessary to capture Middle, even threatening to kill her if they had to.

"They want her dead or alive, Miss Maxi," Ron said, pulling at the ends of his heavy mustache. He leaned toward me to whisper, his mustache tickling my ear.

"He even says he can force you to do it again if he has to."

Jerry was watching us, his eyes narrowed with jealousy. He ran a hand through his hair, then switched off the television set.

Already reporters were starting to converge. We could hear their vans pulling up in front of the house. We closed all the venetian blinds. We could hide out in the cattery for a time, I suggested—stall for time among feline cages.

"You can't just sit here and wait," Jerry said as we all stopped near the cattery steps. I could hear Middle moving from room to room, the heavy thud of her foot hitting carpet. "You've got to make a move."

Suddenly all the rage I'd been burying for the past several weeks rose up in my chest and spewed forth in a great torrent. I pounded my fist on the floor and screamed at Jerry at the top of my lungs.

"And just what would you have me do?" I pushed him so hard in the chest that he stumbled back against Ron. "Maybe if you had been a real man and given me a baby like you were supposed to, I wouldn't be in this mess."

I didn't stop, though I saw tears flooding his eyes. Ron squeezed Jerry's shoulder, but Jerry shrugged off Ron's hand and moved away.

I let my body slump against the counter. The pain in my right foot was unbearable. I cried out and dropped to the floor. "Who the hell am I?" I said.

Before anyone could stop me, I jumped up and ran to the front door and unlocked the double bolts. I threw open the door and spread my arms out wide.

"Here I am!" I screamed, as the flashbulbs popped. "I'm the one who made the clone! I'm the one you want!"

The reporters stampeded over the lawn, smashing my daffodils and crushing the tiny swollen grave of the eyeless kittens. Before they could get to me, Jerry fired a shot above the crowd. More flashbulbs popped as he grabbed me by the waistband and pulled me to the floor. Ron slammed the door and twisted the locks.

"It's time for me to go," I thought I heard Middle say. But when I looked up, there was no one there.

Jerry helped me to my feet and I ran up the stairs to find her. She stood at the window peering out at the crowd through the slats of the venetian blinds. I wrapped her in my arms and held her, the smell of powder in her hair.

We went to bed very late, after Ron assured us the reporters had dispersed for a time. Together Middle and I dreamed that Mother came for us with a crowd of wrestlers behind her. She was dressed as Fergie, with a silky black suit and a wide-brimmed hat, a pair of chunky white heels on her feet. The wrestlers lifted Mother into the air like a queen, twirling her around in their strong hands. She laughed as they passed her from one to the other, her long red hair hanging low over her face.

"I've come to get my baby," Mother said, reaching under her dress and revealing Middle's tattered sneaker. "Has anyone seen my baby?"

She looked straight through Middle and me as if our

presence hadn't registered, then pressed the bloody sneaker to her chest and wept.

"My baby's run away but she can't get far," she cried, slapping each of the wrestlers across the face. She tripped over the white heels. "She can't get far without her shoe."

Middle turned to me and smiled, her bare gums red and swollen. She had yet to grow any teeth.

"Which one of us is her baby?" she asked. Then she screamed, her face contorting in pain, clumps of her red hair falling over her swollen foot.

"Not me," I said. I reached down to check my feet. I had both sneakers on, the laces tied in double knots. "Not me."

When I woke up, Middle was crying, long pitiful shrieks coming from her open mouth. She jumped out of bed and threw herself down, slamming her fist and swollen foot into the carpet.

"It's all right," I said, reaching down to comfort her. "It was only a dream."

"No, it's not," she sobbed. Strands of drool fell from her lips. She didn't bother to wipe them away. I knew a good mother would reach out and scoop them up for her, but the sight turned my stomach, her swollen mouth and the blue veins bulging in her throat.

I sat there on the floor cross-legged as she wept.

Jerry tapped at the door, opening it a crack and peeking in.

"Is everything OK?" he asked. He looked down at her lying there, hair tangled, strings of saliva hanging from her lips.

"It's just a bad dream," I said. "Go on back to bed."

Middle hadn't looked up from her position on the floor, but when Jerry closed the door, she raised her head and wiped the drool away with the back of her hand. I sat there wondering what I might say to comfort her, careful not to be too hasty with my words. It was obvious she did not want Jerry to be her father, and given the fact that he was sleeping in the next room with Ron the security guard, I really couldn't blame her. I knew she hated Mother; she'd said so before. How long would she hold on to this rage as it ate us both up inside?

"You can't protect me," she said, standing up and brushing off her knees with the backs of her hands. "You never have."

She climbed back into bed and pulled the covers over her face. I tried to pry them out of her hands but she had a fierce grip, her fingernails white as she clung to the blanket.

"Middle," I said, reaching out to her. "You mustn't hate Mother. She only wants her baby back. Try to understand. She doesn't know how else to love. That's what all mothers want."

With that she pulled the covers off and shook her foot defiantly in my face.

"Oh, yeah?" she said. "Then why don't you go and be her baby?"

I looked at her for a long time, at the narrow angles of her face, her pointed nose and filmy eyes. She looked like me, that much was true. But she wasn't really me at all. She might have been me at another time, the old me, full of rage and hurt, nursing old wounds and spouting

off at the mouth. That me was gone, long gone. If
Mother were there to see her, I thought, she'd agree that
this was not my true self—or at the very least, that it was
the self I had outgrown.

I let out a long sigh and moved to the window. A
maroon Taurus pulled up across the street. The reporters
parted as Cecilia and Mother walked hand in hand toward the house. I closed the blinds and turned to Middle.
I grabbed her by the shoulders and shook her, hard.

"Because I can't be her baby anymore," I said. "And
neither can you."

Then I wrapped her in my arms and held her as
tightly as I could. Her heartbeat pounded just under my
breast, just as it did when she'd lived for a time inside me.

"You've got to go now," I said, pulling her down the
back stairs and out through the cattery. Already I heard
Cecilia pounding at the door, Mother screaming in the
front yard. "You've got to go before Mother finds you."

We stood shivering in our nightgowns on the back
lawn, huddled by the rosebushes, where Jerry had
buried the kittens. In the moonlight Middle's hair shone
like fire. I reached down and slipped her feet into a pair
of my sneakers, then sat on my haunches to help her tie
the laces.

As she smiled down at me, the smoky film over her
eyes seemed to lift, the milkiness dissolving in the clear
blue of her irises.

"Maxi!" Mother shrieked from the front lawn. "Give
me back my baby!"

I heard cats howling in the house, and the sounds of
Jerry and Ron trying to quiet them. Cecilia's lilting

British accent floated on the air. "You've got to save yourself," someone said, and I wasn't sure if the voice came from Middle or from me, from somewhere deep inside.

With that Middle squeezed my hand and was off, her pale feet almost dancing ahead of her, as if she couldn't wait to go, to get on to the next adventure. She ran as fast as she could, despite the burden of her wounded foot. For a second I stood there breathless at the possibilities.

I didn't try to fight at first when Mother came barreling out the back door and tackled me on the lawn, pinning my arms above my head in a full nelson. The photographers' flashbulbs blinded us as she pulled and tugged at me. We rolled around on the grass, Cecilia with her red wig clipped awkwardly to her head, Jerry and Ron struggling to tear us apart. No matter how hard she tried, though, Mother couldn't hold me still. Once I got going, I thrashed and thrashed until she had no choice but to let go.

"That-a girl, luv," Cecilia whispered, smiling down at me there in the dirt.

When it was over, I crawled to the kittens' grave, stood up, and dusted myself off. Mother still had Middle's sneaker tied around her neck, though it was covered with mud and ripped at the seams, the laces frayed. I motioned to Jerry and Ron to go back into the house, which they did, but Cecilia wouldn't take the hint. Instead she sat cross-legged on the ground and adjusted her wig. She hugged Mother about the waist as Mother started to weep. The reporters were silent.

"You let her go," Mother said as her whole body

seemed to wilt, her glasses hanging from her face. She
looked up at me, tears leaving pale streaks in her heavy
rouge. "You left me there. You didn't even wait for me.
You just left me behind."

I walked over to the cattery door and looked in at all
the pregnant cats in their cages, their swollen bellies
hanging down, nipples puckered through the heavy fur.
Just a short time ago I'd have been waiting for the births
with great anticipation, waiting for that moment when
I'd unwrap the perfect kitten from its sac and all of my
careful planning would come to fruition. I'd assist the
queen in her final push, feel a surge of triumph at something so small coming into the world because of me.

"Yes," I whispered to Mother, though I wasn't sure
she could hear me, "I did. But I had to, Mother. And I am
sorry."

Before she could respond, I went in and closed the
cattery door behind me. The reporters pounded at the
door, Cecilia calling my name high above the crowd. I
knew that leaving Mother would be something I'd have to
live with for a long time to come, and that sending
Middle away was something Mother might never forgive.

The photos of Mother and me wrestling on the ground
appeared the next day on the front of all the major newspapers. CLONE DISAPPEARS AGAIN, the headlines read. TWO
"MOTHERS" BATTLE OVER CLONE. One of the articles said
that Mother had returned home after a sleepless night
on my front lawn, where reporters had circled her until
early morning, praying for a sound bite. But she had
said nothing when asked what she planned to do now
that Middle had escaped.

Norton dodged reporters for a week before the National Institutes of Health finally appealed to the courts to subpoena his medical records. All week images of a sprinting Norton with a lab coat over his head appeared during special bulletins. One reporter caught him while running to his waiting limousine. A picture of Middle was shoved under his nose and held there. "That's not the baby I delivered," Norton mumbled. When asked if he could identify Middle in a lineup, he said, "I don't know who that person is."

The telephone rang day and night with requests for interviews, tabloids offering thousands of dollars for my side of the story. Gary Tate promised to buy thirty Persians if I agreed to go on the show. Even Sophie Sussman, who said she was allergic to cats, swore to let me appear live from the cattery if I gave her an exclusive. She sent a huge bouquet of orchids to the house with a card addressed to me.

"Dear Maxine," the card read. "As a mother myself, I can only imagine the horror of what you have gone through. It is not easy to lose a daughter—or to lose a mother, that is. Let's talk about it. Love, Sophie.

A PS in a scrawling print: "If you were Fergie, I bet the queen would have never let you go."

I wrote my reply on the only piece of stationery I had left with the Bicolor Bliss letterhead embossed across the top.

Dear Sophie,
Thank you for your kind words. However, I must admit I do not know how it feels to lose a daughter, as I have only lost a clone. Only

*real mothers know what losing a daughter is
like.*

   *As for being Fergie, I can only say that I have
no one to be but myself, and that, I'm afraid, is
that. You did bring Fergie into our lives, and for
that alone, Mother thanks you, I thank you, and
even Middle thanks you. Now you can count a
clone among your many fans.*

                                          Love,
                                          Maxine Dublin

After finishing the note, I gathered up all of the newspaper articles that had been written about us and put them
in a box addressed to Mother. If anyone loved mementos
it was Mother; and who better to keep track of all that
had happened than her? I found a stack of tabloids Middle had hidden under the cattery stairs just as I was
about to seal up the box. On the front page of one of the
tabloids was a split picture of Mother's face on one side,
Fergie's in the middle, and mine on the other. In large
black letters the caption read, I AM NOT A CLONE! I folded
the picture in threes, tucked it into the bottom of the
box, and wrote Mother's name in big block letters.

   While I was sealing up the box, Anita called to tell
me that Norton had parked his limousine outside her
house and sent love notes sailing out on paper airplanes
across her lawn.

   "He seems so dejected," she said. "Each note is worse
than the last. He's terribly sorry for what he's put you
through."

   When I didn't answer, she sucked in her breath and
let out a long sigh.

"He'll even say it on television if he has to," she whispered. "This is a broken man."

"And who isn't?" I asked, trying to hide the bitterness in my voice. When she didn't answer, I cleared my throat.

"What about Mother?" I said, twisting the phone cord with my fingers. "Have you heard from her? Is she sorry, too?"

Anita let out a long sigh and said she had to go, that the twins were calling her. She asked if Jerry, Ron, and I would come to Candy and Sandy's tenth-birthday party next week, if we could manage to sneak past the reporters, but I declined. I promised to send them a pair of matching pink sneakers in my absence.

"It's a kids' party," I told her. "Besides, I think the sight of twins might be too much for me right now."

Anita laughed and said she understood. She also said she couldn't promise Norton would be gone by then, anyway, that the steady stream of love notes continued to accumulate on her lawn. She said that once she got rid of Norton she might think about writing a book on the phenomenon of identical twins with single mothers, for whom Candy and Sandy would be the models. She'd dedicate it to me, she said, because after all, she and I had shared our childhood.

"We watched each other grow up, Maxi," she said, before she hung up the phone. "Nobody can ever take that away."

I thought about that for a long time after I hung up. Then I scribbled out my return address on the box to Mother. At first I considered enclosing a note, but now that Middle was gone, I found I didn't know what to say.

The pictures would have to speak for themselves. Mother would come around, Jerry said, in all good time—after all the excitement had died down—though I wasn't sure how long I planned to wait.

When all the cats had finished giving birth, I sold the cattery to Jerry for half of what it had been worth and said good-bye to Jerry and Ron. With all the mismatching that had been done that night, it might take Jerry months, even years, to rebuild my success. I'd miss Jerry, there was no denying that; but I was happy for him that he'd found a way to bring the two halves of himself together. At least, I thought, one of us had been able to.

" 'What's new, pussycat?' " he sang in my ear as we said our good-byes, his arms wrapped tightly around my waist. I laughed and lifted my face to his. Ron slipped one arm through each of ours. His gun poked out from the waistband of his boxer shorts. We laughed and held onto one another's arms as we all sang the chorus together. " 'Whoa-oh, whoa-oh, whoa…' "

With the reporters finally packed up and the cattery sold, I took the Duchess and Bea on a trip out West, bought a pickup truck and a banjo, and started playing on the side of the road. I tied a white sneaker around my rearview mirror the way mothers do with baby shoes. After many weeks, I became quite good; it seemed I remembered a good deal more than the six chords my father had once taught me. The Duchess and Bea slept outside, with their fur blowing in the wind, while I strummed the banjo and thought about Middle—about the comma over her eye, the way she'd run across my lawn as if glid-

ing, how she'd grown inside me and burst forth into the
world, leaving me full of memories and a fuller heart.
Motherhood was filled with losses, I realized, but
women were right about one thing: Nothing else in the
world could match it.

One night while I was strumming the banjo on the side
of the highway, a group of teenage boys in a Volkswagen
stopped behind me and asked to hear "O Susanna." They
were drunk and giddy, tapping their feet and howling
while I played the chorus over and over. When I was finished a boy with a shock of gold hair over one eye
stopped to pet the Duchess and Bea. He looked up at me
with a mischievous smile.

"Hey," called one of the other boys, "did anybody
ever tell you that you look like Fergie, the Duchess of
York?"

I got back into the pickup truck and threw my head
back and laughed, tossed the banjo on the passenger
seat, and started the engine.

"No, no," the boy with the gold hair said, leaning on
the side of the truck, "it's the red hair. It's someone else
she looks like, but I don't know who."

I rested my head against the back of the seat and
thought of Middle, with her swollen foot, the way she'd
smiled at that boy in the drugstore parking lot, the glint
of hope that was in her eye.

"Maybe you've got a twin somewhere," one of the
boys called, "or maybe even a clone. You know, like that
one that was in all the papers."

I just laughed and revved the engine, eager to get away
in case one of them was sober enough to recognize me.

"No, fellas, I'm afraid there's nobody else but me," I said, waving at them as I pulled away. A cloud of dust circled behind me as I sped down the highway.

I thought about what the boys had said, about the long nights I often spent thinking about Mother and our estrangement, how I sometimes stopped at pay phones with my fingers poised to dial her number, but I knew the wounds were still too raw. We all needed time to heal; we'd all been opened up, turned inside out, the way that mothers and daughters often are.

At times I felt sorry that I'd lost a piece of myself along the way, but then I'd touch the sneaker hanging from the rearview mirror and trace the knot in the laces. Sometimes I felt Middle beside me in the dark, her heart beating in time with mine; sometimes I swore it was her voice I heard singing in my ear as I strummed the banjo strings night after night. Other nights I was sure I was alone in the world, with nothing to keep me company but a five-string and a pair of Persians curled up together in the dark. I was alone on those nights but not lonely, and that was what mattered. Some people might have said that I was no longer whole, that I'd lost my child along the way, that I'd let her go too soon. Perhaps that was true; there were parts of my life I might never get back, a fact I would have to learn to live with. In some ways, though, I was wholer than most. I may have lost parts of myself along the way, but I'd gained a new life; and any new life, no matter how short or how diffi-cult, was bound to be worth the struggle.